TRUE BLUE
THE NORTH BROTHERS

AMY KNUPP

CHAPTER ONE

It would be a crying shame if Lexie Gallagher threw up on her pretty white wedding dress.

Then again, the dress hardly mattered now.

She was sure her jaw actually gaped as she watched her fiancé—*former* fiancé—all slim and clean-cut in his charcoal tux, walk away after calling off the ceremony, then turn the corner and disappear from her sight. Her chest felt heavy and tight as the situation sank in.

Now what?

She was standing in a nondescript hallway in the basement of a church she'd been in exactly three times in her life, with close to a hundred and fifty people due to show up in twenty-ish minutes. Alone, stunned, and nauseated as all get out.

She found the wall with her back, leaned into it, suddenly needing its support as her mind went from numb to whirling like a tornado in a matter of seconds.

"Lex?"

The deep, so-familiar male voice resonated through her as Gabe North, her best friend, strode around the corner from the direction Raleigh had gone.

"What did he say?" Gabe said in a low, controlled voice as he hurried toward her. With some measure of relief, she drank in the sight of him, every golden-brown hair uncharacteristically in place, his tuxedo fitting him impeccably.

Lexie reached out and wrapped her fingers around his forearm, maybe subconsciously hoping to prevent him from going after Raleigh when she filled him in.

"We're not…" She cleared her throat to get her voice to work. "The wedding's off," she croaked out.

Gabe swore as his blue eyes, filled with compassion and concern, held hers. He pulled her into his chest and wrapped his arms around her as she came away from the wall and inhaled his comforting scent, let herself wilt a little into his strength.

"I'm sorry, Lexie," he said into her hair. "What the hell?"

She blew a shaky breath into his lapel, where, she realized, she was crushing his boutonnière, the single bloom that signified his role as her honor attendant. *Man maid*, his brothers had teasingly called him.

Instead of answering his question, she said, "Good thing you don't need your flower. I killed it."

"I'd like to kill that son of a—"

"Gabe." She shook her head adamantly, unable to handle thinking too hard about Raleigh at this moment. She angled her chin to look up at him, one persistent thought jabbing at her with spikes of anxiety. "What do I do about all the people?" She could hear a note of hysteria in her own voice.

He seemed to consider that as her own brain ground to a halt.

"He's the one who called it off?"

She lowered her gaze and nodded.

"Then you don't do anything," Gabe said, pulling his phone out of his pocket. "He caused the problem. He can deal with it. I'll let Sierra and Mackenzie know what's going on, and they can talk to anyone you need them to."

He had a point. This was Raleigh's doing. Raleigh's church. Raleigh's family, since she didn't have one. The Norths were her surrogate family and Gabe would tell them. The vast majority of guests were on Raleigh's side, with the exception of a small group from her department, the entire North clan, and a few others.

A wave of light-headedness came over her, and she grasped Gabe's upper arms for balance, grateful he was here for her, like he had been since the first day of kindergarten. "Okay, so…what now?"

He looked both ways, spotted the exit sign at the far end of the hall, took her hand, and pulled her along. "I'm getting you out of here."

She opened her mouth to argue and then closed it.

Escape.

Yes.

"Please," she said, hurrying in her stupid white satin shoes alongside him as he took giant strides toward what appeared to be a back door. "Could you ask Sierra to get my stuff?"

"I'll text her and I'm sure she'll take care of everything."

When they got to the heavy exterior door, he opened it, keeping her behind him. "You might be tiny, but you're hard to hide in the white. Stay here until I come back. I'll get the car."

"Hurry." She was still mostly holding off coherent thoughts, but the need to get the heck out of Dodge before anyone asked her, face-to-face, what was going on pressed in on her as if the hallway was shrinking.

Once the door closed, her forgotten lower-level corner of the church was silent, insulated from above, where she couldn't help but wonder what was happening. Was Raleigh telling the groomsmen? Or had they known before she did? Had he broken it to his parents? What would he tell everyone?

Not the truth—or what Raleigh saw as the truth.

No one but her and him needed to know what had made Raleigh call their wedding off less than an hour before she was to walk down the aisle.

It wasn't true anyway, but as her friend and bridesmaid Kara liked to say, perception was ninety percent of a person's reality, and Lexie hadn't been able to convince Raleigh his was faulty.

Another wave of nausea washed over her and she shoved aside the thoughts. Maybe later she would be able to pick apart the five-minute conversation with her no-longer groom. She squeezed her eyes shut against everything, trying to get through the next few minutes until Gabe got her out of here.

His light knock finally came, and she pushed the heavy door open, squinting against the sudden onslaught of early-afternoon June sunlight.

Weather-wise, it had spruced up to be a perfect Nashville day —low eighties, scattered clouds, slight breeze. She'd worried for weeks whether Mother Nature would pull through for their outdoor reception. Obviously she'd been worried about the wrong thing.

Gabe's white Tesla Model S was right there, pulled up on the double-wide walkway that went from the parking lot to the door, and was shielded by part of the building that jutted out. She glanced around like a criminal afraid of getting caught and exhaled when she realized no one could see her. He walked her to the passenger side, opened the door, helped her get her dress tucked in before closing her in. The simple trainless gown she'd chosen was a plus in clandestine getaways, she thought with another surge of hysteria bubbling up inside.

As Gabe eased into the driver's seat, he was tapping out a text message to someone. "Sierra's going to bring your bag to the main door—"

"I can't go to the main door!" she said in a panic.

"I'm going," he said with a hand on her bare forearm. "I'll get the AC cranked up and leave you here in the car. While I'm gone"—he eyed her hair, which was done up to masterpiece proportions and had a delicate floral headpiece with a short veil in back—"as beautiful as your hair looks, do you think you can get the veil off so you're less conspicuous?"

"I'll see what I can do. Gabe…" She put her other hand over his, still on her arm, stopping him. He looked down at her with his brows raised. "Thank you." Emotion crawled up her throat, and she couldn't say more, could not even begin to pick apart the hornets' nest of emotions.

"No need to thank me. Let's get you out of here."

She nodded as he started the car, realizing, as the cool air blew over her, how stinking hot a wedding dress was, even one that bared two-thirds of her back and had lacy cap sleeves.

As soon as he shut her in and jogged off toward the front side of the building, she flipped the visor down and tried to see how to dismantle her hair. The headpiece wasn't complex, was secured with a built-in comb, but there were pins galore and half a gallon of hairspray holding it and the partial updo in place.

Thankful for something concrete to focus on, she opened the glove compartment and went to work plucking out the bobby pins one by one and tossing them in. By the time Gabe returned, she had her hair clear of everything but hairspray and held the handmade headpiece, staring at the beautiful wisteria flowers in the lightest blush color, entwined with tiny silver leaves and crystals. What a waste of an exquisite piece.

Gabe handed her the small bag with her hair and makeup touch-up tools, her phone, her wallet, and her white reception sneakers. "Sierra and Mackenzie send their love and said to text them soon. They wanted to come back with me and hug you, but I told them we have to go. The sooner the better."

Those two… If she didn't have Gabe, Sierra and Mackenzie were the people she would've turned to. She'd only gotten to know them in the past few months, after she'd asked her college roommate, Kara, and Raleigh's sister, Lauryn, to be her brides-maids. Sierra was engaged to Cole, Gabe's middle brother, and Mackenzie was the fiancée of Drake, Gabe's youngest brother. Lexie had met them at the North family's weekly Sunday dinners. Once Lexie had gotten close to them, she'd asked them to be her personal assistants for the wedding. While she and Kara had been close in college and she and Lauryn got along well enough, the bonds with Sierra and Mackenzie were stronger. They'd become almost soul-sister tight in a short time. For a girl who'd never had a slew of close friends, it was new and different and awesome.

"So here's the plan," Gabe said, his voice calm, reassuring. "Most of the cars are coming in the main entrance to the lot. I'm going to take you out the back route. I want you to put your seat back all the way and lie down so, on the off chance we pass someone on their way in, you won't be seen."

Lexie did what he said with no argument, relieved to avoid people she might know. She'd worry about facing the world later. "Where are you taking me?" she asked from a nearly horizontal position as Gabe reversed down the long walkway and then whipped the car around and took off.

"Haven't gotten that far yet. Where do you want to go?"

Returning to her downtown apartment, where she'd thought she'd spent her last night ever, was unthinkable. She'd left it with so much excitement and hope and joy this morning, and to walk back in now, still single, devastated, feeling like a failure… She couldn't handle that. Besides, Raleigh lived in the same building, six floors up, and he was the last person she wanted to run into.

"Not to my apartment. Not to Europe." She wasn't one of those girls who'd be taking her planned honeymoon trip alone.

"I'm on it." When the car was stopped at a traffic light, he punched in a message to someone on his phone, then set it back on the console.

"Is it safe to sit up now?" she asked. Without being able to see where they were going, all she had to focus on were her thoughts, and those were a combo plate of confusion and ugliness.

"Go ahead."

Lexie raised her seat, then busied herself kicking off the uncomfortable pumps and searching through her bag for her no-show socks and sneakers. When she pulled out the shoes, she smiled and then frowned at the sparkly silver laces Kara had put in, insisting that even though they were practical shoes, they needed bling for her wedding day.

Well, looked like she was going to have bling for her non-wedding day.

To distract herself, she flipped the radio on and searched the satellite streaming service for eighties music. Gabe wasn't a fan, she knew, but she also knew he would indulge her right now. She needed some comfort music, upbeat music, and the second a love song came on, she would punch in something different. Like maybe the heaviest heavy metal.

As Tears for Fears filled the car, Lexie finally took stock of their whereabouts. "You're taking me to your place?"

"I figured you could change your clothes there."

"And then what?"

"I'm still working on it. Trust me?"

"Of course."

She closed her eyes, rested her head back, and focused on the music, only the music, singing every lyric in her mind as Duran Duran and then Bruce Springsteen played. When Queen's "Another One Bites the Dust" started up, she went to jab the control, unable to embrace that lyric, and when she realized Gabe had turned down his street, she clicked the sound system off altogether.

Stupid eighties music.

Gabe pulled into the garage of his sprawling traditional-style home. He turned off the car and pushed the button to close the door behind them, ensuring none of the neighbors would spot Lexie in her wedding dress. Typical thoughtful Gabe, and she loved him for it.

"Let me go in and let Saint out first so he doesn't shed or worse on your dress. Your suitcase is in the trunk, or I'm pretty sure you have some clothes in the spare bedroom."

"I'll see what I left in the house." She knew there were several options, as she sometimes used his pool and left extra swimsuits and clothes there for convenience.

"I'll open the door as soon as Saint's out of the way."

"Hurry," she said as he shut the driver's door, leaving her alone in the cool, quiet three-car garage.

With only the faint light from the garage door opener above, her eyes needed time to adjust again. She closed them, breathed deeply for maybe the first time since Raleigh had left her standing in the church basement, and she couldn't help noticing the shakiness of the breath.

Left at the altar—or close enough.

What a flipping cliché. A humiliating, heartbreaking cliché.

Raleigh was good-looking, successful, two years younger than her thirty-seven, and on his way up the ladder at the large firm where they were both employed, he as an architect and she as a landscape architect. Nearly two years ago, they'd worked on a large shopping center project together, and he'd started pursuing her. Though she'd been reluctant to date someone from work, he'd swept her away with his attention and his determination and his enthusiasm.

Now here they were. Their relationship hadn't been perfect, but whose was? She'd never thought in a million years he would break up on their wedding day.

When the light from the opener clicked off, total darkness descended, and she quickly popped the car door open, which lit up the interior. With a sad sigh, she pivoted on the seat to swing her legs out, struggling because of the formfitting cut of the dress.

The dress that no longer mattered, she remembered, taking less care as she stood.

If she ripped it, so what?

If Saint, Gabe's oversized, overzealous St. Bernard mix, got mud or hair on it, who cared?

There might be a market for used wedding dresses, but who would ever want one from a failed wedding? She wouldn't feel right even giving it away for fear it would curse someone.

She grabbed her bag from the floor of the car, dug out her phone, ignored the gazillions of message notifications, and turned on the flashlight to make her way to the door. As she entered the open kitchen and living area, Gabe was coming inside from the French doors in the back of the house. She caught a glimpse out the window of Saint nosing around the expansive backyard.

"Hey," he said in a gentle tone as he strode over to her. His gaze was assessing, questioning. "You holding up?"

The emotions that she'd held off so far were coming in waves now, and she longed for the numbness of fifteen minutes ago. She merely nodded, battling internally against the storm. "What are our plans?"

"I've got Jalisa working on the details," he said of his executive assistant, "but I'm taking you away. Dress for a flight. Not Europe." He said the last bit with a hint of a grin.

When she didn't even attempt a smile, he sobered and trailed his palm from her upper arm down to her hand, which he held on to. She relished the heat of it, the safety, the caring, and didn't pull away. Just exhaled a slow, semi-controlled breath.

"I don't understand what happened, Lex. Did you guys fight or something?"

She shook her head. She and Raleigh rarely argued. Not even today, as he'd broken up with her. Today they'd debated. She'd tried to make him see his reasons were unfounded. But she wouldn't call it a fight.

"Did he get cold feet?"

"No," Lexie said, recalling numerous times over their ten-month engagement when Raleigh had said how he couldn't wait to be married. "I don't think that had anything to do with it."

"I don't get it," Gabe said. "Is he involved with someone else?" He tipped her chin up with his finger, forcing her to look up at him. "Lex, you know you can tell me anything."

She swallowed and took in those warm, compassionate eyes, knowing he spoke the truth, and yet, half an hour ago, she'd sworn she would never tell a soul.

The truth, though… It weighed her down. And if she was honest, it made her mad, and that anger was bubbling up, starting to boil. The need to let it out burned in her, to have Gabe mirror her outrage, to have him say, *You're right, he's wrong.*

Lexie sucked in an unsteady breath.

"The reason Raleigh called off our wedding is…you."

CHAPTER TWO

Gabe scowled as he wrapped his mind around what Lexie had just said. "*What?*"

She took a step back, broke eye contact, covered her face with both hands momentarily. Then she threw her arms down to her sides and let out a frustrated grunt. "I've told you in the past he felt threatened by my friendship with you."

Gabe let out a harsh, unamused laugh. "What does he expect? We've been friends for three decades. You practically grew up in my house."

She nodded and expelled a shaky breath. "We've been over it dozens of times, and I thought he was finally okay with it. He said *he* thought he was okay with everything, but then apparently, when I had my mini freak-out this morning and you and I were sitting on the stairs, he saw us. He said that moment made him face up to reality."

"What moment?" Gabe tried to stay calm, because Lexie needed calm. "What reality? I was giving you a pep talk about marrying him." Doing what a best friend should do—because it seemed wiser than begging her not to go through with it.

She'd been edgy all morning, ever since he and the rest of her attendants had shown up at her apartment bright and early. Throughout the hours-long getting-ready process, she'd denied anything was wrong, but then, as the ceremony had crept closer, she'd been close to panicking, and Gabe had whisked her away on a private walk through the bowels of the church and ultimately to a deserted back stairwell.

She'd admitted she was battling a pit in her gut ever since she'd woken up, and he'd talked her through it. He'd pointed out it was just last-minute jitters.

It was less than ten minutes after they'd returned to the bridesmaids that Raleigh had insisted on talking to Lexie in private.

"He walked onto the landing above us and saw us sitting there, and something supposedly became crystal clear to him."

"And what is that?"

"He said he and I have never had the strong connection that you and I have. He thinks there's more than friendship between you and me, whether we admit it to ourselves or not. He decided he couldn't live with that for the rest of his life." She closed her eyes and pressed her lips together.

Gabe narrowed his eyes and tried to blank his expression and his thoughts, tried to tamp down the first hint of respect he'd ever felt toward Raleigh Clarke. He tried to bury the thought that the guy wasn't as dense as Gabe had always believed.

Gabe had never let on how deep his feelings for Lexie went— he wouldn't, *couldn't* risk screwing up their friendship with that confession—but if Raleigh had somehow discerned them, well, points for him. If the bastard had backed off Lexie months ago, never asked her to marry him, never gotten her hopes up for a future he ended up unable to provide, then Gabe would be more forgiving.

None of that mattered at this moment. What mattered was helping Lexie get through the day, the next week, the next however long it took.

"I imagine you told him he was wrong," he said.

"Of course I did. In every way I could think of. I couldn't convince him. I don't know if he really believes that or if there's another reason... I guess it doesn't matter in the end. I'm not getting married." Her gaze lowered as if she was ashamed, when she had nothing to be ashamed of.

He gathered her into his arms and muttered, "Damn him," into her hair. Gabe wasn't a big proponent of fighting, not like his brother Cole, but for once, he had the urge to track down that skinny pencil dick and mess up his pretty face.

"It's a good thing, after all, that my mom didn't make it." She buried her face in his chest again, grasping on to his jacket like it was her lifeline.

"Yeah. Good thing."

Good and *Mom* didn't go in the same sentence when it came to Jean Gallagher, as far as Gabe was concerned. Her damn piece-of-work mom. He'd thought inviting her was a terrible idea. The woman had done nothing but fail as Lexie's mom for years. She hadn't bothered to respond to Lexie's email invitation, not even to give regrets, and though he didn't think Lexie had expected much, the woman's silence had still been a major disappointment, he knew.

"It would've been a really long trip for nothing," Lexie continued.

"South America is a long haul," he agreed, fighting to keep his tone neutral. He wasn't sure he could stomach seeing the woman who'd left her family thirty-some years ago to study endangered monkeys, and she sure as hell wouldn't qualify as a reassuring or comforting presence for Lexie if she had shown up.

His phone buzzed in his pocket.

"I'm okay. You should check that," Lexie said.

He pulled his phone out and read the text from Jalisa. "She wants me to call her about our trip. Why don't you go change your clothes so we can get out of town, maybe get you a cocktail."

"Yeah," she said stoically. She sniffled once but her eyes were dry, and Gabe wondered when she would let it all out. Whenever it was, he'd be there. She nodded, inhaled deeply, and went toward the guest room.

Once he heard the door shut, he pushed the number for Jalisa, who answered right away.

"Whatcha got?" he asked.

Three minutes later, he had an itinerary jotted on an envelope on the kitchen island, and he thanked his efficient assistant, then ended the call and went into his own room to pack a bag.

"Gabe?"

He looked up to find Lexie in the doorway of his bedroom, still in her wedding gown.

"The back… The buttons… I need help."

Though he'd given the women privacy when they'd dressed this morning, he'd heard all about the line of tiny buttons that trailed from the middle her back down to her ass. "Come on in." He gestured for her to turn around in front of him.

He already knew what he would be faced with. Though it wasn't right and he wasn't proud of it, he'd stolen random opportunities to check her out in detail from all sides over the course of the day. He couldn't help himself. Even so, when she presented her back to him, he took in a steadying breath and bit the inside of his mouth to keep his mind from going off task. She was beautiful on a normal day, but today, her feminine figure, with that exquisite white fabric hugging it, was breathtaking.

Brushing her soft skin with his big, clumsy fingers was unavoidable as he struggled to unfasten each delicate button. Was this dress designed for a groom's pleasure or his torture?

Maybe for a groom, it would be a pleasure. For the bride's honor attendant who had no right to touch her skin like a lover, no right to anticipate every inch of delicate flesh as it was unveiled to him, definitely torture.

By the time he unfastened the last button, which hit right in the middle of her tantalizing ass and revealed the lace edge of satiny white panties, his fingers were shaking.

"There you go," he managed to get out in what nearly passed for a normal voice.

"Thanks," she said, oblivious to his state, thank God. Holding the dress to her front, she faced him. "What did Jalisa say?"

"The company jet is taking us to Colorado. She booked a two-bedroom condo on the banks of a mountain stream just outside Caribou Creek. Beyond that, you're in charge. We can binge-watch Netflix all day or hike hundreds of miles of trails through the mountains or drive up to the top of the range or whatever you're in the mood for."

Her eyes fluttered shut and her features relaxed a degree. "That sounds perfect."

"Anything for my nature girl." He inwardly cringed at the use of *my* and hoped she didn't think anything of it.

"Thanks again. I don't know what I'd do without you."

"You'd do just fine. You have a lot of good people in your life, Lex. Sierra, Kara, Mackenzie—"

"None of them have a corporate jet though." Her half smile was the first hint of any such thing he'd seen since they'd left the church.

"Or the best executive assistant on the planet." He'd told his assistant they needed something low-key, scenic, and full of nature in Colorado, and the woman had accomplished that in less than half an hour. It was why he paid her so well.

"Jalisa is amazing," she agreed. "I'm going to get out of this. I'll be ready in ten minutes."

"I need to call Connor to see if he can stay here with Saint while we're gone."

Once she'd left, he blew out a breath, shook his head, and picked up his phone. His cousin Connor had been invited to the wedding, as had Gabe's whole family, so he was aware of the situation and easily agreed to dog- and house-sit for the next week. During their brief conversation, Gabe took out a small suitcase and absently threw in clothes and toiletries, then packed up his laptop and other necessities in his work bag.

Before he could take it all out to the kitchen, his phone rang again and he figured it was Connor with something they'd forgotten to discuss. Instead, the caller ID said Mason, and he debated answering. Avoiding his older brother, though, would only fuel the fire.

"What's up?" Gabe said when he connected the call.

"That's my question for you," Mason said. "You're taking Lexie away? Today? Are you sure that's a good idea?"

"She wants to get out of town."

"Why can't Mackenzie or Sierra take her?"

"I've got plenty of vacation time." Gabe hadn't bothered to check his schedule for the next week, just told Jalisa to reschedule everything. He'd told her to notify Mason, who was the CEO of North Brothers Sports and technically his boss, as well, but he'd hoped he could at least get out of town before his brother got the message.

"Work isn't the issue and you know it," Mason said, and those words had Gabe veering from his path toward the main living area, turning back into his bedroom, and heading to the master bath, where he wouldn't be overheard.

"I'm her best friend. I'm going to be there for her."

Mason let out a breath and his tone was more tempered when he said, "She's vulnerable right now, Gabe. Feeling the way you do, do you really think a getaway for two is wise?"

Gabe ran his free hand through his hair, messing it up from its pre-wedding neatness. He could deny his feelings, but it would be a waste of time. Mason knew him better than most, and though this was the first time he'd spoken his suspicions aloud, there'd been signs he knew Gabe cared for Lexie beyond mere friendship. Gabe had simply ignored them. "I'm not stupid."

"You sure about that? Because this feels like a dumb move."

"What the hell do think I'm planning to do?"

"It's not the planned stuff I'm worried about. Shit can happen sometimes. Unplanned fuckups. I know you mean well, but don't you dare hurt her."

"I'm done with this conversation," Gabe snapped into the phone. "I'll be back in the office a week from Monday. You know how to get ahold of me if business requires it." He ended the call and muttered a stream of swear words directed at his nosy, smug-ass brother.

He would never hurt Lexie. That meant keeping his hands off and his feelings in check. Same as always.

Sharing a cabin with her, helping her work through one of the hardest moments of her life, being exactly what she needed and nothing more... Without a doubt, this next week was going to be the challenge of a lifetime, but dammit, he would do it. Even if it killed him.

CHAPTER THREE

The fresh mountain air, breathtaking scenery, and adorable quaintness of the tourist town tucked into the Rocky Mountains helped Lexie temporarily forget she'd been left at the altar today, or close enough to the altar that it counted.

The two lemon drop martinis she'd had at dinner, though… Now that she and Gabe had left the mom-and-pop bar and grill, the alcohol was lowering her resistance to thoughts of the wild, traumatic day. She turned her attention outward, to the sights around her.

Caribou Creek's main street was bustling with people even though it was nearing nine p.m. Shops lined both sides, selling T-shirts, jewelry, souvenirs, chocolates, ice cream, outdoor and hiking gear, and more, staying open late to make the most of their short summer tourist season. The sun had just dropped below the horizon and the town was ablaze with lights. A din of general contentment mixed with the periodic cry of an overtired child. Past the downtown area, the majestic, towering mountains could be seen as dark silhouettes against the dusk sky, and Lexie was struck again with awe and anticipation. Though she'd never been to this specific town before, this part of the country was one of her favorite places in the world.

Once they'd landed, they'd driven a rental car to the condo Jalisa had reserved, dropped their bags off, and gone into town to track down dinner. Since leaving the restaurant, they'd stopped into the outdoor store and bought basic supplies and shoes for a day hike tomorrow, and a T-shirt store, where Lexie had picked up two tees and some sunglasses. If she wasn't so exhausted, there were countless other stores she'd want to go in. She'd hit them later in the week, she promised herself.

As a family of six passed them, Lexie and Gabe moved closer to the storefronts, and she took hold of his forearm to keep her balance. "This is so much better than Europe," she said. Somehow Gabe had known that.

They walked several steps before Gabe acknowledged her comment. "I was wondering when you were going to talk about it."

"Talk about what?" she said flippantly. "There's nothing to talk about. Nothing to see here, folks." She grinned at herself, knowing full well that vodka was making it easier to joke, easier to breathe.

"It's okay if you're not ready yet," Gabe said.

She leaned her head on his upper arm, which was where it hit naturally thanks to their height difference of just over a foot. "I'm not ready to talk about it yet." She popped her head up straight, a spark of fury making its way to the surface. "Except…why in the blazing hell did he wait until today? Why not two weeks ago? Or even yesterday? Yesterday would've been better."

If Raleigh had dumped her yesterday, at least she wouldn't have wasted hours of her life getting prettied up and stuffed into a gorgeous white gown. If he'd really been on top of things and called it off before the rehearsal dinner last night, well, who knew what the refund policies were for that—she'd never once thought she needed to ask—but maybe they could've saved a few dollars and a god's share of embarrassment.

"Last-minute doubts, I guess. And no, I'm not defending him. He should've come to you the second he had any misgivings, and you can't tell me today was the first time for that."

Lexie shook her head, scowling. "He admitted he's been talking himself out of his doubts for weeks. Fool."

Maligning him felt good, even if *fool* didn't do him justice, but deep down, she knew...she was at least as big of a fool as Raleigh. Probably bigger. For sure bigger. Her mistake was in ever believing she would find someone to love her, to marry her, to settle down with her for a lifetime. Hadn't her parents made her fully aware of how tough it was to love her from the earliest years of her life?

"I hate that this happened to you," Gabe said as they slowed in front of a bookstore window paying homage to local authors and touting a vast selection of journals and notebooks, "but I can't help but think you're lucky he flaked now instead of after the vows."

Though Lexie, on some level, suspected he was right, she couldn't process that yet. Wasn't to the point of *thank God, dodged that bullet*. Couldn't fathom that she would be. She'd been ready to marry Raleigh Clarke, *till death do us part*. "Let's go in," she said instead, her itch to shop overpowering her fatigue now. Retail therapy, here she came. With a vengeance.

The inside of the bookstore was vintage but homey and stuffed full of books, gifts, puzzles, and other treasures. As Gabe stopped at a table of paperbacks about the outdoors and the national park, Lexie made her way toward the section in the back corner marked art supplies. All she'd brought with her was what she'd packed for her honeymoon, and though she'd debated briefly when she packed, she'd left her beloved sketchpad at home. Sketching was a solo thing, and she hadn't planned to be solo on her honeymoon. Here, though...

She found the type she liked and picked up two, then located the fine-art colored pencils. They had the good kind here, and it wouldn't be cheap, but she'd been needing to replace some of hers anyway. She discovered some brush pens she'd seen on social media and added those to her pile.

By the time Gabe found her, she'd added two beautiful journals, three packs of colored pens, a trio of cute refrigerator magnets, and a set of moose measuring cups. Instead of giving her a hard time for how much she'd found in such a short time— he knew full well her shopping skills were expert level—he took the vast majority of it from her and carried it while she finished browsing.

"I think that's it for now," Lexie said, avoiding her usual penchant for romance novels, because tonight she wasn't sure she believed in happy endings. "What'd you find?"

His lone book was on top of her tower of creativity tools that were making her fingers tingle with the need to use them.

"A book about hiking in the park. It's the one the guy at the outdoor shop recommended, with maps and trail descriptions, plus safety tips and survival info."

"Sounds like exactly what we need. Cram session tonight?"

"We can pick out a trail tonight and throw the book in my backpack tomorrow morning. Got us covered."

A gentleman in his fifties with a long beard and a friendly smile rang up their purchases, with Gabe treating in spite of her protests, and then Lexie insisted on carrying the bag as they went back out on the sidewalk.

She sidled close and said, "Thank you. For buying me all these pretties. And for agreeing to hike all day tomorrow when you'd probably prefer rafting or rappelling. You're spoiling me."

"This trip is all about you, Lex. Whatever you need to get through the next few days." He put his free arm around her and squeezed her to his side, then released her.

Emotion surged up in her throat and she swallowed it down. "As long as I don't have to bowl, we're good." There was more venom in her voice than she'd intended.

Gabe slowed their pace, nearly stopping. "I thought you liked bowling. You've been on a bowling team with Raleigh for, what, more than a year?"

"I hate bowling," she said, softly but with so much feeling. She'd never told anyone how much she loathed the sport. Had tried so hard to like it.

Raleigh wasn't a sports guy, didn't like football or baseball or hockey or any of the things she'd grown up watching at the Norths' house. He'd never gone running with her or joined her gym, so when he'd had the idea for them to join a couples' bowling team with some people from their company, saying it would give them a social and a physical outlet and something to do together, she'd agreed.

"It hurts my hand. I'll never be able to spin the stupid ball. And the shoes are ridiculous."

"Did he know you hated it?"

She shook her head and shifted her bag to the opposite side. "He bought me my own ball for Christmas."

"Well," Gabe said, sounding like he was amused but trying to hold it in, "we won't go bowling then."

"Ever," she said adamantly. "Or do wine club."

"I thought you liked your wine group."

"I like the people," Lexie said, "but I've been trying to like wine for a year and a half now and…"

"You're a martini girl."

"Martinis, margaritas, mimosas…but no Merlot." She laughed at her alliteration, then sobered. "I'm sorry. I sound so hateful. This isn't how I want to be but…"

"You're upset."

"The numbness is wearing off and now I'm…mad. I'm so mad." Her jaw stiffened, and she clutched the bookstore bag more tightly, until her fingernails bit into her palm.

"Let the mad out, Lex."

They'd reached the last store on this side of the street. Their rental car was parked another couple of blocks down.

"Do you want to cross and check out the other side?" Gabe asked. "The ice cream shop is only half a block away."

Gabe knew as well as Raleigh had that she had a killer sweet tooth. She'd noted the ice cream shop both times they'd passed it. The window proclaimed they had homemade sugar cones and candy-coated caramel apples and forty flavors of ice cream.

But dessert had become a Raleigh thing too. Each evening, even if they weren't able to have dinner together, they'd had a deal that they shared dessert before the day ended, whether it was going out for a cupcake or ice cream or eating cookies at one of their apartments. Raleigh had a quirk about spending the night together on weeknights and didn't allow it, hadn't ever, even though they lived in the same building, so dessert was their means of spending time together each day before saying good night.

Lexie was not in the mood for memories tonight.

Screw dessert.

Raleigh didn't need her? She didn't need a sugar fix.

"I'm good," she said, her jaw tight. "Let's go back to the condo."

Gabe nodded and took the bookstore bag from her as they headed down the sidewalk. The crowd was thinning out rapidly. The leggings and tee she'd thrown on at Gabe's back in Nashville had been super comfy for the flight, but now that the sun was down, she shivered, realizing the mountain air at night was a lot cooler than a June evening in Tennessee. Crossing her arms over her chest, she sucked in the air, trying to cool her Raleigh-inspired ire. It didn't work, and in fact, by the time they reached the car, she'd worked herself up to a wet-hen state and bit her lip to keep a handle on it.

Gabe let her in the passenger side, then went to put the bags in the trunk. When he slid into the driver's seat, he held out the jacket she'd bought at the outdoor store for hiking. "Here. I know you're probably cold."

"You're a godsend," she said, taking it and shoving her arms into it gratefully. "In so many ways. Even more so if you turn on the—"

He'd started the car, and before she could finish her sentence, knowing her well, he had the heater cranked up to high. Then he reached across her legs, flipped a button on the door-side of her seat, and rested his warm hand on her knee. "Heated seats too."

Lexie spared him as much of a smile as she could manage. It was an ongoing thing between them—she was always cold; he was always warm. Temperature battles were a frequent occurrence, but tonight, he'd given her her way. It was a little thing, but that familiarity, that kindness, it eased her turbulent emotions by a few degrees, soothed her a tiny bit.

"Want to stop anywhere? Grocery store? Liquor store, for something besides wine?" he asked as he maneuvered out of the tight parking spot.

She didn't have the energy to either rant some more about wine or smile at Gabe's comment. Merely shaking her head, she sank into the seat, pulled the jacket tighter around her, and closed her eyes, surrendering to her soul-deep exhaustion.

To think that, ten hours ago, she'd had her wedding dress on, her makeup flawless, her hopes running high…and here she was, a bona fide hot mess, still single, still alone save for the best friend who was always there for her.

She squeezed her eyes tighter against a wave of melancholy. Anger was so much easier than sadness, and though her energy was depleted, she clung to the ember of indignation as she thought about the position Raleigh had put her in today. The humiliation.

A few minutes later, Gabe turned the car onto the narrow gravel road that led to the cozy cluster of condos where their unit was. The road went over a short bridge that crossed a rushing stream, full of late-spring snowmelt from the mountain peaks, then curved past the rental office. The property consisted of eight duplexes, all in the log-home style and nestled among tall pines and aspens. It was dark except for a porch light next to each front door. Their unit was the farthest from the office, hugged on one side by a curve in the stream. The soothing sound of the water running over rocks filled the air as they got out of the car, and she decided she'd pile on the blankets and sleep with her window open tonight.

After unlocking the condo door and letting her precede him in, Gabe set the bags down on the breakfast bar. "What do you want to do? Sit on the deck and talk? Play a cutthroat game of Uno? Watch a movie?"

"I think I'm going to bed. I'm not good company."

Gabe crossed over to her, pulled her into a half hug, and pressed a kiss onto the top of her still-hairspray-encrusted head. "I don't expect you to be good company. It's been a colossally fucked-up day and I'm sorry, Lexie. If I thought it would help, I'd fly back and kick his ass."

Lexie pulled him to her, pressed her face into his chest, and tried to soak in any comfort she could gain from his solid strength, his familiar scent. "I just want this day to be over," she finally said as she straightened.

"Go get some sleep. Tomorrow we do nature. Maybe it'll help."

It would help, like nothing else could. Losing herself outside had always been a means of self-preservation and refuge, and she was pretty sure Gabe had taken that into account when he'd asked Jalisa to arrange their trip to this little mountain town.

"Night," she said, leaving the bags on the counter. She stood on her toes and kissed him chastely on the cheek, noting the roughness where it'd been so freshly shaven when this nightmare day had begun.

"Sleep well, Lex."

Leaving him in the open kitchen-dining-living area, she went to her bedroom, the one on the main floor. Both bedrooms were kings, and Gabe had given her this one because it had a bathtub, while the one on the second floor only had a shower. Though she loved bubble baths, taking one tonight seemed like a gargantuan effort. "Maybe tomorrow," she said to the empty room.

She turned on the bedside lamp, which was dim and warm, then went to the window on the back side and opened it a crack. The brisk air smelled of trees and water and earth as she pulled it deep into her lungs and eyed the bed. It appeared it was still made up for chilly nights, with a thick white comforter, a fuzzy blanket, and an extra blanket at the foot.

Anticipating curling up in that pillowy softness, she went to her suitcase on the dresser and unzipped it. When she flipped the top flap open, she sucked in a breath at the sight of the pristine bridal-white baby-doll chemise and matching panties. Her wedding night ensemble. She'd laid it out on top, knowing it was probably all she'd need on her wedding night, and now it felt like a flashing neon sign touting her failed relationship.

Lexie closed her damp eyes and swallowed hard. Pressing her lips together, she opened her eyes and picked up the satiny set and strode to the bathroom. Spotting the trash can in the corner, she marched over to it and stuffed the overpriced lingerie into it, then kicked the wicker basket for good measure.

Then she went back to the bed, kicked her shoes off, but didn't bother to strip down. She flipped the lamp off, slid under the blankets, and waited for a big, ugly cry to start.

She knew she should be bawling her eyes out over the breakup, but the tears wouldn't come.

CHAPTER FOUR

*B*y nine a.m. Mountain time Wednesday, Gabe had taken a panicked call from his employee relations manager about an employee coming to work spaced out on what they suspected was prescription drugs, held an impromptu conference call with his benefits staff, and listened in on the last half of the board meeting. All from the comfort of the king-sized bed in his room in the condo.

He didn't mind a couple of hours of work on vacation when it prevented bigger problems later or hours of extra catch-up when he returned. North Brothers Sports was his livelihood and the center of his existence. Always had been.

His father, Harrison North, had opened it as a baseball specialty shop before any of Gabe's brothers were thought of, even before he'd met his future wife, Faye. In the eighties, Harry and Gabe's uncle Hamilton had expanded into other sports, and today it was a billion-dollar enterprise that supported both of the founders' families plus scores of others.

As the VP of Human Resources, Gabe strived to be approachable and supportive, of both his direct staff and the employees in general. He thrived on solving problems for people, which was a lot of what HR came down to, and if a few minutes of his time while he was on vacation could help someone do that, he was all in.

As he hit send on a follow-up email to the employee relations manager, his cell phone vibrated on the mattress next to him. It was a FaceTime call, and his cousin Connor's ugly mug showed up on the screen. Ugly or, if you asked any female, movie-star handsome, but Gabe didn't hold it against him. He picked up the phone and answered.

"What's up, cuz? I see you're not working," Gabe greeted, grinning. He could tell that Connor was in Gabe's backyard, on the terrace, because he could see the edge of the French doors to his house.

Connor cackled and then seemed to be pushed to one side at the legs, and Gabe knew Saint must be nearby, throwing his weight around. "Not working. Ha. Do you ever *not work*, man? I'm running ragged trying to cover everything for your ass."

An oversized dog snout took up the phone screen and Gabe laughed. "Hey, Saint. You keeping Connor on his toes?" He could hear the jingle of dog tags and a sort of dog "squeal" when Saint heard his voice.

"He's a good boy," Connor said as he rubbed the dog's big head. "I just slipped out of the office to let him out."

"You going to walk him?"

Connor laughed. "Sure. Probably about midnight when I finally have time. Remind me not to say yes next time you take off on an impromptu vacation. When the fuck do you eat?"

"Three times a day, every day. How were the Johansson twins?" Gabe asked of the ten-year-old boys he gave private baseball lessons to every Tuesday evening through his brother Cole's new nonprofit organization, the Harrison North Baseball and Softball Foundation, which offered lessons for kids who wouldn't otherwise have the opportunity.

"Full of energy, man, but ready to work. Those kids have got some talent. Tonight I've got your fourteen-year-old beginners' lesson and then my fan club. Hence the dog walking in the middle of the night."

Connor's "fan club" was a trio of twelve-year-old girls who'd bonded over a love of softball—and a serious preteen crush on their thirty-five-year-old instructor. Jake Nelson, a former MLB player and fellow volunteer, had noticed their rampant fandom when he'd helped Connor with one of his sessions and had been the first to refer to them as Connor's fan club. The designation had stuck. It provided perpetual fodder for teasing from the rest of the volunteers and threatened to make Connor's ego unbearable.

"Thanks for covering for me," Gabe said. "Saint likes morning walks just as much, so that's an option."

"Morning is gym time. Some of us are still exercising regularly, Mr. Vacation," Connor said with a teasing gleam in his blue eyes.

That got a deep laugh out of Gabe. "Try twenty-three miles of mountain trails in three days. And that's not counting the walking we've done downtown."

"How's Lexie doing?" Connor's voice became somber, quieter.

"She's hanging in. Not talking a whole lot about it, but you know her. Introverted on a good day. The scenery and nature are cathartic for her, I think."

"Well, let her know we're all on her side and ready to kick his ass on a moment's notice. All she has to do is say the word."

"Don't think that's ever going to come, but I'll tell her," Gabe said. "Speaking of, I need to go see if she's up yet, see how many miles she's going to make me do today."

"Rough life, dude."

"Did you need anything specific or just calling to whine?"

"Saint wanted to say hi," Connor said. "We've got everything covered. Don't worry about a thing."

"Thanks, Connor. I owe you one."

"You owe me many."

"Get your ass back to the office."

"Too bad the HR VP has no authority over the Operations VP." Connor laughed, told Gabe to put a shirt on, and ended the call.

Gabe hopped out of bed and, without grabbing a shirt, headed down to the first level, overdue for his first cup of high-octane tea of the day. He was curious what Lexie was up to.

There wasn't a doubt in his mind she was out of bed—she'd been getting up before dawn—but he hadn't heard any signs of her. Before he reached the bottom of the stairs, the aroma of coffee hit him. Signs of life, even if he couldn't stand the stuff.

The curtains to the deck door were open, and he saw Lexie sitting out at the high-top deck table, engrossed in something on the wood top. He found a mug of water waiting for him to heat it, alongside a tea bag of his daily black tea.

During the two minutes it took to microwave it, his gaze was glued to Lexie's back as he tried to see what she was so focused on. Her brown hair was in a big pile on top of her head, and she wore an oversized sweatshirt on top. What he could see of her legs were bare, and her feet were in socks with some kind of animals on them. When he spotted the box of colored pencils on the table, he realized she must be sketching.

"Morning," he said as he slid open the door, steaming tea in hand.

She startled at the sound of his voice and gave him a half smile when she turned her head. "Hey, you. I was wondering if you were going to sleep all day."

"Been up for hours. Got caught up by some work stuff or I would've been down sooner. Wow." He took in her drawing as he sat on the chair next to hers. "It's reminiscent of your bedroom growing up. Did you do all that this morning?"

The drawing on the oversized sketchpad had a frame of detailed, realistic-looking light green leaves and hunter-green pine branches that surrounded an imaginative scene of—he angled his head to see better—what looked like a miniature mountain cottage made from a thick tree stump.

"I've been working on it since we got here. It's a fairy house in a fairy garden, mountain-chalet style."

Gabe wasn't sure about the whole fairy part, but the fact was, the details, the colors, the vividness took his breath away. "That's incredible, Lex. You've got some serious skills."

With a self-conscious smile, she shrugged. "I still sketch a lot. It's my therapy when I can't get outside. Always has been."

He knew that better than most. Though he'd rarely been to

her house when they were kids—they'd spent almost all their time at his house—the few times he'd gone in her room, he'd been blown away by the four-wall mural that had grown in scope and detail with each year. Her haven in a house that lacked happiness.

Before Gabe met Lexie in kindergarten, her mom had walked out on the family in pursuit of her blasted monkeys, and her dad…well, the best Gabe could say about him was that he was fairly sure the man had loved his only child. Unfortunately, love didn't always translate into a good parent, and Silas Gallagher had been neglectful and self-centered and a functioning alcoholic for as long as Gabe had known what that was.

Lexie had basically raised herself. Her father had managed to hold on to his job and provide for her financially in spite of his drinking, and he'd never outright abused Lexie either physically or emotionally, but as far as being there for her, forget about it. Though Lexie rarely talked about it, Gabe couldn't not be painfully aware of the situation. She'd never turned down an invitation to the North home, had probably spent more time there than at her own, and any time she was stuck at home, she'd gravitated to the woods adjacent to her house. Her hideaway, she'd called it. In the winter, when it got too cold to spend hours on end in the elements, she turned to sketching and, eventually, painting the intricate floor-to-ceiling forest scene on the walls of her room.

"Whatever happened to your bedroom masterpiece when you sold the house? Do you know if the new owners kept it?" he asked.

"They loved the mural and were planning to make it their meditation room," she said with another modest shrug. "They could've been lying to spare my feelings but I believed them."

"I seriously doubt they were lying. Do you ever think about doing more with your badass art skills?"

She laughed as she shaded the tiny arched fairy door a dusty-rose color. "What would I do?"

"I don't know. Open an Etsy store. Paint murals in children's rooms and nurseries. Give art lessons."

"I already have a good job."

"Sure. As long as you're happy there."

"I mean…yeah. Maybe I don't feel it in my soul the way you do North Brothers, but it's a good job. Good salary. I got a promotion a few months ago. I like my boss. It's going to suck to see Raleigh there, but our departments are on different floors. It probably won't happen often."

"And it'll get easier with time, I bet." He couldn't help but notice how dispassionate her rationale was. But he also couldn't blame her for being practical. She'd spent five years of school prepping to do exactly what she was doing, and she was damn good at it. "So have you decided what trail we're hiking today?"

Lexie picked up a slightly darker rose color from her set of 150 colors and shaded along the top edge of the door. "We're not."

"We're not? Are you too sore?"

Shaking her head, she said, "Much better today. Hiking is my thing, and it's been incredible, every single minute of it. You've done so much for me, always, but especially dropping every-thing in your crazy-train life just to whisk me out of town. Today you get to choose what we do."

"I want to do whatever you want to do."

"Nope. I'm not playing that game today." She set her pencil down, the tips of her mouth curving up, and met his eyes. "I mean it, Gabe. You're always giving, giving, giving. To me, to your company and brothers, to your mom. You never put you first."

With a half laugh, he said, "I didn't know that was a bad thing."

"It's not, sometimes. But sometimes I wonder if you're even capable of putting yourself first."

Her tone was gentle but her statement made him uneasy. She wasn't the first person to accuse him of it. His mom had taken him to task more than once, particularly in the months after her heart attack last year, when she was starting to feel good and developing her new normal. She'd said he was the kindest person she knew (mother's bias, he realized) and considerate above all else and that she was eternally grateful for his thought-fulness, especially as she healed, but that he needed to take care of himself too. She'd said it all in her mom tone, the one that brooked no arguments.

He'd tried to take half a step back, not wanting to make his mom feel like he didn't trust her to take care of herself or like she wasn't independent, but beyond that, he'd waved her message off. That was the way he was wired. Taking care of others was how he rolled, what he liked to do. It wasn't all selfless either. He could easily admit he received plenty of gratification from helping people.

"I can see you're about to argue with me," she said lightly and shook her head. "This is easy. And I'm not backing down. You're choosing something for us to do today. Anything you want, within reason. I know you looked through the tourist magazines in the living room. There's a thousand things to do. So what will it be? White-water rafting? Miniature golf? Boating on the lake? I think I even saw a tour of a brewery or a distillery somewhere..."

He raised his brows at her and crossed his arms, keeping a straight face even though a smile was poking at him hard. She was using her don't-argue-with-me tone. As shy as she was, she only ever used it with a handful of people, and fucked up though it might be, he loved being one of them.

"What if I want to hike?" he asked.

"Not allowed. Anything but. We can hit the trails again tomorrow if you want, but today, we're doing something Gabe-ish."

That made him laugh. "You sure you don't want to do that trail to Lotus Falls? We could take a picnic dinner and make it back by dark."

"Gabe."

"You're not going to let this go, are you?"

She gave him a determined shake of her head and stared him down.

He leaned back in his chair, narrowing his eyes, deciding to test her. "Okay then. Let's go axe throwing."

Lexie's brows shot up. "Axe throwing," she repeated. "You want to go throw axes?"

"I saw it in one of the magazines."

She nodded, which told him she'd seen it too. "Is it safe?"

"I'm sure they have rules to keep everyone safe." Picking up one of the shades of green pencils—Prussian Green, according to the silver etched letters on it—he gave her an out. "Or I could beat you at a round of mini golf."

She swallowed, holding eye contact. "Let's go learn how to throw axes. That, you can probably beat me in."

Gabe laughed as he stood. "You just going to roll over like that and let me win?"

"Not on your life. I'm just saying I've never held an axe in my life, but I'm thinking they're heavy."

"I bet they have a mini axe for the five-foot-and-under crowd," he teased as she slid down from the elevated chair to the floor of the deck, driving home his comment.

"I'm five one, and if they want to give me a handicap, I might take it."

Her smile was the widest one he'd seen since Saturday morning, and it elicited a carnal reaction in him. He resisted the urge to pull her in for a side hug or to touch her in any other way. Though he'd never hesitated in the past and they'd always had a casual affection between them, now that Lexie was single and they were on a trip together, it felt…different. A little dangerous.

Or maybe that was all in his head.

Regardless, his aim was to give Lexie whatever she needed to start to recover, to deal with going from nearly married to alone in the blink of an eye. While he didn't know exactly what that was, he knew for certain his deeper feelings had no place in anything. His problem to deal with and he was.

Come to think of it, it was going to feel damn good to throw axes.

CHAPTER FIVE

When Gabe had chosen axe throwing two days ago, Lexie had had to work to keep the dread from her face. Winging weapons around was never a good idea, right? But she'd thrown the gauntlet out to Gabe, so to speak, so she'd swallowed down her doubts and learned how to throw an axe at a wood target.

It turned out, to her surprise, axe throwing was fun and therapeutic in a vastly different way than nature or art was. When that sharp metal wedge made contact with the wood—and stuck—the satisfaction was immense and immediate.

After a lesson and a bunch of practice throws, she'd gotten the hang of it and had gone on to defeat Gabe—big, athletic Gabe, who was a foot taller and a ton stronger—in their friendly competition. She'd only gloated a little.

Today, after a second session, in which Gabe had prevailed and gloated excessively, he had proclaimed her previous victory as beginner's luck. They'd wagered lunch, and Lexie was treating him at a locally owned pizza place on the main street with outdoor tables on the backside, overlooking the mountain stream that flowed through town.

As much fun as they'd had throwing axes, and as calming and breathtaking as the scenery was, none of it was enough to wipe out her dread of tomorrow. Of going home.

The lunch crowd was thinning as Gabe finished the last slice of pepperoni. Lexie was watching a chipmunk on a boulder near the stream, trying to imprint the idyllic scene to her memory—the car-sized boulders and picture-perfect footbridge arching over the water, the incessant soothing sound of the ice-cold water burbling and splashing over the rocks, the earthy, crisp smell of the pines and the mountain air. If she could bottle it up, she would, because she was going to need it once she was back in Nashville.

"What's on your mind, Lex? You've gone quiet." He shoved the last bite of pizza in his mouth and wiped his hands on a napkin, his eyes piercing her all too perceptively.

"I'm a quiet person," she said, fully aware the dodge wouldn't work.

"You are a quiet person, but this goes beyond Lexie quiet. You thinking about Raleigh?"

She looked up at him in surprise—because she wasn't. Not exactly. "I don't want to go home. Can we just…keep doing this? Hide away here in a little mountain cabin forever? You could work remotely and I'll"—she shrugged—"open an Etsy store and paint murals."

A look overcame Gabe's face, an intense one, just for a moment, and it almost seemed to be…longing? Was he not as satisfied with his job as she'd thought? Or was something else back home making him less than happy? Before she could think about it further, he relaxed and grinned and said, "And we can grow our own vegetables and give guided hikes on the weekend."

"I'm so in. Except the vegetables." She took a drink of soda. "I don't want to face anything back home. Not my job in the same building as Raleigh, not my lonely apartment, also in the same building as Raleigh, and not my coworkers, who are either going to bombard me with questions and sympathy or just act weird and avoid the topic. That is the epitome of awkward."

"The first day back to the office might suck." After pushing his plate out of the way, he leaned his elbows on the table, looking thoughtful. "You know, you could stay with me for a while. Maybe until you find a new place if you still want to move."

The plan had been for her to move in with Raleigh after the honeymoon, and they'd stay there for the few months remaining on his lease, and then they'd buy a house together. Her lease was up in three months, but she luckily hadn't yet given notice that she was leaving. So she had time to mull her options.

It seemed to be time for her to plan her own future. Alone.

"I think I need to finish out my lease while I decide what to do."

"You could have the back bedroom with the big window and the en suite bath," Gabe said. "You'd have your own space on the opposite side of the house, plus the pool and the dog. Saint would love it."

The idea was tempting. Not as tempting as hiding in the mountains, but Gabe's place sounded better than the apartment where she'd spent so much time with Raleigh, planning her future life with the guy. Tempting but cowardly.

"Thanks for offering, but no. I need to face up to everything, get it over with. But I'll be over to use the pool."

"You're welcome anytime, as always. For the pool or as a roommate."

"You don't mean that," she said, waving off the idea. "But I do mean the part about facing the crap storm. The next few days will be the worst of it. I'm coming to terms with some things, like being alone. I need to be by myself. I'm not good at relationships. I don't know why I thought this one was different."

"I don't think 'relationships' is a skill set a person has or doesn't have."

"Says the guy who hasn't had a relationship ever."

"I've had plenty."

She tilted her head and raised her brows at him, knowing full well the longest he'd ever stayed with a woman was a couple of months. "I suppose, technically, yes, if you count a handful of dates as a relationship. How many women have you loved?"

"We were talking about you," he said with a chagrined grin. She knew as well as he did he'd never been remotely serious about a woman. Like his brothers, Gabe had always been more about quantity of women than quality. "A person isn't necessarily bad at relationships just because they don't last forever. If that's the case, we're all bad at them. How many relationships actually end in marriage?"

"I was left at the altar, Gabe," she said in a low voice.

"Which means he wasn't the right guy."

"I'm never the one who breaks up. Always the one who gets dumped." If she was honest with herself, the problem went a lot deeper than boyfriends and breakups. It went all the way back to a day when she was four years old and her mother left. And probably a bunch of days leading up to that as well.

"What about that jackass who cheated on you?" Gabe said.

"You're right." She thought back to close to ten years ago. "Danny. I broke up with him. I'd be a fool not to."

"He's a waste of oxygen," Gabe said, his dislike evident.

"Not going to disagree with you on that." She sat up straighter. "Are you ready to go?"

"Did you want dessert from here?"

She hadn't had dessert all week because it had become such a Raleigh thing and it made her sad, not to mention, she'd mostly stuffed herself extra full at every meal to replace the calories they burned hiking each day. But doing away with one of her favorite things in life was stupid. It was time for her to take her dessert status back into her hands.

The front counter, where they'd ordered and paid for their pizza, was full of tempting cheesecakes, cookies, and cakes, but if she wanted to do this right, she had something else in mind.

"I do want dessert, but not from here."

"You want ice cream," he stated, not a hint of question in his tone, because he did indeed know her that well. He stacked their plates and napkins on the pizza tray. "Let's go do ice cream."

———

THE SIDEWALKS out front of the businesses along the main street were chock full of people, but behind the buildings, there was a meandering walkway that was more peaceful, less populated. Gabe suggested they take that route to the ice cream shop. He had more to say about her and her relationships, but he was debating whether it was the right time or not. Maybe it was too soon.

Lexie was quiet, thoughtful, likely still going over and over her breakup, as he knew she had been on and off all week. She'd asked out loud more than once in the past few days what she'd done wrong, what she could've done better, and Gabe had kept most of his thoughts to himself because they weren't what she needed. But after hearing her say she wasn't good at relationships, he felt compelled to point a few things out to her.

"Hey, Lex, I don't think you're bad at relationships," he said as they walked.

She let out a scoff-laugh. "History proves otherwise."

He hated that she was so down on herself. Though he'd tried to like Raleigh, tried damn hard for Lexie's sake, the guy had always rubbed him wrong.

Knowing what he knew now, Gabe suspected their relationship had been doomed from the start because Raleigh could never accept Lexie's closeness to the North family and specifically him. When he thought back to Lexie's arguments with Raleigh, there were multiple that stemmed from his hang-up with the Norths. The most recent one had been less than a month ago, at Drake and Mackenzie's engagement party at Clayborne's. Raleigh had walked out, pissed off, and left Lexie there. When Gabe had driven her home at the end of the party, she'd said only that Raleigh wasn't happy about spending the evening with the whole North family.

Whether he'd said it out loud or not, the guy had wanted Lexie to choose, him or the Norths, and Gabe thanked fuck he hadn't lost her as a friend.

After a few steps, he said, carefully, what he'd been thinking all week as he learned more about the ins and outs of her relationship. "You never let anyone see the real you, Lex," he said gently. "Not only guys but women too. You don't let anyone really know you."

Her scowl was instant. "How do you know how well Raleigh knew me?"

The question struck him in the gut, because that had been tormenting him for months.

She veered from their route, stalking over to one of the multiple footbridges that spanned the river and led to more shops as well as some parking lots. Since they'd parked on the opposite side of the main street, behind the kite and toy shop, he was confused until she planted herself at the center of the bridge and looked out over the rushing water. He sidled up next to her, following her gaze to some kind of blueish-black jay splashing around in a bird-sized pool to their right.

"He's loving life," she said, nodding toward the bird.

Gabe watched it distractedly, then said, "Hear me out, Lex."

"Translation: I'm not going to like what you have to say."

"Maybe not but I need to say it."

She exhaled loudly. "Fire away."

He sorted his words out quickly, trying to find the best way, the least inflammatory way to say it. "I know you better than just about anyone in the world, and there are things you won't even tell me." About her mom leaving, for example. It had happened before they'd met, and all he knew was that it was a forbidden topic. But that wasn't a safe subject for today either. Instead, he said, "Take the bowling thing with Raleigh."

"I tried to like it, Gabe. It was important to him."

"And I give you full credit for that. That's compromising. But then you hated it and it didn't get better, and instead of telling Raleigh and coming up with something you could both be happy with, you kept pretending to like it. Am I right?"

"Well, yeah."

"You didn't let him know that the real you hated it. Same with the wine club."

"Just because I told you the things I didn't like doesn't mean it's okay for you to use those against me."

"What about the guy who turned you into a temporary Cubs fan? What was his name?"

"Julian," she said, sounding resigned.

"Right." Gabe worked to not let his dislike for Julian show. "You've been a Cardinals fan your entire life. We've hated on the Cubs together. Along came Julian, and as soon as you two started getting involved, you turned into a Cubs fan."

"I was trying to get along with him. Giving us something else in common."

"But you're not a Cubs fan. You *didn't* have that in common." His frustration came out in his tone, even though he was trying to temper it. Probably due to years of holding back his innermost thoughts on the subject. That and wondering how anyone could cheer for the Cubs.

"What happened to compromising?" she snapped.

"Compromising would be not hating the Cubs. Compromising would be watching Cubs games with him and maybe even cheering for them when they're not playing your team." He watched the water below them as a duck paddled its way out from under the bridge. "Compromising means giving a little, not giving up yourself completely. Not hiding the true you. Did you ever tell him that you were a lifelong Cards fan?"

"It was only baseball," she said quietly, which told him she hadn't.

"Lex, you're an amazing person all the way around, but if a guy can't get to know that person, there's no way he can love the real you. Maybe he can love the you he knows but…"

He dared a glance her way, and her eyes narrowed the slightest bit in agitation as she continued to stare straight ahead at the stream. Realizing he'd hammered in his point far enough, probably too far, he gritted his jaw, locked it. Gabe watched the duck flap its wings, spraying water before settling back down on the surface.

When a couple of minutes had ticked by with Lexie frowning, looking pensive and unsure, he decided it had been too soon for this conversation, after all, and was about to backtrack when she leaned her elbows on the top rail of the bridge, averting her gaze downward.

"You want to know something about me that nobody

knows?" she said so quietly he had to strain to hear her over the din of the water. "My deepest, ugliest fear?"

He leaned on his elbows to bring his head closer to hers and waited, curious.

"Ever since I was a little kid," she said, "I've been scared that I'm…" She shook her head, ran her hands over her face. "Scared I'm unlovable."

Gabe's head snapped back slightly, as if he'd been slapped. Lexie's hands were over her face again, so she missed his reaction, but when he went to say something, his mouth opened and he just stood there in silence. Shocked silence.

He glanced in her direction again in case he'd missed a sign that she wasn't serious, like the corner of her mouth twitching up in a grin, but no. Face still hidden. Shoulders slumped. She was serious.

Still at a loss, he straightened and put his hand on her opposite shoulder, squeezed it, trying to somehow convey what he wouldn't—couldn't—tell her. That he knew her and loved her the way Raleigh never could.

He'd never dared to jeopardize their friendship by admitting to his attraction. Every time she started dating a new guy, it killed Gabe a little more, made him think he was an idiot for not speaking up when he'd had the opportunity. Then, with Raleigh, when it had turned into an engagement with a supposed forever attached to it, Gabe had nearly choked on his regret. He'd spent the past ten months trying to make peace with his loss while being the supportive friend Lexie needed. Now, his main concern was what was best for Lexie. He knew without a doubt that was not having her best friend pull the rug out from under her by admitting to certain feelings.

"Lex…you are lovable. Lots of people love you. Every single member of the North family loves you, and that's just for starters."

She sniffed, removed her hands from her face, blew out a breath. "I love your family back, Gabe. Even Cole," she said of the black sheep who'd been hard to love for quite a few years, pre-Sierra. "And I know they love me. Your mom loves me almost as if I was her daughter, and I love her just as much. I know all of this rationally, but there's this part deep inside of me that can't seem to get the message. That rattles off certain truths like machine-gun fire. My mom couldn't love me enough to stay. My dad couldn't love me enough to stay sober. All my exes couldn't love me enough to make it work..." Her voice cracked and she shook her head, overcome. For the first time all week, he saw the tears filling her eyes and quickly overflowing to roll down her cheeks.

Gabe's heart ached for her at the same time he wished he could go back in time thirty-plus years and beat some sense and compassion into her worthless parents. He pulled her into his chest and let her cry. It was a quiet flowing of tears and sniffles, no sobs, but at least she was letting some of it out.

When, a few minutes later, she sniffed a couple more times and swiped at her eyes, as if the worst of it was over, he kissed the top of her head, wanting to do more. Show her so much more. But this wasn't the right time. "No kid should be subjected to parents like yours, Lex. They did wrong by you in every way possible. But look at you. You've turned out pretty damn amazing in spite of them. They're the losers."

"I know that in my mind." She straightened and wiped her eyes again. "Believe me, I've worked through so much of this logically. It's just hard to heal the damage."

It had never, in all the years he'd known her and loved her, been harder to be just her best friend than right now. Fuck, how he longed to love her so hard, so thoroughly that she unlearned every negative thing her worthless parents had instilled in her.

"You're right," she continued. "I don't let people know me. Not past the surface. It's...hard." She leaned her head on him. "Scary."

"From where I'm standing," he said, his voice rough with restrained emotion, "you are one hell of a person. Kind, funny, creative, talented, successful..." *Gorgeous, sexy, enthralling.* "There's a lot to love. You should own it, embrace it, work on loving yourself."

She laughed softly. "And you should do pep talks for a living."

"I sometimes do," he said, relieved the mood had lightened some. He had no idea if anything he'd said really got through to her. How could he undo the damage from a parent, both her parents, that had been embedded for decades? He couldn't just talk her out of it, and he wasn't in the position to show her. For now, all he could do was what he'd been doing—be there for her, listen to her, buy her ice cream.

Straightening, he entwined his arm with hers. "Are you ready for that ice cream?"

"More than. And sugar cone."

"Always."

They made their way off the wooden bridge, back to the walkway, arms still laced together, talking not necessary now. After they crossed a side street, Lexie pointed to the back windows of one of the businesses.

"Check it out. Mountain cabins. Maybe it's a sign," she said with a half grin.

The business was a real estate office, and the windows were filled with printouts of listings. They went to it to browse, Gabe's interest roused.

Real estate investing was something he'd gotten into a few years back, thanks to a college buddy who'd developed a luxury lakeside community on Dragonfly Lake, just outside of Nashville. In addition to investing in the project as a whole, Gabe had purchased three of the vacation homes and had a property management company handling them. They'd turned out to be solid, profitable investments, and he intended to invest in other properties as he found them. He just hadn't had a lot of time to explore options.

"Ooh, look at that one," Lexie said. "Not a cabin. More like a chalet." She pointed at a stunning, sprawling lodge-style house nestled in a pine-covered mountainside.

He moved closer to read the details. Five bedrooms, five baths, over four thousand square feet, brick terrace with a hot tub in the back...a true mountain escape that proclaimed to have an excellent vacation rental history, and that sparked his investor self.

"Do you mind if we go in?" he asked, and Lexie whipped her gaze to him.

"You want to buy a house?"

He shrugged. "Maybe as an investment property. I don't know. I'd like to learn more."

She eyed him, then looked down the walkway at the ice cream shop's back entrance. "Here's the thing. I happen to be taking my dessert destiny back into my own hands as of right now. So how about we compromise? First we get my ice cream, then we can buy you a house."

He laughed. "I like that you have your priorities straight."

"Don't get between a girl and her sugar fix."

"Wouldn't dream of it." He snapped a photo of the contact info for the real estate agent. "I'll call the agent, ask some questions, see if it's remotely a good idea."

He glanced at the time on his phone, saw that the afternoon was getting away from them. "What if we stayed an extra day, maybe looked at some properties tomorrow?"

"I already told you I don't want to go home. Another day here in paradise? Sign me up." She flashed him a genuine smile, the first one since they'd left the axe-throwing place, and after her quietness at lunch and the tough conversation they'd just had, he was damn glad to see it.

In fact, whether the real estate opportunity panned out or not, he decided then and there that an extra day in Colorado was in order if it would make Lexie happy.

CHAPTER SIX

Since Lexie liked her job most days, she didn't necessarily adhere to the Monday Sucks school of thought. However, the first Monday back after a trip? Reentry was always a challenge.

The first Monday back after a trip preceded by a failed wedding? No sugarcoating it—it was going to suck.

The first Monday back after a trip preceded by a failed wedding when you worked at the same company as the almost-groom?

Pass the vodka.

On this clear, temperate June morning, she'd elected to walk the eight blocks from her apartment to work, something she'd done regularly before Raleigh, or BR as she'd started to think of it. She'd stopped the walking habit because Raleigh preferred to drive, and riding together was something they'd done most days, as long as they didn't have client meetings or site visits that required separate vehicles.

As she took a sip of her steaming coffee—third cup of the day, thanks to being wide-awake, worrying about reentry, since roughly four a.m.—she halted suddenly on the sidewalk. Was walking versus driving to work yet another example of what Gabe had been talking about? Another way she'd hidden herself in order to be what Raleigh wanted?

She hadn't liked Gabe's suggestion at all, even as it had rung true. Had spent some time since their discussion trying to come up with someone who she'd let see the real, deep, true Lexie. She hadn't been able to do it—no men she'd dated, and probably no women either, not even Kara, who she'd known since freshman year of college. She was an introvert, an only child, a lonely only child, and keeping things to herself was a long-standing habit. And, she was starting to realize, probably a protective measure as well.

Yes, she was the queen of compromise. She'd always let herself believe it was a strength, what people did to make relationships work, but Gabe had forced her to be honest with herself. It was more of a cop-out. When she'd tried to think of something Raleigh had sacrificed for her, a compromise where he'd given something up, anything… Yeah. She was still trying to come up with an example.

If she was brutally honest, she could admit to a dose of defiance this morning when, during her two-mile run, she'd had the idea of walking to work. She might've even said out loud, "It's stupid to drive on such a beautiful day." Because the real Lexie loved the outdoors, loved fresh air, and driving when she could walk went against the things that mattered to her.

Shoving the disconcerting line of thought aside, she turned her attention to the world around her, took in the details as she hoofed it the last couple of blocks to her office building—the large sidewalk planters outside the bank filled with bubblegum-pink summer snapdragons, pink hybrid petunias, and sweet potato vine, the pair of rock pigeons picking at a treasure in the street near the curb, the window boxes overflowing with lavender geraniums, pink dianthus, and white sweet alyssum that lined the front of the cafe that served the best cheesecake in the city.

Most days, she loved the city she lived in, had lived in her whole life except for her college years, but today, it was hard not to wish herself back in Caribou Creek, hiding away courtesy of Gabe.

For the hundredth time, she thanked her lucky stars for that man. Not only had he rescued her from the scene of the non-wedding but he'd stretched their trip out an extra day and a half so he could buy a rental property or two.

She laughed to herself. Who did that?

She'd grown almost used to Gabe's wealth, which, she knew, he'd had a large part in building up through both the family business and investing, but his real estate investment habit had only started two or three years ago, and it still boggled her, as an apartment renter who'd never owned a home, that he could plunk down the cash for multiple properties.

She hadn't hesitated for a second when he'd asked, Friday afternoon, if she minded staying in Colorado until Sunday and visiting a few properties. The less time she had to spend alone at home, anticipating this Monday morning, the better. The extra time had been beneficial for Gabe too, as he was making an offer today on the lodge-style home they'd first seen in the window of the real estate office.

Before she was ready, she'd reached the twenty-story building that housed her company along with a handful of others. Martin and Baines had offices on the second through tenth floors.

Once she was in the main-floor lobby, she stopped at a chair tucked out of the way, pulled off her sneakers, and switched them out for the three-inch wedges in her bag. She always felt frumpy wearing walking shoes with her work clothes—mushroom-colored ankle-length pants and jacket with a white camisole this morning—and today of all days, she needed every bit of confidence she could get.

After stowing her sneakers, she stood and skimmed her gaze over the dozen or so people making their way toward the bank of elevators, ensuring the coast was clear. No sign of Raleigh, so she stepped back into the fray.

Her chances of running into him today were fifty-fifty. The company was big enough that, if she was really lucky, she might be able to go days without seeing him. They'd spent so many months seeking each other out, meeting for lunch, or visiting the other's office, and sometimes even working on projects together, that she was no longer sure how often they'd meet up without planning it. Her fingers were metaphorically crossed that she would get through the day Raleigh-free.

One elevator opened and almost everyone got on. Lexie elected to wait for one of the others, as there were additional people already on the first one, coming up from the basement cafeteria and coffee shop, and it was impossible to ensure that her ex wasn't among the crowd with a quick glance in.

Another elevator dinged, and she and a woman she recognized from Accounting greeted each other and went toward the doors as they slid open. A large man strode out, hurrying toward the main door, blocking Lexie's view of the three occupants of the car. She was already stepping in when her eyes met Raleigh's and her lungs stopped working.

She darted her gaze to the right of him and saw two of Raleigh's friends and fellow architects, Jim and Cyrus. They'd been on the wedding guest list.

Time stopped and she froze with what had to be a deer-in-the-headlights expression. The three men stared at her in silence as the doors closed behind her, trapping her.

Her eyes returned to the man she was supposed to be married to, the man whose brown eyes she knew so well, whose clean-shaven jawline was as familiar to her as her own reflection, whose small, almost unnoticeable scar below his right ear she'd run her finger over a thousand times.

What was she supposed to say? She'd been freaking out about this moment for days now, trying to prepare herself for it, and still, she had no idea what to say to this man who'd been a crucial part of her daily life for nearly two years. The man who was looking at her as if he barely knew her. As if he'd never been in love with her or planned to marry her. As if she were merely a coworker sharing the elevator.

"Good morning," he said formally, coolly, then raised his foam coffee cup and took a drink, signaling he had nothing else to say.

"Hi, Raleigh," she said haltingly as her recent past crashed with her current reality in a painful way.

Normally, Jim and Cyrus would have greeted her warmly, as

she knew them well and had worked with them both on a large commercial project recently, but it seemed that the awkwardness permeated the entire elevator and affected everyone.

As the lift started moving upward in its old-building, slow way, Lexie was shaken out of her stupor and turned and hit the button for the sixth floor, where the landscape architects worked alongside IT. She noted that four and eight were lit as well, for Accounting and the design/architect floor.

Never in her life had she felt as awkward as when she turned to face the elevator doors and watch the floors light up in silence with Raleigh standing less than three feet away. And then the doors opened on four, and she was reminded of the saying *never say never* as, once the accountant disembarked, dear Judy Robards from HR stepped on, along with one of the HR interns.

Lexie had spent nearly an hour in Judy's office just two weeks ago, preparing for her marital status change. Judy, who was nearing retirement age and had been with the company for many years, was a wealth of information and a matronly woman who considered the younger employees her brood.

As she and the intern entered the elevator, her face lit up and she nearly pounced on Lexie. "Welcome back, Mrs. Lexie Clarke."

Lexie thought for a couple of seconds she might actually pass out from the embarrassment. Passing out would be a welcome escape from this morning of torture, come to think of it. Sweet baby Jesus.

"Um," Lexie said, and her expression must have tipped off Judy that things weren't right, because the woman's wide smile flipped into a frown of concern in a heartbeat.

"What is it, honey? Are you not well? Did you get sick on your honeymoon?" For seemingly the first time, Judy glanced over at Raleigh and company and her eyes got bigger. "Raleigh?" She looked back and forth between him and Lexie as Lexie tried to find words.

"We aren't married," she finally said, managing to sound matter-of-fact about it if she did say so herself.

Judy gasped and her hand flew to cover her mouth. The

elevator was dead quiet until Judy's gaze jumped to Raleigh again, then back to Lexie, and the metal chain on her glasses jingled. "My heavens. I'm so sorry," Judy said.

Lexie forced a grin and said, "It's okay, Judy."

And maybe it would've been relatively okay, maybe they could've made it the thirty seconds until the elevator let Lexie out at the sixth floor, but Judy's eyes filled with tears, and she still had her hand over her mouth.

"I'm just..." Judy shook her head and the tears spilled over, and Lexie might've been even more mortified than the older woman. "I feel terrible," Judy said in a wavering voice.

Raleigh, who Lexie was starting to want to punch just because, leaned over and touched Judy's forearm. "You didn't know." He stepped back to his side of the elevator, avoiding Lexie's gaze.

The intern shrank to the side and hit the nine button several times even though it was already illuminated, as if maybe that would speed things up, and Lexie was all for it.

In spite of her own bone-deep humiliation, Lexie put her hand on Judy's shoulder and squeezed supportively, wondering why she hadn't gotten a job at a building with modern, fast elevators.

"Do you have a meeting on nine?" Lexie asked somewhat unnecessarily, because the ninth floor was where multiple conference rooms and the auditorium were located.

Judy nodded morosely as she swiped a finger under one mascaraed eye.

Finally, finally, they reached the sixth floor. The elevator stopped, and then it sat there for its usual three never-ending seconds that, today, seemed like a full minute before managing to open its doors.

"Why don't you step out with me," Lexie said to Judy. "I'll get you a tissue." When Judy nodded mutely, Lexie told the intern, "She'll be right up," and then she and Judy exited the godforsaken elevator from the nine circles of hell into a blessedly deserted hallway.

"Mercy, Lexie," Judy said, "I'm such a heel."

Thankful she had something to do besides fall apart, Lexie steered the older woman toward the window at the end of the elevator bank, digging in her bag for a tissue. She pulled one out, handed it to Judy, and reassured her in a quiet voice, "How could you know? What were the chances I would blindly walk onto the same elevator as him on our first day back after we were supposed to be honeymooning?"

What were the chances indeed?

She sucked it up for now, again turning her focus to comforting Judy, aware on some level how whacked that was and yet glad for it.

"I am so sorry to hear your news, honey. What on earth happened?"

Lexie bit her lip against the surge of emotion, then managed, "He called it off."

Judy seemed to have a little more control of her emotions as she pulled Lexie into a hug.

The genuine kindness and concern of this woman nearly did her in, and in a New York second, her own eyes were threatening to overflow with tears, and her throat ached with sadness and loss. She squeezed her eyes shut, willing the tears not to fall, the cries not to escape, and held on to the woman who smelled like coffee and flowers.

A few seconds later, they both straightened, and Judy said, "I better hustle it up to that meeting. Are you going to be okay?"

Wiping the corner of her eye as they walked back to the elevators, Lexie nodded. "I'll be fine. I've got a busy day."

"What a start to the week for you. If you need anything, you just holler." Judy pressed the up button, dabbing under her eyes with her tissue yet again.

"I will. Thank you. Have a good meeting," she said stupidly, in a hurry to exit the area before someone else hopped off an elevator.

She heard the ding behind her as she turned the corner and made a beeline for the ladies' room. It was thankfully deserted, and she took a look in the mirror to see how much repair was necessary. Her mascara was intact, her hair was windblown from the walk but not too bad, and all she really needed to do to her face was add some fresh lip gloss.

She might be hiding everything on the outside, but her insides were a different story. It wasn't quite eight a.m. and she was already a disaster.

After adding a layer of color to her lips, she pulled out her phone and sent off a quick message to Sierra.

SOS. Any chance we can do drinks tonight? Monday SUCKS.

CHAPTER SEVEN

abe considered it a victory that he made it home
Monday evening in spite of the crippling temptation to
join two of his brothers at Clayborne's for dinner—his
brothers who were with their fiancées, Mackenzie and Sierra, *plus
Lexie*.

Drake had come into Gabe's office at quarter after five with
the invitation to join them. Apparently Lexie had had a tough
day at work and had instigated the get-together with the girls.
Drake and Cole had invited themselves.

It had taken every damn ounce of willpower in Gabe to not
go with them. The excuse he'd given Drake was legit—he had
indeed needed to read the report his Employee Incentive
Committee had put together and jot down some feedback and
questions—but it wasn't the whole story. The bigger truth was
that he needed to give himself some physical space from Lexie
before he lost his damn mind.

The past week with her in Colorado had been incredible and
torture at the same time. For twenty-four seven, he'd been straddling a line between being a supportive friend and wanting more
—lots more. Lexie needed his friendship now more than ever,
and coincidentally, all the one-on-one time with her had only
strengthened his more-than-friendship feelings. When she'd

wistfully suggested they stay in the mountains together permanently…

Getting through the report had taken twice as long as it needed to because his concentration was shit, but he'd finished it, sent his feedback, and managed to steer his car home instead of to the Hale Street bar and grill where Lexie and the others were.

Now he sat on the edge of the patio table in his backyard, watching Saint sniff around to find the right place to relieve himself, wondering how Lexie was doing. For her to reach out to the girls and ask them out for drinks said a lot, because it wasn't her usual MO.

He ached to make sure she was okay. She'd texted him around lunchtime to ask if he'd talked to the real estate agent yet. They'd exchanged a few messages, and then she'd had to rush off to a meeting, and he hadn't heard from her since.

Screw it.

As soon as Saint finished his business, he took the dog inside, gave him a thorough ear-scratching, and fed him his dinner. As he hadn't had a chance to restock the refrigerator after his trip, he was going to Clayborne's for a burger—and to check on Lexie.

Twenty minutes later, when he walked up the stairs to the second level of Clayborne's, still in his suit and tie, it was easy to locate his people. They'd scooted three tables together and were loud enough he'd heard them seconds after entering the building. In addition to Drake, Cole, Sierra, Mackenzie, and Lexie, Sierra's friend Hayden was there, as were Sloan McGuire and Micah Sullivan and another couple he wasn't familiar with.

The instant Gabe took in the scene, he was hit with a pang of jealousy so potent he paused in his tracks. All these people were here for Lexie, *with* Lexie, because she needed it, and he'd selfishly chosen to distance himself from her?

He was a dumb fuck in more ways than one.

One look at Lexie and he could tell she wasn't sober, from the dopey grin on her face to the way she leaned on the table as if it was the only thing holding her up. Her hair was tousled and her jacket was slightly askew on her shoulders. She was fucking adorable in all her intoxicated imperfection.

He headed toward the table, realizing her day must've been all kinds of awful if she was in that state, as she wasn't a big drinker and he could count on one hand the number of times he'd seen her truly wasted.

"There's the workaholic," Drake announced above the din as Gabe approached. "About time you joined us."

"That would be Mason," Gabe said, "who's still at the office."

"Of course he is," Cole said. "It's not even dark yet."

Several at the table called out greetings to him, and he returned them.

"Gabe! You made it!" Lexie's voice wasn't overly loud in general, and with all the racket of the bar and the others at the table, it didn't stand out now, except to Gabe. He heard her exclamation loud and clear, and it reached deep inside of him and pulled at him something fierce.

Before he could do more than smile at her, she'd launched herself up and, holding on to the back of each chair on her way, made a path around the tables and ended up at his side. She threw her arm around him and leaned her head on his arm—her head and all hundred pounds of her. He wound his arm around her, as much to support her as greet her, and pressed a kiss to the top of her head.

"Hi, Lex," was all he could manage to say now that she was at his side.

"Hey, Gabe, we're glad you could make it," Sloan said. She was the entertainment manager here at Clayborne's and in on the planning of Mackenzie and Drake's engagement party.

With Lexie still plastered to him, Gabe went to Sloan and hugged her with his free arm, then shook hands with her boyfriend, Micah, who played drums for Steele Hearts, a country band that was currently topping the charts.

"Have you met Lena and Ash?" Sloan asked, pointing to the two Gabe didn't know. He shook his head and moved with Lexie toward them.

"Lena is my BFF and my sister-in-law. My brother, Ashton, somehow suckered her into marrying him, and I'm going to be an aunt in three months."

When the brunette woman turned to shake his hand, Gabe couldn't help but notice her pregnancy on her otherwise small frame. "Nice to meet you, Lena. Congratulations." He moved on to Ash and narrowed his eyes. "Wait a second…you're familiar."

Ash stood up, laughed, and shook his hand. "You a hockey fan?"

"Rampant one." Holy shit. He knew who this guy was. "You're Ash McGuire of the Penguins."

"Formerly. Well, still Ash McGuire. Been retired a couple of years."

"Injury, if I remember right," Gabe said. "So now you live here and have a family. Congratulations. We'll have to talk about the upcoming season sometime. It's looking like it could be a promising one."

"Love to. Finley's going to do great things," Ash said, retaking his seat as Gabe made his way around the table with Lexie still glued to his side, which was more than okay with him.

He poured her into her chair as Sierra, who was sitting next to her, scrambled to move her chair over. As Ash grabbed an extra chair from an empty table, Gabe leaned down and said into Lexie's ear, "You doing okay?"

She craned her neck to look up at him awkwardly, her neck bending as if it were boneless. She sank into a laugh and said, "I'm gooood."

Gabe lowered himself to the chair to her left, and he couldn't help it—he pulled her into him for another side squeeze. As he was helping her to straighten again, because she did need an assist, he noticed Drake raising a brow at him, but he ignored it.

Sloan passed a menu to Gabe, and he glanced at the burger section and ordered when the server came to his side. Talk at the Sloan-Micah-Lena-Ash end of the table centered around babies and country music. The other end, which he couldn't hear quite as well, was focused on wedding talk, with both couples engaged and planning their big days and Hayden deep into helping them. It left him and Lexie in the middle, and when he looked down at her to gauge which conversation she was following, he was pretty sure the answer was neither, based on the way she was circling her finger around the top of her empty martini glass and gazing into it as if it held the secrets of the universe.

"I heard you had a rough day," he said so only she could hear.

"Was a Monday-ish Monday," she said, mushing her words together.

"Work stuff?"

She seemed to consider that for a few seconds, narrowed her eyes, and eventually said, "Raleigh is work stuff now. Nothing else."

"We can go with that. Wanna talk about it?"

"Huh-uh. I want"—the server set his plate in front of him at that moment, and Lexie looked it over—"french fries."

He laughed and told her to help herself, thinking she really didn't understand that he'd give her anything she wanted.

Of course she didn't. He'd never told her.

For good reason.

Having her suddenly single and technically available was fucking him up six ways to Sunday. Over the years, she was frequently involved with a guy, had almost seemed to go from one to the next perpetually, and Gabe had always told himself it was better that way. Then there was no temptation for him to pursue his attraction to her, and thus, no way for him to screw up their friendship.

Over the past almost-year since Raleigh had popped the question, Gabe had been coping, dealing with it, trying to make peace with his gargantuan loss. He'd told himself he would start dating soon, after the wedding, because he didn't want to be alone for the rest of his life. He hadn't been able to see how the hell it was going to work out, but he'd known he had to make it happen somehow.

And then suddenly, in the literal blink of an eye, everything had changed again. Lexie was wrecked over it. Understandably. He himself ached for her loss, her heartbreak, and he couldn't help but think how satisfying it would be to smash Raleigh's mediocre face in. Satisfying but not helpful to Lexie, and that's what had to rule everything. Not his own damn feelings, which kept surfacing and trying to sway him.

The time wasn't right, and for him and Lexie, maybe it would never be right. If so, he'd have to figure out how to deal with that again.

Lexie had devoured at least half his fries as Hayden, who owned Henry Interiors down the street, regaled the whole table with a story of one of her current design clients, an elderly society woman who insisted on a design theme for her entire house that consisted of the color purple and cats.

"They just don't go together," Hayden said. "There are ways to make purple work and ways to make cat decor work, but together?" She made a pffft sound and threw a hand up. "And she wants it classy, not kitschy."

The whole table was laughing, less about the story than at Hayden's dramatic delivery of it.

"She wants kitty, not kitchsy," Drake quipped.

As Gabe finished the last of his burger with a laugh, Lexie leaned her head on his shoulder and closed her eyes.

"Oh, sweetie," Mackenzie said from across the table. "You're going to be hating life tomorrow."

Lexie didn't even register that she'd become the center of attention.

"How many lemon drops did she have?" Gabe asked.

"Only three, I thought," Sierra said, sounding concerned. "It was probably the tequila sunrise that did her in. Pierce is making them strong tonight."

"That's a lot for a half-pint-sized human," Drake said.

"Not a half-pint," Lexie declared, grinning but not bothering to open her eyes.

"I think I better get you home," Gabe said, pushing his empty plate out of the way.

With some effort, Lexie straightened and opened her eyes. "I'm good."

Sierra laughed gently and said, "You're so not good. But if you get lots of water and sleep, there's hope for tomorrow. It's still early enough."

Lexie groaned at that and glanced at the faces around the table. "Thanks for helping me put Monday out of its misery. I gotta go now."

There were supportive laughs and well wishes around the table as Gabe helped her locate her work bag, hanging from the back of her chair, and threw some cash on the table for their tabs.

He guided her down the flight of stairs and out the side door that opened up on Hale Street. As soon as they were outside, Lexie stopped in the middle of the brick sidewalk, and for a moment, Gabe wondered if she was going to throw up. Instead, she lifted her nose to the air and drew in a deep breath.

"Ahhh, smells amazing!" she said with gusto. She peered across the street, then started heading straight for Sugar Babies bakery. "Cupcakes. We need some."

Gabe grabbed her arm before she reached the traffic-less street. "They're closed, Lex. It's going on nine o'clock."

"The light's on."

"In the back." It was undeniable someone was in there baking something magnificent. "See the closed sign?" He pointed to the window.

Lexie's brows lowered as she stared at the sign, looking slightly incensed, and Gabe smiled to himself.

"Come on, Lexie Lou, let's get you home." The nickname was what his parents had called her when they were growing up. He used it sometimes but only to prevent himself from speaking his private name for her, Sexy Lexie. He couldn't ever let that one slip.

Putting his arm around her, he guided her down the sidewalk to where he'd parallel parked his car as she muttered to herself about cupcake flavors she wanted right that instant.

After helping her into the passenger seat, he jogged around, started the car, watched in amusement as she sat up intently as if to adjust the station on his streaming radio service, but one look at it, and she shook her head and rested it against the headrest, as if it was too much trouble. They listened to a country station for the short drive to her apartment.

As he turned into the driveway of the high-rise building, he glanced over to find her eyes closed, her lips parted just barely, her breaths coming evenly. Looked like he'd be parking in the underground garage and getting her safely up to her apartment and to bed.

All in a day's work for sorry-ass fools like him.

CHAPTER EIGHT

There were times when a guy knew full well he was doing something ill-advised and he did it anyway. Gabe offered his wiser self a mental *cheers* as he scooped Lexie out of the front seat of the Tesla into his arms.

When he stood up, swinging her with him a little awkwardly, she let out a howl of surprise, even though he'd said her name three times when he'd opened her door, trying to rouse her. Luckily she laughed instead of screamed.

"Gabe, whatcha doing?"

"Getting you home, my little drunkard. You were out cold."

"Was only resting," she mumbled. She laid her head on his shoulder and slipped back asleep, or at least to a state where she was vastly unaware of anything around her.

Gabe couldn't avoid breathing in her faint honeysuckle scent or feeling the softness of her feminine thigh beneath his fingers where he held on to her. Of course, he knew her scent well, but the feel of her slender leg wasn't something he normally got to experience. He knew he wouldn't easily forget the sensations of having her so close and vulnerable.

Thank God he'd decided to go to Clayborne's. He knew the girls would've gotten her home or to one of their places, as would his brothers, but this way he could be certain she was taken care of, safe, not passed out in an elevator or choking on half-digested french fries.

Her bag was slung over his shoulder, and when they got to the elevator, he had to stand her up next to him so he could find her key card to activate it. She found her legs, grasped on to his upper arm, opened her eyes, and tried to focus. "Oh. We're here."

He grinned to himself. He'd never in all his years seen her this intoxicated. She was normally cautious with alcohol, happy to have a drink or two, but backed off as soon as she started to feel tipsy, which didn't take much. Her first day back to work must have been stellar for her to consume so much.

Finally, he located the card and summoned the elevator. When the doors slid open, they entered the empty car, with him supporting her to the back wall. She held on to his arm as she took off her heels one by one, then handed them over to him.

"What time is it?" Lexie asked, squinting against the relatively bright light of the elevator.

After stuffing the abandoned shoes in her bag, he pulled his phone from his pocket. "Nine oh seven."

She seemed to ponder that for a couple of seconds. "What day?"

"Monday."

"Oh," she said instantly, as if that brought everything back. "I hated this Monday. So I needed happy hour."

"I'd say happy hour was a success," Gabe said.

"It made me happy," she said with a relaxed grin. The grin disappeared almost instantly. "Tomorrow's gonna suck."

"There are some things we can do to ward off a hangover." Or lessen it. In her condition, there was no way around tomorrow being rough. "The longer you can stay awake and sober up, the better tomorrow will be."

"Voice of experience?" she asked, not quite getting all the syllables in *experience*.

"Been a while, but yes," he said. The elevator stopped at her floor, and they exited as soon as the doors opened. "Coffee, lots of water, Tylenol, shower."

"I loooove coffee," she said with emotion.

"I know you do. You can pick your favorite flavor."

"Caramel vanilla creme," she said with no hesitation.

"Dessert in coffee form," he said as they reached her door. "I'll start the Keurig. You should take a shower."

She let him unlock her door as she leaned on it. He held on to her when he opened it, certain she would've ended up on the floor otherwise.

"You going to be able to stand up in the shower?" he asked.

With an uncharacteristic giggle, she said, "There's a seat."

He flipped on the light in the living room, set her bag aside, and tossed his jacket on the arm of the couch. The apartment was a small box, with the kitchen on the left, open to the living room on the right, with a breakfast bar and stools separating the two. Adjacent to the living room was Lexie's bedroom, and the only bathroom was across from her bedroom door, nestled next to the kitchen.

The decor had always had a feminine, romantic flair to it, with evidence of her love of nature throughout—floral, chenille, and neutral-colored animal-print throw pillows, soft-toned forest-scene paintings over the couch, a polished light wood coffee table with distinctive natural grain patterns. Now, however, some of it was in boxes, stacked by the door to the small balcony, next to a dozen potted plants and trees.

Lexie managed to walk into her bedroom without help, and Gabe headed to the kitchen to start her coffee and fill a tall cup with water.

The coffee was just finishing brewing and he was reaching for a mug from her mug tree when movement at her bedroom doorway caught his eye, and he turned his attention that way. He lost his grip on the empty mug, and it clattered on the granite counter as Lexie froze midway between her bedroom and the bathroom door—wearing nothing but flowered bikini panties, her breasts bare, beautiful, impossible to ignore.

He was stunned stupid for what seemed like several seconds, not moving, not finding any words, not breathing.

"Oopsss," she said as she belatedly crossed her arms over her chest, looking genuinely embarrassed. "Forgot you were here." After a heartbeat, she said. "My body's not the kind guys like anyway."

Before he could unfreeze his tongue and respond, she was in the bathroom, out of his sight, and he heard the door close. He leaned his hands on the counter, supporting his weight, trying to recover.

Wait. What had she just said? *My body's not the kind guys like anyway?*

On what fucking planet?

Her body was goddamn perfect, and he wasn't likely to get that image out of his mind for the next hundred years. Sure, he'd seen her in a swimsuit countless times and done his best not to imagine what the parts under the fabric looked like, for his own sanity and the sake of their friendship. Her breasts weren't large, were barely a handful, but his hands itched to palm them, play with them, pluck the rosy nipples until she was squirming underneath him.

He sucked in a slow breath, trying to re-center himself, and heard the shakiness of it. There was hard proof in his suit pants that her statement was unequivocally false. What kind of poison and lies had the shithead she'd been engaged to filled her mind with?

More importantly, how was Gabe going to get his shit back together and be able to face her as if nothing had happened when she finished her shower? He noticed the water had turned on, and he wondered for a moment if she was sitting on the shower seat while the water flowed over her...

Nope. Wrong direction for his thoughts.

Coffee. Water. Extra-strength pain relievers. He set to work getting the items ready, adding creamer to her coffee, lining them up on the counter. A crash came from the bathroom, and he took two steps in that direction before he heard a laugh and, "'M okay! Hit my elbow," hollered out to him and then a quieter, "Stupid door."

He caught himself smiling and then shook his head.

He'd told her the best thing was to stay awake for a while to sober up, and that was valid, but it'd be easier, safer if he could tuck her into bed, turn the lights off, and let himself out. Go home and take the longest cold shower of his life.

The water turned off and he heard the glass door rattling. The exhaust fan turned on, and then, seconds later, he heard her retching, and all concern for himself vanished. He went to the closed bathroom door and knocked lightly.

"Lex?"

Her reply was more heaving, and he cringed.

"You okay?" he asked, realizing what a dumb question that was.

He heard a faint groan and the clatter of the shower door again but no verbal response.

"Lexie? I'm opening the door."

He stuck his head in the room and saw, with simultaneous relief and regret, that she'd wrapped herself in a fluffy pink towel. She was literally hugging the toilet, her eyes closed. Her hair was dripping wet, as if she hadn't had time to wring it out before her stomach emptied. He went to her side and pulled the strands back, then reached for a second towel and wrung her hair into it.

"Thanks," she breathed out into the toilet.

Her skin was still damp and water was puddling on the floor beneath her. He squatted down behind her and dabbed the towel over her arm and shoulder. Standing again, he searched for a hair band and found one in a drawer. He pulled her wet hair behind her head and awkwardly worked the band around it to keep it out of her face.

"Sssorry," she slurred out.

"Nothing to be sorry about."

"Ssstupid."

"Not stupid," he reassured in a low voice. "Do you feel any better?"

She shook her head slightly.

Gabe rubbed her shoulder, wishing he could take the bad feelings away, then busied himself finding spare towels. A few minutes later, he had both Lexie and the floor reasonably dry, and he lowered himself to sit next to her. As soon as he settled, Lexie leaned forward and emptied her stomach again, and he helplessly put a hand on her back.

When she'd finished and flushed, he located a washcloth, dampened it with warm water, and handed it to her. "Wipe your face down. It'll feel good."

Lexie sat up straighter and let go of the bowl, opening her eyes for the first time since he'd come into the bathroom. They were red and watery. She took the cloth from him and, with both hands, swept it over her face with a groan that sounded more like pleasure than misery.

"Do you think you can stand?"

She handed him the washcloth and nodded. Gabe held on to her shoulders and helped her up, ensuring she was steady before he released her. He eyed the towel she'd tucked into itself under her arm to see that it was secure.

"How are you feeling?" he asked.

Lexie sucked in a slow breath, making her chest and the towel rise. She let the breath out and met his gaze. "So much better."

He smiled and brushed a strand of hair out of her face. "We need to get your hair a little dryer."

She closed the lid of the toilet with a thunk, then plunked herself down on top. "Hair dryer's under the sink."

Gabe located it, plugged it in, and reached behind her to remove the loose band and free her wet hair. It was still wet enough to drip onto her shoulders, so he picked up the towel he'd used on it before and was about to take it to the ends again when Lexie held her hand out.

"I can do it."

He let her, glad to see she was more alert now. It seemed purging the poison had helped.

When they had her hair mostly dry, she stood, still wearing the towel over her body.

"Where do you want your coffee?" he asked, keeping his eyes from dipping to her cleavage.

"In my bed." She put toothpaste on her toothbrush and then

brushed her teeth, leaning her shoulder against the wall as she did.

"You're supposed to stay awake for a while," he reminded. "So you don't feel as bad tomorrow."

Once she'd spit toothpaste in the sink, she said, "I'll stay awake in my bed."

He laughed. "Right."

"I will," she insisted, sounding like a stubborn little kid. She rinsed her mouth out, then wiped it with a hand towel. "If you stay and talk to me."

"In your bed?"

She nodded. "I just need to rest. While we talk."

"You'll fall asleep." And he'd die of temptation.

"Keep me awake." She made her way toward her room.

He hung up the towel she'd used on her hair, refusing to let his brain go to the ways he could keep her awake.

Talking, dumb ass.

Once he'd straightened the bathroom and hung up the damp towels, he glanced into her mostly dark bedroom and saw she wasn't in her bed yet, heard her moving around out of his sight. He went to the kitchen and grabbed the coffee, water, and pill bottle, then headed back toward her room, the light above the stove, behind him, the only illumination in the apartment.

"You decent?"

She didn't immediately answer, but he heard her to the left, still out of his sight, and then she appeared in front of him wearing a satin chemise in a delicate shell pink, with white lace along the neckline and the hem. It wasn't revealing or risqué. The fabric wasn't sheer, her cleavage was hidden, and the length covered everything that needed to be covered. But the vision she made, the sheer femininity of the floral lace and the expanse of skin it did reveal, had his blood heading south and his male instincts pounding through him.

Gabe swallowed hard as he drank in the sight, and then, in an effort to get his head right, he took two steps to her nightstand and set down the water and Tylenol bottle. He turned back toward her with the coffee between them, as if it could protect him, and held it out to her.

"It's cooled enough. Take a few swallows," he said.

She did as he said and let out a throaty *mmm* as she handed the mug back to him. He turned and set it down, and before he could brace himself and turn fully back around, she was right there, reaching up and throwing her arms around his neck. Instinct had him holding on to her sides, the silky fabric a tactile kick in the libido he didn't need, and yet he couldn't make himself let go of her.

"What's this?" he managed in a gravelly voice.

"Just…thank you," she said, peering up at him with those pretty brown eyes.

Before he could respond in any way, she was dragging him down to her mouth and clumsily pressing her lips to his. It was a quick buss, could definitely fall into the friendly category, but before he could reassure himself of that and take a step back, her gaze flitted down to his lips.

Gabe stopped breathing, couldn't seem to move as her lashes rose again and their eyes met, and then she kissed him again, this time not so friendly. This time, lingering. This time, a little moan escaped from her throat, turning him inside out in a flash, and though he knew full well he should, he couldn't make himself end it, couldn't pull away. He couldn't keep himself from responding, kissing her in return, running his hands up her back until his fingers hit her baby-soft flesh above the edge of her pajamas.

He relished the feel of her heated skin, and then, without his brain's okay, his hands trailed back down to her butt and hoisted her up his body so their mouths were better aligned. Her legs wrapped around him and the kiss deepened. She tasted of caramel and sugar, coffee and mint, a conglomeration of sweetness and heaven. He was on the verge of losing every semblance of self-control.

God help him, it was the most overpowering kiss of his life.

And if he didn't end it now, he was going to lower her onto

the bed that was inches away and strip her pajamas off and cover her body with his.

With a profound effort, he ended the kiss and put a few inches between them.

Lexie's eyes fluttered open and met his gaze again. He could practically see the sluggish progression of her thoughts as different expressions crossed her face—pleasure, then confusion, then realization. Her eyes popped wider finally, and she let out a quiet, "Whoopsss. Party foul."

He laughed, and some of the tension lightened. Some of it.

"If there was any doubt you were overserved…" he said. He brushed his finger down the tip of her nose affectionately and then stepped away, deciding the best thing to do was ignore the kiss that had rocked him hard and made him rock hard. "We need to get you sobered up. Want to take your coffee to the couch?"

"In here," she said, and she crawled into her unmade bed and pulled the blankets up.

Climbing into the other side of her bed right now would be the dumbest thing he could do. He knew his limits, and they were currently being pushed to the edge.

"You're going to fall asleep," he said.

"I'm wide-awake." She sounded much more alert than she had at any point since he'd sat down next to her at Clayborne's.

"Take another drink." He handed her mug to her, and she propped herself up on her elbow and complied. When she'd gulped down half of it, she handed it back.

"Happy now?" she said with an adorable, still-not-sober grin.

Loaded question.

"You want me to let you go to sleep?" he asked.

"Want you to sober me up. I don't want to have a hangover."

With another laugh, he said, "You should've thought about that a few hours ago."

"Stay, Gabe. I'm awake. Gonna sober up."

He stared down at her eager, wide-open eyes, thankful the rest of her was hidden under a thick floral comforter, and came up with a solution. After kicking his shoes off, he lowered himself to the floor right in front of her, leaning against the bed and stretching his legs out. He was still there for her but not in her damn bed, unable to see her tempting self without turning around.

It turned out his plan wasn't foolproof. A few seconds later, he felt her fingers burrowing through his hair at the back of his head, just a light, soothing movement that connected them. He closed his eyes and held back any expression of contentment.

"Did you know that Drake and Mackenzie set a date?" Lexie asked. "They're planning a destination wedding in the South Pacific. Also Sloan and Micah got engaged a couple weeks ago. So along with Cole and Sierra, more than half the people at the table tonight are getting married. Not me though."

She sounded sad for about three seconds, then picked back up on the chatter about her friends' wedding plans and engagement party plans and whatever else came to mind, content with Gabe's replies whenever she asked a question. Apparently she hadn't been lying when she'd said she was wide-awake. He paid attention as much as he could, fighting off thoughts of that kiss.

"It seems like they'll all have good marriages," Lexie said after sitting up to drink more coffee. She took several audible swallows, then held it out for him to set back down. "At least they're having sex more than once or twice a month. That's a good sign, right?"

The comment was odd, and he narrowed his eyes in the dim light, puzzling over it. Between that and the bit about her body earlier…

He bit his tongue to keep from asking. As well as they knew each other, as much as they shared, they didn't normally discuss their sex lives, and it was another line he knew he shouldn't cross. But the silence in the room grew, and his curiosity was overwhelming—as was his concern.

"You and Raleigh…didn't?" he finally dared to ask.

"No," she said with zero hesitation. "Raleigh wasn't very into physical affection. He was weird about a lot of things."

"Like what?" he asked, frowning.

"We couldn't spend the night together on weeknights. He

said he slept better alone and needed to be rested for work. The weekend nights we did stay together, it had to be at his place, never mine, and…" Her voice grew quieter and now she seemed to hesitate. "I guess he just didn't find me that appealing."

"That's insane," he said without thinking, straightening at the same time and turning partway to make eye contact. "Lex, you're beautiful. Ninety-eight percent of heterosexual guys would kill to be with you. The other two percent…" He tried to imagine what the hell might prevent someone from being attracted to her, with her pretty, soulful eyes and gorgeous mane of hair, her easy, if quiet, laugh, and her pure-as-gold heart. He shook his head. "The other two percent are on life support or clinically dead."

"Raleigh isn't in either group," she said, her voice somber and matter-of-fact, as if she bought into that prick's worldview, or at least his Lexie view.

"He was all wrong for you." He'd thought it a thousand times, but never had he been more sure of it.

If that asshole had gotten into Lexie's head and made her think she wasn't appealing…

"Or I was wrong for him," she said.

Gabe pulled his knees up and locked his arms around his legs in an effort to staunch the overwhelming need to pull Lexie into him and show her exactly how appealing, desirable, sexy as fuck she was.

"He's an idiot," he muttered through gritted teeth.

When a minute or two had passed with him lost in his thoughts and incredulity, he realized Lexie had gone silent. Her eyes were closed, her face relaxed, and when he strained to listen, he could discern quiet, even breaths.

She was supposed to stay awake for longer, get the rest of her coffee and some water down. He pulled his phone out to see that it was nearing ten thirty.

The way he was feeling, he'd be a bigger idiot than Raleigh Clarke if he woke her up and revved up his own frustration and temptation even more. He stood, watching Lexie to see if she stirred. She didn't.

Only once he was on his way out for the night did he dare to bend down and press a platonic, chaste kiss to the top of her head. Then he slipped his shoes on, crept out of her bedroom, turned off the kitchen light, grabbed his jacket, and got the hell out of her apartment.

When he'd used his key to lock it and stood there by himself in the bright hallway, he didn't feel a damn bit of relief.

CHAPTER NINE

The truth burned at Lexie before she even opened her eyes the next morning.

She'd kissed Gabe.

She had locked lips in a non-friend way with her best friend in the world.

Her best friend, who she couldn't bear the thought of losing.

The idea was more excruciating than the pain in her head or the desert-dryness of her mouth. Tenfold.

Refusing to crack her lids open, she rolled to her stomach, burrowed her arms under her pillow, and full-on hid from reality. Except reality kept working its way into her head in spite of her efforts.

She'd never been that intoxicated in her life, and she vowed she never would be again. Alcoholism was in her genes, and she couldn't live with herself if she ever ended up like her dad, so she normally made sure there wasn't a chance.

A more immediate issue, though, was the memories that filtered through her head. Gabe had taken care of her, from getting her home to holding her hair while she—*cringe*—puked to making her coffee and trying to keep her awake. She was ashamed of all of it, deeply ashamed. While he would likely say it was nothing, because that's the kind of person he was, for her, it was too similar to her childhood, when she was on the other end of it.

And sweet baby Jesus, she was pretty sure she'd flashed him.

Humiliation blazed through her, and she kicked the tangle of blankets off, understanding for the first time what a hot flash must feel like. Pure slice of hell.

She mostly didn't have body image problems. Her metabolism was blessedly fast, and she stayed in shape by running. People called her body type athletic, which was to say, in her opinion, not feminine. When it came to being with a man, she knew her body wasn't sexy. At five one and a hundred and five pounds, she was the size of a child, and her A cups did nothing to convince a person otherwise. One of her exes had told her she had a "little girl body," and she knew it was true.

And she'd showed that to Gabe last night—and basically admitted to him that Raleigh hadn't found her sexy, in case Gabe hadn't made that conclusion on his own.

Maybe she could still do the hiding-in-the-mountain-cabin thing—by herself.

She grabbed her phone to check the time, realizing in that instant she hadn't set her alarm, and yep, she'd overslept. She had exactly twenty-nine minutes to shower, get presentable, and get her butt to work.

First things first, she opened the bottle of Tylenol and swallowed two down with the room-temperature water Gabe—bless that considerate man—had left on her nightstand. As she raced to the bathroom, stripping off her nightgown on the way, she swore to avoid Gabe for the next ten years, minimum.

———

By the end of the workday, reality had set in, and Lexie knew avoiding Gabe would never work. If she was going to be able to live with herself, she needed to apologize.

He'd texted her late that morning to check on her. She'd told him she was fine, had made it into work, and had to rush off to a site check, the latter two of which were true. She was still working her way to fine.

It was nearly six thirty p.m. when she finally finished the longest workday of her life and sank into her Subaru. Thankfully, she was no longer hungover but merely exhausted and perpetually dehydrated. Without starting the car, she considered what to do next. Apologizing to Gabe was at the top of her list, and as much as she dreaded it, she needed to get it over with.

On Tuesdays, he usually went straight to Cole's foundation and got home after seven. She decided to head toward his house and swim while she waited, picking up a ready-to-bake lasagna from an Italian deli on the way. Dinner would be part of her apology.

It'd been a long time since she'd let herself in to use his pool —Raleigh had refused to spend time at Gabe's, and she'd cut down on her time there, as well, in order to keep the peace. But the thought of the refreshing water on this humid evening was hard to resist. She couldn't seem to drink enough fluids to make up for the alcohol last night, but maybe she could absorb it through her skin and start to feel half-alive again. Osmosis, like a plant.

Knowing his smart home would notify him when she used her key to get in, she didn't bother texting him. Saint greeted her at the door, tail wagging, and once she'd loved on him and given him his dinner, she changed into one of the swimsuits she'd left there. She and Saint headed to the backyard, and she dove into the deep end. The cool, refreshing liquid went a long way toward bringing her back to life. She glided to the edge of the pool to watch Saint nose around the yard and to figure out what to say to Gabe when he arrived.

He was, frankly, the most important person in her life. Had been for as long as she could remember. Despite the strength and longevity of their friendship, there were still moments, all these thirty-ish years later, when she felt like the tagalong who was lucky to be in his life. It was hard not to feel that way sometimes, as their friendship had started when he came to her defense against a couple of bullies the very first day of kindergarten.

Lexie had been the shortest in the class, by a lot, and they'd teased her from the moment they'd seen her—until Gabe had stepped in.

Gabe had invited her to his house that day, and she'd been welcomed into the North family ever since. Thank God for that. She'd been included for dinner more evenings than not, had learned to play baseball from Mr. North just like all his sons, had been treated like a little sister by Mason, and had known Cole since he was an infant and the twins, Drake and Zane, since they were newborns. She'd stood beside Gabe at his father's funeral and helped his mom during her heart attack recovery.

Gabe, of course, had always been popular. He was the golden-child type, the kid everyone liked, who got along with the smart kids and the athletes and the popular crowd equally. Lexie had been on the fringes, shy and perpetually self-conscious but accepted on the surface because of her status as Gabe's best friend.

There'd been those who had accused them of being more than friends, and not in a kind way, but Gabe had blown them off, and Lexie had learned to ignore them. Though Gabe was the catch of the school and any girl would be lucky to be loved that way by him, Lexie had never let herself go there in her mind. If she wanted to maintain their friendship, and God, did she, Gabe as anything more than platonic was strictly off-limits.

Drowning in regret, she buried her face in her wet hands as she remembered kissing him less than twenty-four hours ago.

When she pulled herself out of the pool a few minutes later, Saint had sprawled on the covered part of the patio, and she found a text from Gabe that he was on his way home. After a quick dry off, she padded into the kitchen and turned on the oven. She shivered in the air conditioning but refilled her extra-large insulated cup with more ice water and relieved herself in the bathroom, thinking maybe she was finally getting enough liquid.

The oven was ready when she returned to the kitchen, so she put the lasagna in, set the timer on her phone for an hour, and headed outside to the hot tub. Between being in a damp swimsuit in the air-conditioned house and aching from the hangover, she was more than ready for the soothing heat and massage of the jets.

She turned the motor on and slid into the warm water, thinking she wanted a hot tub in her own house someday.

When Saint sat up and cocked his ear, she was sure Gabe had arrived, and her heart picked up speed, her dread like a tangible cloud of steam hovering around her head. Sure enough, after a few minutes, he came out to the patio wearing nothing but swim trunks. As always, she couldn't help noticing how fit he was, how perfectly muscular his chest was, what a pretty picture he made without a shirt. She was human and not blind, and she often gave him a hard time for it, but today she didn't say a word, feeling all kinds of awkward.

This was why you didn't go and kiss your best friend.

Under the surface, she pulled her knees into her and shrank into a ball, as if she could protect herself from the embarrassment.

"Hey, Lex," he said, sounding as if she hadn't made a total fool of herself last night. "It smells fantastic in there," he said, pointing toward the kitchen as he approached the hot tub.

If he could do normal, she could try to do normal.

"Secret family recipe," she joked. "Just not my family."

"How're you feeling today?" He hopped into the hot tub and sat across from her.

"Swell," she said. "Ish. The pool helped. And now the jets. How was baseball?"

"The Johansson twins are a handful some nights, but we finally got some good time in. Connor spoiled them last week. Let them get away with no running at the beginning."

"That sounds like Connor."

While he told her more about the ten-year-olds who required much more energy than she could've summoned today, she half listened, half gave herself a pep talk for the apology she needed to spit out. She leaned her head back on the edge of the hot tub, her eyes closed, wishing she could just relax and find comfort in the familiarity of Gabe's voice.

"You asleep?" he asked after a pause where she must not have responded as necessary.

Lexie shook her head and opened her eyes, then forced out the words. "Gabe, I'm so sorry about last night."

"Stop," he said, waving her off above the water surface. "You were fine."

"Are you kidding me? I was as far from fine as I've ever been."

He shrugged. "You were lit, for sure. Turns out you're a happy drunk. Best kind."

A happy, stupid, kissy drunk was more like it. "I remember what I did. I'm so embarrassed—"

"Don't be."

"And scared it will screw us up."

Gabe pushed himself over to her side of the six-person tub and faced her, up close and personal. "It's not going to screw us up, Lexie." He grasped her hand and turned her slightly toward him. Brushing her wet hair behind her ear, he said, "We go back more than thirty years. One night of a drunken Lexie isn't enough to change all that. Not even close."

She met his eyes, seeking reassurance. It was there in his compelling blue gaze—sincerity, steadfastness, and concern...for her. It was the concern that nearly did her in. No one else in her life had been there like Gabe had, for so many years, in so many ways, and the feelings that evoked in her, that his ability to overlook her bad parts and her stupid moves evoked...

Gratitude was only the beginning of it. Relief, affection, love... Her love for him had been a constant—*he* was her constant—but after last night, she felt almost embarrassed by it, like maybe it wasn't quite as platonic on her end as it was supposed to be. But that would be pointless and detrimental, so she shook the thought off and put a little space between them, forcing a grin to lessen the intensity of the moment.

"Thanks, Gabe." She blew out a breath of relief, in part because he was so understanding and she hadn't ruined them, and in part because she'd increased the space between them.

She debated what she said next. It'd be much more comfortable to skip it, but there were things she needed to say, to confess to. "I also remember what I said about Raleigh."

Gabe was quiet for an extra-long moment. "Was it true?"

"I'm afraid so. All this thinking lately has made me realize that our relationship was really not very good." It explained why she hadn't cried that first night or for several days afterward.

"Based on what you said, he seemed to have a lot of rules."

"I tried to be understanding," she said, thinking this was yet another example of what Gabe had pointed out to her in Colorado. "I didn't want to be too demanding or needy or…" She inhaled deeply, struggling to be open about an uncomfortable, personal topic but needing to put words to some of the thoughts that had been going through her head lately. "I don't know."

"Wanting to be loved isn't needy. Wanting your fiancé to show you he loves you isn't demanding." Gabe's words weren't any louder than necessary to be heard above the whir of the jets, but there was a hard edge to them, a hint of anger. Toward Raleigh, she understood.

"I'm not so sure he loved me," she said, averting her eyes as her body temperature suddenly shot up to a boil again. She rose and sat on the rim, unable to stand the heat of the water for another second. Gabe's gaze swept over her bikini as the cooler evening air hit her.

"He's a fucking idiot then, Lex."

She laughed again, still not feeling any true amusement. "Not the first time you've told me that."

He looked like he was about to say more, but then he just shook his head resolutely, and she knew he considered the failure of her engagement Raleigh's fault, but he didn't have all the info.

With a pivot of her body, she climbed off the edge of the tub and turned the jets off, in need of the quiet.

"The thing is," she said once she'd returned to the side and taken her place on the edge again, "I thought, all those months, that I loved Raleigh. But now?" She shook her head and dared a look at Gabe. He was staring at her intently, patiently. "I don't think I ever did." When Gabe didn't say a word, she continued,

"I don't know how I got it so completely wrong, but after turning everything over and over in my mind for the past week and a half…" She shook her head. Hated to admit this out loud and yet needed to. "It hit me that I don't miss Raleigh so much as I miss having someone in my life."

Gabe opened his mouth, closed it again.

"What?" she said. "Just say it."

He studied her for another few seconds. "I had that thought when we were in Colorado. Of all the things you said about him and your relationship and the breakup, you never once mentioned missing him. You were sad, but I wouldn't call it brokenhearted."

Lexie considered that and said, hesitantly, "I think I was more in love with the idea of being married than I was with Raleigh. It's awful of me. But I didn't love Raleigh, at least not the way I should love the man I'm going to marry."

Gabe turned and rested his elbows near her feet on the edge of the tub. "Not awful. Just honest. You didn't deceive him on purpose."

"No. I wanted to love him. I thought I did." She shook her head. "Which just goes to show how messed up I am. Who gets that wrong?"

"A lot of people."

"I need to make peace with being alone, start moving forward as a single girl, figure out how to be truly okay with it."

"Taking some time to get over a broken engagement seems smart."

"I don't just mean a few weeks or months. I've been"—she searched for the right word—"trying for years. Trying to meet the right guy, trying to make relationships work, trying to find my other half. I'm tired, Gabe. I think I need to quit the guy hunt and spend time on me and what makes me happy."

He put his hand on her ankle and squeezed supportively. "What makes you happy?"

She frowned as it struck her that she needed to ponder that. It also struck her that the temperature outside had dropped a few degrees as the sun had lowered in the sky, and she slid off the hot tub edge, walked over to the towel cabinet, and wrapped a thick towel around her shoulders as she thought about the question. Distractedly, she wandered back to the tub and leaned her butt against it, facing the yard.

"I've got new girlfriends I really like in Sierra and Mackenzie and Hayden and Sloan. That's, like, two or three more than I've ever had at one time."

"Drinking buddies," Gabe joked.

"No." She flicked him in the side of the head without looking at him.

He pulled himself out of the water and went to get a towel for himself.

"I've got my art," she continued. "Someday, when I have a place I can paint, I think I'll create an enchanted forest room. Four walls of murals. Full of lush greenery and bright blooms and maybe even some creatures."

"Like your bedroom growing up."

"But even better. In the meantime, I'm going to stay in my apartment. And redecorate," she decided. New color scheme, new decor pieces, new look that wouldn't remind her of the years she'd wasted with Raleigh Clarke. With a little online shopping, she could transform her place in a week.

Gabe leaned against the tub alongside her, his thigh against hers. "I like that you're looking ahead instead of behind and figuring out how to move on from that guy who didn't deserve you."

She wanted to believe that last part, but she'd be lying if she said she did. However, she merely nodded and said, "It sounds like there's a *but*."

He shook his head. "No *but*. Just...I don't think you should rule out future relationships just because one guy was the wrong guy."

"More than one guy. All the guys."

"So far." He crossed his arms over his chest, making his biceps bulge. "But if the right guy comes along..."

"And how will I know if he's the right guy or just another wrong one?"

"They say you just know," he said lightly, like he didn't quite buy into it.

"Who is *they*, Mr. Kismet?"

Gabe laughed. "Some mythical creatures. Maybe you can paint them in your forest." When the timer on her phone went off, he said, "Please tell me that's food time."

"That's food time."

"You are amazing." He affectionately tugged at a strand of her wet hair. "Maybe I'll ask you to marry me."

"Haha, funny guy. In case you haven't heard, I'm swearing all guys off."

She preceded him into the kitchen, ignoring the fact that her heart skipped a beat at his off-the-wall, non-serious suggestion.

CHAPTER TEN

$\mathscr{B}$y Wednesday evening, the only thing Gabe needed more than a beer was a decent night of sleep, and based on the past two nights, he knew the sleep wasn't happening. So a beer it was, and maybe a sandwich or two to go with it.

When Connor had invited him and Cole to grab a drink after their coaching sessions at the foundation, Gabe had accepted instantly, relieved to avoid his empty, lonely house for an extra couple of hours. Cole had insisted on Sunshine's, the dingy, unassuming bar downstairs from his apartment, because he was meeting Sierra at his place when she finished a party-planning session with the girls for Drake and Mackenzie's engagement. The dimly lit, seen-better-days interior of Sunshine's suited Gabe's state of mind just fine.

The place was about half-full when they walked in, and Connor led them past the pool table to a booth against the far wall. Winona, the straight-shooting, good-hearted owner, was behind the bar, talking to a couple of rough-looking older guys sitting at the counter.

Gabe slid onto the duct-taped upholstered bench across from his cousin and brother and picked up a no-frills menu photocopied on a vertical half sheet of paper. The choices were few—Winona didn't have a fryer or cooking facilities beyond a toaster oven and a microwave, and she unapologetically offered simple sandwiches on bakery bread and chips to go along with whatever adult beverage your heart desired.

Within seconds, the black-haired proprietress slid up to the table. "How's the GQ Crew tonight?" She didn't get a lot of suits here and had adopted the moniker for the North brothers and cousins, who, she claimed, classed up the joint. "No ties. Must be a baseball night," she said, taking in their athletic shorts and Harrison North Foundation T-shirts.

"It's a baseball night," Cole confirmed. "Looks like a busy evening for you."

"This keeps up, I'm gonna have to hire help."

"Might not be a bad idea," Cole said. "I know you think you're invincible and all, but when was the last time you took a night off?"

"Just last month for your engagement party." She crossed her arms over her chest as if she'd, in fact, won that battle and didn't even blink at having only a single night off in a month's time.

"Don's a saint," Cole muttered, shaking his head, referring to her live-in lover.

"Don's a lucky guy and he knows it. You want a draft?" she asked.

"Usual. Sandwich included."

"Beef and cheddar on sourdough, barbecue chips," Winona recited as she turned her attention to Connor.

"Ham and cheese, please, Winona. You have any corn chips?"

"I might. Beverage?"

"Same as him," Connor said, flinging his thumb in Cole's direction.

"I'll have the same as Connor," Gabe said.

Winona turned to him and frowned. "You look like you're having a rough day, hon. You sure you don't need something harder than a beer?"

Gabe shook his head and forced a smile. "I'm good."

As soon as Winona hurried off to make their order, Connor said, "You do look like shit, man. Been trying not to tell you that all day, but since she brought it up..."

"I didn't sleep well is all," Gabe said.

Cole scrutinized him from across the table, and his brows shot up his forehead toward his closely shorn hairline. "Is this related to taking Lexie home Monday night?"

"Wait, what?" Connor piped up. "What happened between you and Lex?"

"Nothing happened between me and Lex," he said automatically, instantly realizing it for the lie it was but not taking it back.

"She was schnockered like I've never seen her before," Cole said. "Gabe had to take her home. Practically carried her out of Clayborne's."

Connor narrowed his eyes at him. Gabe had never admitted to him how he felt about Lexie—what good would that do?—but the way Connor was eyeing him right now, he was pretty sure he, like Mason and apparently Cole, suspected.

Thank God for Winona's excellent timing. She showed up with three cold mugs of beer, slid them around the table, and scurried back to the kitchen to make their food. Gabe buried his face in his mug and gulped down half the cold ale in one go.

"So you took Lexie home and…what?" Connor asked.

"She threw up. She chattered about weddings and engagements and babies." *She flashed me. She goddamn kissed me.* "She passed out."

When both assholes across from him continued to stare him down, he said, "What the hell do you think? I took her home and climbed into her bed and took advantage of her? Lexie? Do you understand how fucked up that would be?"

"You'd never in a million years do that," Connor acknowledged. "Doesn't mean it wasn't a tricky situation. Am I right?"

Hell. *Tricky* didn't quite cover it. Gabe took another swig of beer.

"We'd have to be blind not to know how you feel about her," Connor said.

Winona delivered their double-decker sandwiches along with ice waters and asked if they needed another round.

"This one might need some Johnnie," Cole said, pointing to Gabe.

"I'm good," he said again. He was straddling a fine line. On one side was having a beer or two and avoiding his house for a little longer. On the other was drinking a bottle of the hard stuff and trying to shut his damn brain down from its never-ending Lexie loop.

Once the bar owner was gone again, the three of them ate a few bites in silence. Gabe didn't taste much, didn't really notice what he was eating. He was yet again lost in his thoughts, wondering how much to say. Because while he mostly preferred to handle his shit himself, if he didn't get some of this out of his head, he was going to drive himself fucking nuts.

"She opened up about her relationship with Raleigh," he said after swallowing a bite. "Last night she admitted she doesn't think she ever loved him and he didn't seem like he loved her."

"I always thought he wasn't worthy of her," Connor said. "That just proves it. What's not to love about Lexie?" When Gabe shot him a sharp look, he added, "Like a sister for me, dumb ass."

"That son of a bitch did a number on her mentally," Gabe said. "Made her think she's not attractive or lovable or some shit. Only let her spend the night on weekends. I get the impression their sex life was almost nonexistent."

"Meanwhile, here you are, dying to be with her," Cole said quietly, astutely, somehow without judgment.

Gabe didn't bother to confirm, just shoved another bite in, wishing he could bury that need.

"Seems to me," Connor said as he wiped his hands on his napkin, his sandwich already gone, "opportunity might be knocking."

"What the hell are you talking about?" Gabe set his mug down hard without taking a drink. "She just got dumped on her wedding day. She might not have lost the love of her life, but she lost the future she thought she was going to have. There's no opportunity there beyond being what she needs, and that's a friend."

"I was there when you found out she got engaged, man," Connor said. "It killed you. You going to deny that?"

Gabe merely shoved some chips in his mouth and studied his plate.

Connor had nailed it. Lexie's announcement of her engagement had gutted him. She'd told his family at their weekly Sunday night dinner. Cole hadn't been there but Connor had, along with Mason, Drake, their mom, and their aunt Liz. Lexie had joined them, as she frequently did, but left Raleigh at home, maybe knowing on some level the North family wasn't sold on him. Gabe's mom had handled the announcement with grace and love, he remembered, while he had sat stunned and devastated. He'd done his best to hide his reaction, had thought he'd recovered enough to pull it off. Evidently not.

"I'll take that as a no," Connor continued.

"I'm not going to deny it," Gabe finally admitted.

Lexie's engagement had been crushing and also eye-opening. With that news, the kernel of hope that had nestled in his head, the one that said, for all those years, that while the timing had yet to be right, maybe someday it would be… Yeah, that kernel had been pulverized into dust, and he'd had to accept that he'd missed his chance. He'd had to choke down, over the past nearly year, that more with Lexie was not in the cards. That's what was necessary to be her friend, and being her friend, having her in his life in some capacity, was as vital to him as baseball, his job, and oxygen put together.

"I can't just bulldoze my way in because I want something more from her," Gabe said. "That's the last thing she needs."

"What if," Cole said as he pushed his empty plate toward the center of the old, scarred table, "what she needs is the same thing you need?"

Gabe couldn't deny the lurch of hope in his chest at that thought. But he didn't have to admit it out loud, either, because this wasn't about hope or his happiness. It was about what was best for Lexie.

"What if," Gabe parroted, "Lexie has no interest in being more than friends with me? What if I pursue something beyond friends and she doesn't feel that way about me? Then I've fucked up one of the best things in my life. Pretty sure there's no coming back from that."

"So you're saying you'd rather play it safe and have second-best than take a risk and maybe have it all?" Connor asked.

"What do you think I've been doing for half my life?"

"If that's enough for you, then keep on keeping on," Connor said with a shrug Gabe knew was meant to goad him.

It fucking worked. Because it wasn't enough for him.

The three of them were silent for seconds that stretched into minutes, Gabe lost in his thoughts, turning things over and over. Risks, timing, possibilities.

"You're right. I don't want to lose the chance again," he finally admitted when a loud Kiss classic finished playing on the jukebox. "I want her in my life. As more than a friend. So how the fuck do I do that? And more importantly, when?"

"Time to grow a pair, cuz," Connor said. "Go after what you want."

"My advice?" Cole said. "Don't waste too much time. I fought and fought with myself over Sierra and look where that got me. I hate to think if she'd given up on me and moved on. And all that time I wasted?" He shook his head. "Now that I'm with her and know what I was missing? I wish I wouldn't have wasted a single second."

Decent advice, maybe, but Cole hadn't been dealing with a woman who'd just been dumped on her wedding day. Lexie needed time to recover.

She might've said she was giving up on guys, but he knew how she was wired, and she wanted nothing more than someone to love her fully, completely.

The way he could.

So while these two schmucks might be right about growing a pair and going for it, he had to bide his time. Had to tune in to Lexie so he could discern when she was ready to start the hunt for Mr. Right again. And then he had to take a big-ass risk and let her know how he felt.

CHAPTER ELEVEN

riday after work, while the rest of the world probably went to happy hour, Lexie had come home from the office, shed her work clothes, thrown on some shorts and a tank, and was camped out in the living room chair next to the balcony doors.

The boxes were mostly unpacked, and the place was starting to look different from before, intentionally. The curtains, new ones in a vivid coral to coordinate with the rest of her décor makeover purchases, were wide open to let the early-evening light in, but the heat and humidity were too much to open the doors. Her AC had yet to take a break since she'd gotten home.

Another run-in with Raleigh at work today had her lost in a heap of thoughts she hadn't really entertained before—specifically that her job satisfaction wasn't nearly as high as she'd thought before her failed wedding.

When they'd first started dating, it had been exciting and fun to work at the same company. Now that she dreaded running into him, she found she kept one eye out for him any time she strayed from her desk. But she was beginning to suspect her discontent ran deeper than just trying to avoid her ex.

Her job as a landscape architect kept her challenged with a variety of projects, some more interesting than others, but the most recent promotion had added to her administrative and stuck-in-meetings duties, and even before that, the balance between the technical side, which she was fully competent with but didn't love, and the creative side, which she thrived on, skewed far to the tech side.

Ah, well, it was a good job. Right now, her art was bringing her joy, and she felt lucky to have both. Lucky, too, to have time to herself on a Friday night so she could indulge her creative urges while sipping ice-cold lemonade.

Ever since she'd gotten home from Colorado, she'd been spending more time drawing. She'd started this colored-pencil piece last night, inspired by her honeysuckle-scented body lotion that she'd been using for as long as she could remember. The drawing was of a single close-up honeysuckle bloom with its tubular corollas and distinctive anthers, a ruby-throated hummingbird hovering midair and sipping its nectar. Yesterday she'd sketched the details and started to add color, but today was her favorite part—deepening the layers of colors in such a way that it started to look more like a photograph than a drawing. The outline of the distinctive bloom was dramatic already, and she couldn't wait to add the greenery behind to give the flower even more visual impact.

For the dozenth time, Gabe's question about doing something with her art circled through her mind. She'd been thinking about the bins of finished works from over the years. Some of them were crap that would never see the light of day, but some of them... If she matted them, they might be something she could sell online.

She'd been researching Etsy all week as she had spare time, from how to use it as an artist to what others were selling. Though money wasn't her main goal, the idea of sending her art out into the world piqued her interest. From what she could tell, it was a low-stakes venture that she could do for fun, with no pressure and only opportunity to find some fulfillment her job didn't provide.

Maybe soon she could tell Gabe she was looking into doing more with her "badass art skills." She caught herself smiling at the thought of him. Then she sobered. If she was honest, she'd caught herself thinking about him more than usual the past few days, and she knew exactly why.

That kiss.

That ill-advised, bad-decision, earth-shattering kiss.

That kiss that, in spite of her drunkenness and embarrassment, she could remember all too well. She could still recall the look in his eyes as they'd seemed to drown in each other's gaze. His hands had felt large and strong and hot as they trailed over her cool, silky chemise and onto her skin. His body, when he'd lifted her into it, had been wide and hard and…

Swallowing down on that, she realized her thoughts had once again gotten away from her and she'd stopped coloring, the Marine Green pencil dangling from her fingers. Those kinds of thoughts could start to erode their friendship by making things weird between them.

Forcing herself back to her project, she took the pencil to the hummingbird's back, varying the pressure to get a bolder hue in some places and to blend in others. As she set down the Marine Green in the pencil tray on the end table and searched for a complementary gray shade, a knock at the door startled her.

When she brought her focus to the room around her, setting the lap desk and drawing on top of the pencil tray, she realized the natural light had faded significantly. As she hopped up to answer the door, she checked the time and was shocked to see it was after seven thirty.

There was a distinct, inappropriate jolt in her chest when she saw Gabe out the peephole. That was what thinking about kissing him did, and she needed to ban those thoughts permanently. After giving herself a moment to breathe in and re-center, she opened the door with a welcoming smile.

"Tell me you haven't eaten yet," he said in greeting, lifting a plain brown carryout bag.

"I haven't eaten yet," she said, identifying the aroma as Thai food. "And you're not only the best friend in the world but possibly psychic as well."

"I do my best," he said, flashing her a smile as she let him in. "Sorry I didn't text first."

"You know you're welcome anytime."

Before Raleigh, they'd not hesitated to drop in on each other without warning. Raleigh's dislike of Gabe had made that ill-advised.

"Isn't it your volleyball night?" she asked.

He played on the North Brothers league teams, both volleyball and softball, and volleyball had been on Fridays in the summer months for as long as she could remember.

"The other team canceled. Which is just as well, because we need to celebrate." As he set the bag on the dining table, he looked up at her, beaming. "The lodge is mine."

"The lodge? In Colorado?"

"I got the call less than an hour ago. We finally reached an agreement. Closing will be in about a month."

"Congratulations!" She threw her arms around him, genuinely happy for him. Laughing, he hugged her and spun her around.

"I loved it so much when we went through it," she said, making a point of pulling away, out of his tempting arms. With a final squeeze of both of his hands, she stepped toward the table, then busied herself opening the bag and taking out the containers one by one while Gabe got plates from the kitchen cabinet.

"I'll need help furnishing it," he said as he handed her a plate. "The previous owners are taking everything. That's a shit ton of square footage to fill."

"Of course. I'll do what I can, but for a place that big, have you thought about hiring Hayden Henry? I bet she's better at mountain-lodge style than I am."

"That's a good thought. I'd still want you involved though. I trust you."

The statement warmed her more than it should, and she told herself it was relief that she hadn't screwed up that general trust by being drunk and stupid on Monday evening.

One by one, she opened the containers, verifying he'd gotten their usuals—drunken noodles, which was her favorite, pad Thai, and red curry with chicken. They filled their plates family-style, and Gabe headed toward the couch. On the way, he veered to the chair in the corner and the end table where she'd left her honeysuckle work in progress.

"Wow," he said, standing over it, his head tilted at an angle. "That flower looks almost like a photo. That's incredible, Lex." After studying it for a few more seconds, he went to the coffee table, set his plate down as he sat on the couch, and leaned over it to dig in.

"It's not done yet," she said unnecessarily. She carried her plate to the near end of the couch and curled her legs under her, her dinner balanced on her lap. She took a bite of drunken noodles, closing her eyes to evaluate the spiciness level. "Definitely a four tonight."

Gabe sampled some noodles from his own plate, blinking as the flavors likely exploded on his tongue. "A five bordering on cook-had-a-fight-with-his-girlfriend level."

Lexie laughed at the familiar dialogue. They both liked spicy, but her tolerance was higher—or, as Gabe said, her taste buds were deader—and they never agreed on where on the spice scale of each dish fell.

As she scooped up a bite of pad Thai to give her tongue a break, she worked up the nerve to ask some business questions. She could research herself, but Gabe had the knowledge she needed. Her hesitancy was in speaking the words out loud, because that would take her one step closer to going for it.

"What would I have to do to set up a business to sell some of my artwork?" she finally asked when her mouth was empty.

Gabe set his chopsticks down and angled a look of surprise in her direction as he chewed and swallowed. "Really? You're thinking about… What are you thinking about doing?"

"Nothing major," she insisted. "Just setting up a shop online. Kind of for fun. But I thought it would be smart to have a business set up. Make it official. Wouldn't that be easier for taxes? I mean, assuming I ever sold a thing?"

"You'll sell," he said with more confidence than she felt, and then he launched into LLCs and EINs and a host of other uncomfortable business setup topics, explaining what he'd done when he started his real estate investment company. "I can help you.

It's not as difficult as it sounds. Pretty easy, when you get down to it."

"Do you know much about Etsy?"

"I bought my mom a teakettle on Etsy once," he said with a grin.

"Helpful."

"Actually, I think I know someone who does a lot of business online with her photography. Sierra's soon-to-be sister-in-law Asia."

"Asia from Clayborne's?" she asked of the pretty blond assistant manager who sometimes waited tables when they were swamped.

"That's her. You should definitely pick her brain."

"I will." She would text Sierra to see if she could get the name of Asia's online shop to take a peek. "I was thinking about choosing a dozen or so pieces to start with. Post them so I can see how it works, how much time it takes, what's involved. A big challenge will be getting good photos of my work."

"And maybe Asia could help with that," Gabe said.

"Excellent idea. I might have to hire you as my chief operations guy. But the pay is not competitive."

"I'll help you however I can. You know that."

An hour and a half later, Gabe had indeed helped her locate the online forms for setting up a business. She'd filled them out and paid the fee, and before she could even think too hard about it, she was a business owner.

Riding the excitement from that milestone, she'd dragged out the plastic bins from under her bed, where she stored years' worth of artwork, some in colored pencil, some in watercolor. The vast majority were nature-oriented, some of them realistic, drawn from her deep knowledge of botany, and others were fantastical and completely make-believe.

She and Gabe were in her bedroom, he on the floor with a large, shallow bin in front of him and Lexie on top of her bed, sorting through a deeper container. They'd decided to choose twenty pieces, and so far, they had fourteen that were definite yeses and another ten that were maybes.

"These," Lexie said, perking up as she neared the bottom of her bin, riffling through the last few sheets of sketch paper, markedly different from the professional grade she'd switched to sometime in her teen years. "These were some of my very first nature drawings. I sketched them sitting in my tree fort when I was probably six or seven years old. They're what gave me the idea to paint my bedroom walls back then."

Fort was a bit of a misnomer, as it had been crafted by nature, an old cedar tree that hadn't been cared for for decades. The heavy lower branches had grown downward, creating a crawl-space near the trunk, where Lexie had been able to sit up straight. She'd spent many an hour in the refuge of the fragrant evergreen branches and had eventually taken to sketching the view.

"Where it all started," Gabe said, studying the pieces she held up. "Your talent was raw then but still there."

Lexie didn't see talent in those early attempts, but what she did see was a little girl searching for an escape from a lonely house, a lonely homelife. She wasn't sure if she'd been born with some kind of innate artistic talent or just spent so many hours at it that she'd honed some skills.

"Lex? What's this?"

She tore her focus from her earliest drawings to see what had Gabe's voice going quiet, almost reverent.

"Oh." She put a hand to her chest and sucked in a breath, as if the colored-pencil drawing had made a physical impact. Setting everything aside, she slid to the floor and kneeled next to Gabe, taking in the image.

"Is that my mom's chair?" he asked.

Surely he didn't need to ask. The slate-blue Adirondack chair with fading paint had been on their patio for decades now, repainted countless times but always slate blue. In the drawing, a wooden bat was propped up against the chair, and a baseball mitt lay on the concrete beside it. Hanging from the opposite chair arm was Mr. North's red St. Louis Cardinals trucker hat, worn and well loved.

Lexie couldn't help smiling at the memories that rushed in as she nodded. "That was a big day for me. It was the very first time your dad invited me to go to the baseball field with you and Mason. That's the day he taught me how to swing a bat and hit a ball."

With a reminiscent smile, he said, "I remember it. You were so determined to do everything he said and make him proud."

"It wasn't every day I had a former pro baseball player give me lessons," she said. "Your dad made me feel like I was a part of your family. All the time, but especially that day. He was such a good human being." Her voice had gone thick with emotion, the joy evoked by the memory mixed in with the sadness that he'd died so young.

"Yeah." Gabe's voice was heavy with similar emotions. "You know he was buried with that hat?"

When she glanced up at him, his eyes were damp. Lexie entwined her arm with his, drawing him into her side, resting her head on his shoulder for a moment. "I remember he was buried with a hat, but I didn't know it was that one."

They sat there for a long moment, staring at the drawing, wrapped up in the memories, until Gabe seemed to snap out of it.

"Is this a yes for online?"

Lexie shook her head. "This one I'm keeping."

Once he'd flipped through the remaining few pages in the bin, she put it on the top of the stack to figure out what to do with it later.

It only took a few minutes longer for them to narrow down the selections to twenty. It was nearing midnight, and as they'd both offered to help Sierra and Cole move into their new home tomorrow, they needed to sleep.

As Gabe gathered the bag of trash from their dinner to take out with him, Lexie congratulated him again on buying the mountain lodge.

"I'll probably fly out for the closing," he said, "and to take possession. You should come with me. We can get organized on furnishing it, see what we're dealing with. I'd like to have it ready to stay in by fall."

"Give me some advance notice and I might be able to take a

couple of days of PTO," she said, hoping she could make it work. At the door, she hugged him like she usually did, keeping any improper thoughts at bay.

"Want me to pick you up in the morning?" he asked.

"If we can grab some pastries on the way."

"Only way to do a move," he agreed. "See you about seven thirty."

"Night, Gabe."

As she closed the door, she reflected on the evening with him. Not only had it been productive but it had been comfortable. Nearly back to normal, both between them and in her mind.

Nearly.

CHAPTER TWELVE

exie wasn't an overly spiritual person, but sometimes she couldn't deny when the universe was sending her a signal.

Like today, for example.

Today, that signal came loud and clear in the form of Asia from Clayborne's. When Asia and Jackson, her fiancé and Sierra's brother, had shown up at Sierra's apartment this morning to help with the move, it had perked Lexie up like her coffee couldn't. Lexie had promised herself she'd look for an opportunity today to ask Asia about her photography business.

The entire North clan, cousins Connor, Logan, and Miranda included, had turned out to help, as had Sierra's siblings and their significant others—Hunter and Kennedy in addition to Jackson and Asia. Mrs. N, Liz North, and Geraldine Fleming, the clan matriarchs, had been charged with supplying lunch and dinner, which served the purpose not only of feeding the fifteen or so people who were doing the hard labor but also of keeping the older generation from joining in on the hard labor. After Mrs. N's heart attack last October, her pack of big, overgrown boys made sure she barely lifted a finger anymore.

With all the people and all the chaos of first emptying Sierra's apartment on Hale Street and then cleaning out Cole's place above Sunshine's, Lexie hadn't had the chance to catch Asia in a small group—until now.

Now it was early evening, all the couple's belongings had been transported to the new-to-them hundred-year-old farmhouse-style home on the edge of the city, and the two North moms and Geraldine had just left after serving up a huge quantity of spaghetti and meat sauce along with garlic toast.

Lexie, Asia, Kennedy, and Sierra had decided to work for another hour or so on the kitchen before quitting. Mackenzie, Hayden, and Miranda were upstairs unpacking linens and towels, making beds, and setting up the bathrooms so Sierra and Cole could shower before collapsing into bed if they so desired. Some of the guys were installing appliances, and others were assembling various pieces of new furniture. Tito, Cole's black-and-white cat, was wandering the house, nose going full tilt, as if he was trying to figure out what had happened to his world.

As Lexie and Asia unpacked boxes, Sierra and her sister figured out where to store everything they unloaded.

"Question for you, Lexie," Asia, who wore cantaloupe-colored capri-length sweats and a periwinkle tee, said as she pulled tape off a medium-sized moving box. "Are you and Gabe involved?"

Sierra let out a quiet laugh from the other side of the island, and Lexie shook her head, endeavoring to act nonchalant. "Nope. We've been best friends for years."

"You're not the first person to ask," Sierra said, and Lexie remembered the night not too long ago when both Sierra and Mackenzie had questioned her.

"I just wondered because you showed up together before eight a.m. and…" Asia shrugged.

"And let's be honest. He treats you like a goddess," Kennedy said as she unwrapped some canisters from white packing paper.

"What?" Lexie said with a self-conscious laugh. "He's thoughtful but—"

"The man came in first thing this morning and made sure he set a lemon poppy seed muffin aside for you because he knows that's your favorite," Asia said, her eyes sparkling, hands on her hips as she gaped at Lexie between unpacking items. "You were barely even up the stairs yet."

Lexie waved the comment away. "It's just the kind of guy he is. He's unselfish to an extreme and has looked out for me since kindergarten."

"And treats you like a goddess," Sierra repeated.

"Maybe you should give him a chance to be more," Kennedy said carefully. "They don't grow 'em like that every day."

Lexie thought for half a second about confessing that she'd kissed him just days ago—and that it hadn't ended well. It would surely end all the *are you guys a thing* talk. But she bit down on the words. Sharing such personal info didn't come easily. As someone who'd not had close girlfriends until Kara in college, she didn't have a lot of experience baring her insecurities. It didn't get much more embarrassing than kissing Gabe when she was drunk—unless she counted getting dumped an hour before her wedding ceremony.

She'd had enough mortification for one lifetime, so instead, she smiled, reiterated that they were just friends, and changed the subject as they returned to unpacking full steam.

"So, Asia," Lexie said, "I heard you're a photographer?"

"I am, yes," Asia said.

"A gifted one," Kennedy said.

"Aww, thanks," Asia said humbly.

"What kind of photos do you do?" Lexie asked, relaxing a bit now that she wasn't the one being questioned.

"I do what's called fine-art photography. I take photos and manipulate them to create art. As opposed to, say, a portrait photographer or a landscape photographer or a photojournalist, who all use a camera to capture what's in front of them. I do that and then mess with it."

"Intriguing," Lexie said, meaning it. It sounded like they might have even more in common than she'd thought. "So you might take a picture of a flower, but then you alter the color or the lighting or something?"

Asia pulled out a coffeemaker and set it on the island and

nodded. "Exactly. A lot of my pieces are black-and-white with a single item colorized."

"I have one of them," Sierra said as she removed packing paper from assorted glassware. She glanced toward the dining room and the great room and shrugged. "Somewhere in this mess. She took it on Hale Street, actually, on the brick sidewalk. It's a black-and-white shot looking down the empty sidewalk, where a purple umbrella is sitting upside down, open, on the bricks."

"Ooh, maybe we'll come across it before the day's over," Lexie said as she pulled a stack of wrapped dinner plates from the bottom of a box. They were making good time between the four of them. "So you have a store online?"

"I do. I have an Etsy store as well as a website. I've been able to cut down on my hours at Clayborne's because my photography business is building."

"That's exciting," Lexie said, "and encouraging. I...set up a business last night. Well, Gabe helped me. Because we're friends and that's what he does," she threw in before they could make a big deal of it. "I formed an LLC and was thinking I might start an online store for my artwork." She held her breath, waiting for their reactions, nervous. Not a lot of people knew about her art, and it was a little freaky to put herself out there.

"Do you do photography too?" Kennedy asked.

Lexie shook her head. "I draw and paint. Some watercolors, but colored pencils are my favorite. I do a lot of nature stuff."

"I'd love to see it sometime," Asia said.

"Same," Sierra said. "I had no idea you're an artist."

"You're a landscape architect by day, right?" Kennedy said.

"I am."

"Are you wanting to go full-time with your art?" Asia asked.

"Oh, no. I mean, I don't think so. My job is good. I went to five years of school for it. I just want to do a little more with my art, see if it catches anyone's eye. If not, no big deal," Lexie lied. If no one bought anything ever, she'd be more than a little crushed. She straightened from the box on the floor and gathered her nerve. "I, um, have some snapshots of the pieces I thought I'd start with on my phone. Not good photos, mind you. I took them last night to keep track of which ones I want to mat and put online."

"Oh, let's see," Asia said, popping up from the box she'd been digging in.

With a stronger round of nerves, Lexie dug her phone out of the pocket of her denim shorts. Wiping her hands together to dust them off, Asia came around the boxes to Lexie's side, and once Lexie had swiped to the first one, she handed her phone to Asia.

"Try not to cringe at the photo quality. I was hoping to ask you for advice on how to get good enough shots to put them online. If you guys think I could sell any." Lexie bit her lip and stuck her hands in her back pockets to keep from fidgeting.

"Wow." Holding the phone, Asia turned and leaned against the island, still studying the first one, which was a rendering of a lilac branch and bloom. "This is…paint? It looks like a photo."

"That's colored pencil," Lexie answered.

"It's so realistic I can almost smell it," Asia said, shaking her head. "You've got some serious talent, my friend."

"Thank you," Lexie said, finally allowing herself to exhale.

Kennedy and Sierra hurried over to steal a peek.

The realistic drawings were first—the lilac, a single poppy bloom with an unopened bud beside it, a lush light pink peony, and others.

"Lexie, these are stunning," Sierra breathed after a few moments of silence. Her reaction to the trio of zinnias was a gasp. "My god. You drew that? With colored pencils?"

Feeling lighter, Lexie laughed. "Yes, ma'am."

Kennedy was quiet while all three of them swiped through the realistic ones and into the whimsical pieces.

"These are completely different and yet still fantastic," Asia said. "They could illustrate a children's book."

"God's truth," Sierra said.

Kennedy's eyes had narrowed and she looked thoughtful. "You have two distinct styles there. Which one is your preference?"

"I don't know," Lexie said slowly. "I started with the realistic ones when I was a kid. I drew everything I could find outside, and nature interested me more than man-made things. Flowers, especially, and leaves, as you can see. After several hundred drawings on paper, I got the idea to paint a mural on one of my bedroom walls, and it started out realistic, with vines and leaves and flowers and stems everywhere. By the time the wall was filled with plants, I decided it needed some critters and different colors and added insects and butterflies and…well, the one wall grew to four, the critters expanded to include fairies and their houses and hideaways, and now I guess it just depends on my mood."

The last shot on her phone was the one she'd drawn in Colorado, of the mountain-chalet-style fairy house surrounded by greenery.

When Asia finally handed her phone back, she said again, "Wow. Yeah. You can sell those. Whatever became of the four-wall mural?"

"It was in my dad's house, which I sold when he died." She'd had no attachment to the house—except for the mural. No warm memories of holidays or family meals. No reason to hold on to the place. Even the mural hadn't swayed her. While she loved it and had found so much refuge in her indoor fairyland forest, it was bittersweet, painted during the loneliest years of her life, and she'd hoped someone else would find value and serenity in it instead. "You know, I think I still have photos of it."

She flipped way back in years on her photo collection, to the time period when she'd sold her dad's house and had photographed each of the four walls in detail, to document them for herself. Finally, after endless scrolling, she found them and passed her phone around.

"Imagine this kind of thing in a nursery," Kennedy said.

"What?" Sierra whipped a look toward her sister. "Married for less than a year and already you have babies on the mind? You?"

"I don't have babies on the mind," Kennedy said with an odd expression. "But can you imagine it? Even if you only did one wall… I think a lot of moms-to-be would love the idea. You could market that."

"Kennedy's a marketing consultant," Asia said. "She's helped me a ton."

"And me," Sierra said. "She does the marketing for my remodeling business too."

"Impressive," Lexie said. "You do marketing for two-thirds of the room." She laughed. "Maybe three-thirds one day if I get that far. I'm overwhelmed and don't know where to start other than slapping these"—she pointed to her phone—"up online. Once I can figure out how to photograph them. Do you have any tips?" she asked Asia.

"Hundreds. Or I could just do it for you for a bargain and teach you along the way. The key thing is lighting. Maybe eventually we can promote each other online."

"There's all kinds of opportunities like that on Etsy," Kennedy said, "and some basic things to do during setup that will optimize your visibility and help to get sales."

It sounded like a foreign language, and Lexie's enthusiasm shrank while her doubts rolled in. What was she doing, really? A business? A business had to be successful to survive, and she had no idea how to make a business successful.

"You look like you're going to throw up," Sierra said.

"I might." Lexie returned her phone to her pocket. "I'm not a businessperson. Just a girl who likes plants and colored pencils." She laughed at herself to cover her nerves. Somehow this was easier to talk about than Gabe, but still uncomfortable. She'd been a lone wolf for so long that, now that she'd started to connect with these girls, especially Sierra and Mackenzie, she was realizing just how much she kept to herself. How much Gabe was right, not that she'd rush to him and admit it. She wanted to get better at opening up.

"And a girl who can rock the hell out of a huge technical landscape project and who has some serious art chops," Sierra said with conviction.

"The business end of art is intimidating," Asia said. "I get it. But you're in a great position. You have a full-time job and don't have to pay the bills with your art, right? So for as long as you choose, it's low-stakes financially."

Lexie let out a breath. "You're right." She bent down to reach into the box again and pull something else out, and Asia came up alongside her. Lexie rose and set a wrapped item on the island.

"Something that helped me when I took that first leap was breaking it into baby steps," Asia said. "If you think about running a successful business and all the things it entails, it's overwhelming. But if you think about doing baby steps, like establishing your LLC, picking out your first products, taking the pictures, setting them up online, those are less scary and all you need to worry about right now."

"And you've already done two of those." Kennedy made a sweeping gesture, complete with sound effect, of drawing two large checkmarks in the air.

Lexie busied herself unwrapping the item she'd set down, a toaster, as she worked at setting aside her doubts. "So next up would be photos, and you'll help me with those?" she asked Asia. "I'll pay you for your time."

"In a heartbeat. Discounted rates," Asia said.

"And if you want help setting up your online store, writing the descriptions, incorporating the best search terms, I'm your girl," Kennedy said.

"Yes, please," Lexie said, feeling less intimidated knowing she had these competent women to help her. "You guys... I never expected this. You're inspiring. As exhausted as I am, I have half a mind to go home tonight and get to work."

"That's crazy talk," Gabe said as he wandered into the kitchen. Parking himself behind Lexie, he rubbed her shoulders, massaging some of the sore muscles from all the lifting earlier, drawing an *ahhh* out of her. "How are you girls doing in here?"

"Making progress," Sierra said as she looked around. "We've unloaded a half dozen boxes and put the stuff away pretty quickly. Only a hundred or so to go."

"Drama queen," Kennedy said. "There's maybe twenty kitchen boxes max. And we've got a good start on the things you'll want tomorrow—plates, glasses, toaster, coffeemaker. Really, what more do you need?"

"Fresh-baked muffin delivery from Sugar Babies?" Sierra's brows rose in a plea to her sister, who was part owner of the bakery.

"Maybe if you still lived down the block." Kennedy shrugged as if to say, *Tough luck.*

"Are you guys done for the day?" Lexie asked Gabe, still relishing the feel of his strong fingers digging into her shoulders with just the right pressure.

"Hunter and I finished assembling the last of the shelves. Jackson is just about done with the desk. Cole and Mason are finishing up with the washer and dryer. And Drake… I suspect he disappeared to find Mackenzie."

"Those two are either adorable or nauseating," Sierra said.

"You have no room to talk." Kennedy rolled her eyes, grinning at her sister as she broke down an empty box.

"I'm thinking that, as soon as you're done here, we should go for some ice cream," Gabe said to Lexie.

"Mmm," Asia said. "This is a good man." She bobbed her eyebrows at Lexie, making her laugh.

"He knows how to treat a girl," Sierra added.

"Like a goddess," Kennedy chimed in.

"So is that a yes?" Gabe said.

"Have I ever in my life said no to ice cream?" Lexie asked, moving away from him reluctantly. She hated to end the shoulder massage, but she wasn't pulling her weight while the others kept working. Besides, she wanted to get to the ice cream.

"I'll go see if the guys need any more help. Let me know when you're ready."

"Just a few more minutes," Lexie said.

"Let's finish the boxes we have open and call it good for the day," Sierra said.

"Be back in a few then," Gabe said as he headed down to the basement.

When Lexie stood again with two serving bowls in her hands, the other three were staring at her with wide, teasing grins.

She set the bowls on the island, flustered. "Oh, no. You guys are engaged, married, in love, and crazy! Just erase all those thoughts from your heads right now," she said, laughing.

"Mmm-hmm," Sierra said.

Kennedy added, "Like a goddess."

CHAPTER THIRTEEN

The following Friday evening, as Gabe sped home after the weekly NBS volleyball game, he tried to tell himself Lexie had nothing to do with him skipping dinner and beer with his team. Tried to convince himself it was just that a thunderstorm was threatening and it was smarter to come home.

It didn't work.

Lexie had everything to do with it.

He let out a breath of relief when he saw her Forester in his driveway as he turned down his street. After pulling past her car, into the garage, he shut the door behind him and sat there for a moment, trying to get his shit together before he went inside.

One brief, well-intended conversation with Connor after the first set at volleyball was all it had taken to send Gabe into an all-out panic.

"I saw Lexie today," Connor said as they walked from one side of the net to the other on the outdoor court at Jimmy's Sports Bar. "She was at Cadence having lunch. With some guy."

Gabe somehow didn't slow his step even as his goddamn heart felt like it stopped beating.

"She was dressed professionally," Connor continued, "so I assumed it was a business lunch, but then when she got up to leave, he stood and they hugged."

"Hugged? Who the hell was she hugging?" Gabe couldn't quite

believe she would go on a date so soon after Raleigh, but a hug was not business.

Connor shook his head as he wiped sweat off his neck, then tossed the sport towel to the ground next to his water bottle. "No idea. They were all the way across the restaurant, so I couldn't hear anything and I didn't know the guy. And then she was out the door."

"Did he go with her?" Gabe asked.

"He stayed and paid the tab. I'm sorry, man. I thought you'd want to know if there's some dude homing in on your girl."

Gabe had forced himself to shrug it off—at least on the surface—and finish the rest of the match. Once they'd claimed their victory, which had unfortunately taken all three sets, he'd checked his phone as he, Connor, and Drake were heading toward the bar to order food and beer. His security system had sent a message that Lexie's key had been used for entry to his house. He'd made a snap decision, and here he was.

"Calm the fuck down," he coached himself out loud. "You don't know that it was a date, and even if it was..."

He shook his head, yet again confused, because Lexie hadn't said a thing about being ready to date yet or meeting someone new. The last he knew, she'd sworn off men forever. Of course, he hadn't talked to her as much as usual this week. They'd both been busy, he with his work and sports and she with her new business undertaking on top of her job. He knew she'd met with Asia to get some professional photos of her artwork, and she'd been hard at work getting all the pieces posted. But beyond that, he felt out of touch with her.

He'd never liked feeling out of touch with her, but if there was another man involved, he hated it even more. If he'd missed his chance with her yet again...

Fuck.

Sitting here wasn't doing a damn bit of good, so he climbed out of the car, shut the door, and headed inside, reminding himself the whole way to reel it in.

When he opened the door, Saint showed up, but it took a few seconds, as he came from...one of the extra bedrooms? Where was Lexie?

"Hey, boy," Gabe said distractedly as he rubbed the dog's head. "You got company? Where's Lex?"

Saint's wagging tail told him she wasn't in danger, and his fear dissipated but his curiosity did not. He set his keys, wallet, and phone on the kitchen island and headed toward the hall to the spare bedrooms. He found her in the doorway of the middle bedroom, the room next to the one where she kept swimsuits and clothes.

"Lex?"

She startled as she turned and saw him, and he realized she had earbuds in, which she promptly removed and stuck in the pocket of her shorts.

"Hey. What are you doing here?" she asked, her hand going to her chest as if to calm herself.

He let out a half laugh. "I live here."

"It's Friday night. Volleyball. You never get home this early."

That was true normally. Midnight would be an early night. It was a weekly tradition that everyone who showed up for their games, usually ten to fifteen people, stayed, ate, drank, socialized. Sometimes others from work joined them.

"I saw you were here and wondered what was going on." Partially true.

"It was so hot and humid," she said as they walked toward the great room. "I needed a swim. Then the wind picked up and I got out and checked the weather and saw we're under a storm watch."

"And you didn't want Saint to be alone during a storm," he said, grinning at one of their inside jokes. Lexie was the one who hated storms, not Saint.

With a sheepish smile, she crouched down and hugged the giant gentle beast. "Poor dog would be terrified."

"You know you're welcome anywhere in my house, but what were you doing in the extra room?" He had a mental flash of her waiting in his room for him, in his bed, wearing nothing but sheets...

"Oh." She sat on the floor next to the dog, her back against the inside corner of the L-shaped sectional. "I was looking at your walls. You and the girls got me thinking about murals, and I'm itching to try one."

"And you need a canvas," he said as he stepped toward the kitchen part of the open-concept living area to check Saint's bowls.

"I fed him," Lexie said, which he'd figured, otherwise the dog wouldn't have been content to lie next to her. "I obviously can't use the walls in my apartment, so yeah."

"What kind of mural are you wanting to paint?" he asked as he lowered himself to the edge of a cushion on the opposite end from her, anything but relaxed.

"I'm open to trying anything. I'd just like to start building a mural portfolio in case I eventually decide to market that service. I could paint over it when I'm done, once I've had Asia shoot photos of it, so you wouldn't be stuck with a nursery wall in your spare bedroom."

"No."

"No? To a mural? Or…?"

"Well, no to painting over your artwork, first off." An idea sparked, and he narrowed his eyes as he considered it. "You know where your nature stuff would really fit? The Outdoor Department at the store."

"At North Brothers Sports?" She tilted her head and looked far from convinced.

He sat up straighter, imagining the possibilities. "Think about it. East-side store. Do you remember what Outdoor looks like?"

"I usually go to the west-side store." He could see her racking her brain to remember the other local location.

"There's the wall where the Outdoor sign is… What if you did a woodsy mural across the top and down both sides of the opening to the department? It would be big…"

"I was thinking more of a practice mural," she said. "That's intimidating."

"We'd pay you, of course." He didn't have a single doubt in her ability to pull it off.

"Wow, that's…that's a big deal. You can't just offer me that. Mason would kick your ass."

"He might try," Gabe said, not scared in the least of his CEO older brother, but she had a point. There was a process for making a change. But the east-side store was due for a cosmetic update in the next few months, as they prepared to open a brand-new location on the west side. The older store needed a spruce-up. Paint was part of that. He made a mental note to pursue the idea with his brother. "Lex, you're welcome to paint any or all of the spare bedroom walls. Paint to your heart's content."

"Really?" Her pretty brown eyes came alive, and she popped up off the floor, hurried over to him, and threw her arms around him. "Thank you, thank you."

Gabe closed his eyes and inhaled the scent of her—clean, honeysuckle, not chlorine. She must have showered after swimming. She straightened too soon, and as the urge came over him to pull her back down, he remembered why he'd rushed home in the first place. As she sat down a few inches from him, pent-up energy had him shooting off the sectional. He strode to the kitchen area again, to buy some space and time, try to get the logical side of his brain fired up. Casual. He needed to be casual, not possessive or jealous.

He went to the refrigerator and pulled out a beer for him, a can of lemonade for her, carried both back to the sectional, and held out the lemonade.

"Thanks," she said, taking it.

"Connor said he saw you at lunch today," Gabe said, striving for casual and conversational as he sat back down, popped open his beer.

Her head jerked up to meet his gaze. "I didn't see him."

"At Cadence. He said you were with some guy."

She nodded and said, "Jonah Varga. Why didn't Connor say hi?"

"I guess he didn't want to interrupt your date," he said, fishing hard, congratulating himself for keeping his tone even and nonchalant.

Lexie laughed. "Jonah's not a date. I went to school with him at Iowa State. He was in the landscape architecture program too.

He just moved to Nashville and wanted to connect. He doesn't know anyone else in town."

"Maybe he thought it was a date," Gabe said, recalling that the guy had treated her to lunch.

"I highly doubt that, as he likes to date boys instead of girls," Lexie said. "Besides, I'm not dumb enough to go out with someone right now. It hasn't even been a month since I got dumped at the altar."

Gabe allowed himself to sag back against the cushions, closing his eyes.

Thank fuck.

Out of nowhere, a roll of thunder, off in the distance, broke into the silence, and even though the windows were all closed, a strong gust of wind was audible as it hit the house.

Lexie frowned and pulled her legs up to her chest, trying to hide her nervousness about the weather, but he could see it. He put his hand on her knee.

"It's okay, Lex."

"I know," she said, but she patted the cushion and said, "Saint, come here, boy," anyway. The big, protective dog did her bidding and curled up on the other side of her, his large body stretching along the other side of the sectional.

Gabe bolted off the cushion not because of the weather but because of the storm inside of him—the lingering jealousy, the relief, the need, the fear that it would only be a matter of time before Lexie *was* ready to go on a date with someone. He went to the double doors that opened onto the patio and looked out. Though it was nearly dark—prematurely thanks to the weather—he could see that Lexie had put all the outdoor cushions into the storage bin in preparation for the storm. A flash of lightning revealed tree branches swaying in the wind.

Tonight was it. He needed to level with Lexie before she did find someone new to date. He didn't expect her to fall into his arms or confess she felt the same about him. In fact, he suspected his confession would stun her. But he had to do it anyway, had to put it out there. Because if he missed the opportunity again…

He shook his head, still gazing out the window.

He couldn't miss the opportunity again.

She might not feel the same way, which would devastate him, but then at least he'd know. He'd have taken the chance.

"Lex," he said, still facing the window, gathering his courage as the wind picked up intensity.

"Yeah?" she said from behind him.

Gripping the beer bottle tightly, he lifted it to his mouth, downed a good half of it in one go, then turned to face her. "I need to talk to you."

Still huddled up next to Saint, she turned to face him, her eyes on him, concerned. "If it's about the walls, it's okay to change your mind."

"It's not about the walls," he said distractedly, working out how he could possibly say what he needed to say without ruining a thirty-plus-year friendship. "I… Shit. I don't know how to start."

"Just say it. Gabe, what's wrong? Are you okay?" She sat up straighter, one hand still buried in Saint's fur.

"I'm fine. For the moment…"

"Are you sick? Your mom?"

"What? No. Nobody's sick." He strode back over to her, his instinct always to comfort her, and lowered himself to the cushion near her but not touching her. "It's nothing like that—"

"What is it? You're freaking me out."

Setting his bottle on the end table, he pushed all the air out of his lungs and slid his hands from his thighs to his knees. "You know I never liked Raleigh, right?"

"Yes," she said, drawing the word out into a question.

"I tried to like him, Lex. I swear I did."

"Okay. This is all ancient history now, you know?"

"He wasn't the right guy for you at all."

"Um, I know. We've had this conversation."

"The reason I didn't like him is that I was jealous." He sensed her going still beside him but was too chicken to look at her as he barreled forward. "I want to be the right guy for you, Lexie."

The only sound was the wind gusting. Gabe closed his eyes,

didn't breathe, didn't move, wondering if he'd just delivered the words that would kill their connection forever.

"What are you saying?" she finally asked in a quiet voice.

He swallowed and did a half turn on the couch so he was facing her. Looked her in the eye. Took her small hand in his and forged ahead with the raw truth. "I'm saying that my feelings for you go deeper than just friendship. I'm attracted to you, Lexie. Crazy attracted."

CHAPTER FOURTEEN

exie pushed herself up to a sitting position from her slump as she stared into Gabe's intense crystal-blue eyes and tried to process his words.

"I know the timing is wrong," he said in a rush. "You're still getting over your breakup and coming to terms with not getting married, and I get that. I don't expect anything from you."

"What… Whoa." She still struggled to catch up. "You…"

Gabe let go of her hand, ran his through his hair, and re-situated himself a couple more inches away from her. "I just needed to tell you," he said, his gaze averted. "To be honest with you, because we've always been honest with each other. Except for this. I've hidden it because I don't want to ever screw up our friendship." His gaze popped back up to hers. "Have I screwed up our friendship?"

Lexie expelled a sort of half laugh, half nervous exhale. "You've got to slow down. I'm still trying to understand. You… You're attracted to me? Like, sexually?"

He blew out a breath. "Sexually, romantically, more than friendly." With a shake of his head, he took her hand again, palm to palm between them, their fingers entwined, and continued, "I'm not asking for anything from you right now, but I needed you to know. I needed to tell you before you decided to find some new guy. I didn't want to miss the opportunity yet again."

Yet again? "How long have you felt this way?"

"A long time. Years."

"You never let on. Ever." She frowned, thinking back for any sign. Had she been missing signs for…years?

"It wasn't always easy, but I didn't want to lose you, Lex. I still don't want to lose you. I meant what I said about the timing being bad." He let out a self-deprecating laugh. "The timing is terrible. All I'm trying to say is, once you're ready to get involved with someone again, whenever you're done working through Raleigh and the breakup and all that, just know that I'm throwing my name into the hat. Because too many times, I didn't, and every damn time, I regretted it like hell."

He kept going, talking, giving her outs, pleading his case, but Lexie barely heard any of it. She was stuck back a couple of miles ago, letting it sink in that Gabe was attracted to her. Sexy, beautiful, golden-boy Gabe. She studied the hand that was locked with hers, his fingers long, thick, so very strong and capable. It dwarfed her hand and his touch warmed her clear through to her heart.

Her gaze moved to his face, his scruffy jaw, his symmetrical nose, his lips, still talking, the lower lip slightly thicker than the upper one. Then fell into the depths of his light blue eyes that were filled with so much earnestness and emotion—and insecurity.

That's what finally cut through to her, drove her to action. Big, gorgeous, confident Gabriel North was baring himself to her, letting her see his vulnerability, his fear, his self-doubt, and God, this man had nothing to doubt.

He'd stopped talking and was staring back into her eyes expectantly, as if waiting for her to respond, but she hadn't heard the question, so lost in her own thoughts and feelings, so many feelings. So to answer whatever it was, she leaned forward as she squeezed his hand and pressed her lips to his, grabbing his nape with her other hand and pulling his head closer, holding him to her, making it clear this was no friendly peck.

As their breaths mingled hotly, she felt his hand at her waist, and she poured herself into the kiss, telling him without words that she was attracted to him too, sexually, romantically, more than friendly.

———

THE LAST THING Gabe had expected was…this. To have Lexie in his arms tonight. To taste her sweetness, to be engulfed by her feminine scent, to have her baby-soft skin under his fingertips.

Though he'd dreamed of this moment for years, it was better than he ever could have imagined. A hundredfold better. And it was just a kiss. A slow, exploratory, tantalizing-as-fuck kiss.

As one, they reclined, him on his back, her halfway on top of him. It could've been awkward, with one of his feet on the floor and Saint partially in the way, but none of that mattered. All that mattered was that Lexie was kissing him, her breasts pressing into his chest, and the sensual purr that escaped from her nearly did him in.

His blood pounded through him, centering below the waist, and he found himself conflicted, torn between ravaging the ever-loving hell out of this woman as if the very fate of humankind rested solely on them and revering her like the precious gift she was.

He settled for somewhere in the middle, running his fingers through her loose, long locks of silky hair, luxuriating in the feel of it draping over him as their tongues tangled and teased and tormented. It went against everything in him to not flip her over and take control of the kiss, but he was still half expecting her to end it, apologize, and say she'd made a mistake. If this was a mistake, he wanted it to last for as long as possible so he could log it all in his brain and remember it forever.

But Lexie wasn't acting like it was a mistake as she pressed her hips into him and her fingers found their way under his T-shirt, onto his flesh. As she explored his chest, her mouth trailed slowly along his jawline toward his ear, and the nips and kisses combined with the caresses of her fingers had him burning, need-ing, aching to be skin to skin with her. At this rate, they were thundering toward that do-or-die point, and he didn't want to go the wrong way with her.

"Lex," he whispered as her tongue toyed with the lobe of his ear, and damn if that wasn't erotic as hell.

"Mmm?"

His lips curved upward as he lay there savoring the sensations of such a seemingly simple moment, the tickle of her breath on his damp skin, the sporadic contact of the tip of her tongue with his needy flesh. It shouldn't be this provocative, but this was Lexie. This was what she could do to him.

"Kills me to say this," he said, his voice all kinds of rough and full of need, "but stop for a second. Because if you don't…" He let out a low growl.

She did stop and lifted her gaze to his, then dragged her finger along his lip in a light caress. "You liked that?"

With a lust-filled half laugh, he said, "I'm liking everything you do. Liking it so much that if we need to stop and be rational, then we need to do that now, before it's too late."

"Why would we need to stop?"

He raised his brows at her, scrutinized her eyes, her face, looking for any kind of doubt, any sign she wasn't as into this as he was. He found none. But still, for the sake of the future between them, of their friendship, he needed her to reassure him. "I want you in my bed, Lex. Naked. Writhing. Needing. And if that's not what you want, we can quit right now and we're okay. We'll be okay."

It might take him a two-hour cold shower to be okay, but he'd get there.

"If you think I'm going to shy away from that, then you don't know me as well as I thought you did," she said, grinning, then pressing another kiss to his lips.

Gabe fought not to fall into her, into what he wanted more than anything in the universe. "I know the friend side of you better than I know myself, but this other side, this sexy, seductive Lexie… I'm still learning. And trust me, I'm loving every fucking bit of it and then some. But I need to make sure you're sure."

"I'm sure. Are you sure?" she said flirtatiously.

"Lexie Nicole Gallagher, I'm going to show you exactly how sure I am. If you'll let me."

"Try me."

He pulled her head down to his, kissed her soft, swollen lips like the starved man he was. The leisurely sweetness of their previous kisses went up in smoke, and urgency pulsed through his veins and spilled into the way he devoured her mouth, her lips, her tongue.

He was about to roll from under her and switch their positions on the suddenly too-narrow sectional when Saint let out a sort of sigh/whimper sound and shifted his oafish body, infringing farther on their side of the L shape. It was enough to bring Gabe partway to his senses. He propped himself up onto his elbows and ran his palm over Lexie's cheek.

"Bedroom," was all he had to say, and she slipped off him, onto the floor, and stood, looking alluringly rumpled and so damn ready for him. It didn't matter that she was fully clothed in an old tee and some worn cutoff shorts, her hair in complete tangled disarray. He'd never seen a more beautiful sight in his life.

Saint lifted his head and glanced at them, as if he, too, had noticed everything was all of a sudden different between them, as if their chemistry was a tangible thing. Gabe patted the dog's head and said, "You're staying out here, big guy."

He took Lexie's diminutive hand in his and tugged gently at her, leading her toward his room. The lights were out and he didn't waste the time to turn any on. He couldn't wait to feast his eyes on every inch of her body once he had her naked, but for now, the frequent but distant flash of lightning would have to do. Because the one thing he wanted to do more than see Lexie was feel her.

At the side of the bed, he sat on the mattress, pulled her between his legs. He ran his hands beneath her tee, up the sides of her slender torso and back down, then lifted the shirt off her, tossed it aside. Her hand went to the middle of her back, and she unfastened her lace-trimmed bra and let it fall down her arms to the floor as he went after the snap and zipper of her shorts. Once they were unfastened, he dipped his fingers in both sides, beneath shorts and underwear, and rid her of both at once, leaving her standing in front of him, bare and so fucking beautiful he could weep.

As if God was looking after him, a series of lightning flashes lit up the room at that moment, giving him an eyeful he would never, ever forget.

A sudden crash of thunder shook the house, and Lexie jolted slightly. Gabe palmed the backs of her upper thighs, then ran his hands upward, to her tight, perfect ass, drawing her even closer. "You okay?"

With a gusty, sharp exhale, she said, "So okay. You need to strip down."

He was reluctant to take his hands from her even for a minute, but after rubbing his fingers over her flesh for a few seconds and circling his tongue around her navel, he pulled slightly away and whipped off his own shirt.

As he swept Lexie up in a cradle hold to put her on the mattress, another boom of thunder rattled the house, and she threw her arms around his neck. Having a naked Lexie cling to him might be one of his favorite things in the world…and yet he knew it would pale in comparison to burying himself inside of her.

After a quick kiss on her lips, he set her down, removed his shoes and socks, and threw his shorts and boxer briefs off in record time. He crawled in next to her and rolled to face her, and she was right there welcoming him, pulling him into her, seeming as eager as he was.

Thank you, God.

Their lips met again, and their hands were everywhere, caressing, teasing, exploring, as if trying to make up for so many years of missing out on each other's bodies. As he toyed with one of her nipples, she arched into his touch, silently begging for more.

He trailed his way from her lips to her breasts with his tongue, tasting and nibbling along the way, catching his breath as he felt her leg wrap around his, her toes crawling up his calf, opening her to him even more. But he was afraid to move, afraid if he didn't slow this down, slow himself down, he'd blow it for both of them and embarrass himself.

He devoted himself to learning every millimeter of her breasts and her nipples and what made her squirm the most, which turned out to be a light tug of her tip with his teeth and tongue. As he continued to lavish attention on her responsive breasts, his fingers sought out the apex of her thighs and found her wet and ready for him. Fuck, his sexy Lexie was turning him inside out.

It wasn't going to be long before he sank into her, no matter how much he wanted to make this last forever, and he realized with a start that he needed a condom.

"Lex," he said as he felt her small hand close around his cock. He moaned as his eyes rolled back in his head, and he bit his lip against letting go. If he let go now, there would be no birth control and probably it would be less than awesome for Lexie. Reaching down for her hand, he twined their fingers together and pulled her away, resting their joined hands alongside her shoulder as he kissed her. "Need to get a condom."

"Mmm," she said as she arched her hips upward and rubbed against him, killing him. "Good idea." She made no move to let him go, grabbing his ass, pulling him into her.

Summoning every last ounce of willpower, he pulled away and climbed off the bed, his blood pounding painfully to his heavy cock as he made his way to the master bath, racking his brain, praying he still had some condoms. It'd been months since he'd gotten laid. He'd done his share of oat-sowing over the years, but compared to his brothers, he was a saint. He'd learned early on that no one was Lexie. The older he got, the less appealing a one-night thing became, and he hadn't been with anyone since the night he'd learned of Lexie's engagement. *Former* engagement.

He rushed into the bathroom, flipped the light on, and yanked the top drawer open, encouraged at the sight of the condom box at the bottom and thanking God out loud when he saw there were a few packets left inside. After ripping one open, he slid it on and went back to Lexie, not bothering to turn off the bathroom light, loving the sight she made, waiting there in his bed, looking semi-ravished and needful and gorgeous. He set out to ravish her the rest of the way.

As he walked to the bed, Lexie's gaze roved up and down him and stopped in the middle of him. If it was possible, even more blood pounded into the body part she stared at. Crawling over her, he asked, "Like what you see?"

Her fingers wrapped around him as she said, "I trust you can make this work somehow."

"I won't hurt you. I promise."

"Trust you completely," she whispered as she pulled his head down to her and kissed him again, her other hand still stroking him, and he wasn't sure which did it for him more, her words or her actions. Hell, who was he kidding? The sensation of having Lexie's fingers on him, her hands all over him was heaven.

Without another thought, he lined himself up at her opening and nudged into her wetness, trying to be careful to not go too fast or too hard, when all his body wanted was to be buried so deep he couldn't tell where he ended and she started. He tried to read her gasps and groans as he inched farther in. Her hands clasped on to him, and her legs wound around him, and when he felt her fingers at his butt, pulling him deeper into her, he asked, "You okay?"

"Mmm," she said. "Super okay."

Once he was in to the hilt, he paused, overcome by the utter bliss of finally being inside of Lexie. After a few seconds of trying to reel himself in and get control, he began to move, a little at a time, gently, making sure she was with him.

"Gabe?" she said in a gasp.

"Yeah?"

"I may be small but I'm not fragile." She squirmed under him.

"Meaning?" There wasn't a whole lot of blood moving through his brain right now.

"Meaning either go faster or flip over and let me try."

With a laugh, he said, "Oh, so you're going to turn bossy during sex?"

"If I have to." She moved her hands from his ass, up his sides, to his nipples and pinched them both, rubbed them, toyed with them, as if she was trying to incite him to lose control.

"See, that just makes me want to take my time even more," he said, gritting his teeth and pulling out of her oh so slowly, realizing instantly that that kind of teasing would only backfire.

Still playing with his nipples and his chest, she caught his mouth in a possessive, persuasive kiss, and there was no way he could hold back any longer.

He pushed into her, drew another gasp from her along with a drawn-out "Yessss" that made him feel like he owned the fucking world. And then it was no use trying to control anything, as he lost himself in her, in the sensations, the climb, the quickening rhythm, the heat, and eventually, the release, just seconds after she clung to him and contracted around him and called out his name like a prayer. His orgasm shook him to his soul and had his arms shaking and his toes cracking and his head spinning.

Eventually, as he caught his breath and blood started trickling back into his brain, he lowered himself to the side of her, pulled her into him, unable to form words yet. She nestled against his chest, her skin damp like his, her breathing not back to normal yet either, and all he could think was that he'd been waiting half his life for this. For Lexie.

She—all of her—was exactly what he needed.

He only hoped it wasn't too soon for her.

CHAPTER FIFTEEN

*L*exie was reasonably certain she'd never experienced the true meaning of bliss until she slowly, deliciously woke up in Gabe's bed.

Before she opened her eyes, she relished the feel of his fingers draped over her arm, as if he couldn't bear to sleep without touching her, and she nearly pinched herself to make sure this was real. The little aches in weird places were proof enough. As her mind gradually replayed their night, she knew it had all happened, because it was so much better than she ever could've imagined.

She cracked her lids open, noting that the room was lit by the sun, the storm having ended at some point in the night. He lay on his side, facing her, the sheet covering his bottom half, affording her the opportunity to drink in the beauty of her lover, her sinfully sexy best friend.

His skin was bronzed from the sun, the hair on his chest closer to blond than brown, and his chest and arms were solid and sculpted from his morning workouts at the gym. Her fingers itched for a pencil and sketchpad so that she could transfer the image to paper and hold on to this slice of beauty forever. Not that her brain would ever let go of it.

Her gaze roved upward, to his handsome, so familiar face, his jaw covered with a day-old scruff. His light brown lashes rested peacefully on his cheeks, and she could swear his mouth tilted the tiniest bit upward at the corners as he slept. Because of her?

It was a little bit hard to wrap her brain around that, but last night, he'd left no room for doubts. She'd been stunned stupid for several seconds when he'd admitted his feelings, but once she'd reassured herself he was for real, she'd done something she'd never in her life done before—she'd jumped in with both feet and made the move on him. Without thought. One-hundred-percent impulse. She was neither overly cautious nor impulsive in anything, more middle-of-the-road, but last night, she'd shut her brain off and leaped at the chance to get closer to Gabe.

It was probably better that she hadn't thought too hard, hadn't let her lifelong insecurities rear their heads. Because the payoff… Good lord, last night had been unreal, in a mind-blowing, magical way. Making love with Gabe, sharing her body with him for the first time, was unparalleled. Not that she'd had a super-long list of lovers, but she'd had enough to use two hands to count, and none, not one, ever, had tended to her body and her pleasure so thoroughly.

It hadn't been long after the first round that they'd gone for a second, and Lexie had been a little shocked, and not disappointed one bit, that he was good to go so soon after.

Later, they'd shared a late-night snack in bed, and then Gabe had rolled toward her and announced his goal of lavishing every inch of her body with his attention. She'd laughed and had the absolute pleasure of him keeping his word. When he'd finally buried himself inside of her a third time, she'd had so many orgasms she'd lost count. She hadn't known her body was capable of anything close to that.

As much as she was tempted to roll him to his back and crawl over him and go for round four right now, her bladder was telling her otherwise, so after another admiring gander, she slipped her arm out from under his hand and slid silently out of his bed.

Saint lifted his head from his dog bed at the foot of Gabe's king-sized bed as she stood, and she ruffled the fur on his head as she walked by. Before hitting the bathroom, she veered over to

Gabe's nightstand, where both their phones were, to grab hers. As she picked it up, a message popped up on Gabe's phone, and she couldn't help reading it.

Nancy Callahan: Good morning, Gabe. Please call me when you can. Thx, N.

Lexie froze for a moment. A woman was texting Gabe at—she checked the time—6:42 in the morning? A woman who seemed to know him well and be used to him calling her? Was it someone he'd dated? Slept with?

Every insecurity she'd ever had burst to the surface.

With a guilty glance at Gabe that verified he hadn't stirred, she escaped to the bathroom and closed the door without a sound. Her mind spun as she went about her business.

Who was Nancy Callahan? The name seemed familiar, but she couldn't place it. Nancy wasn't a common name for a woman their age. Also, Lexie wasn't aware that Gabe had gone on any dates for some time. It wasn't something he normally hid from her, so she tended to believe she'd know if he had.

She started to breathe easier as she splashed water on her face and helped herself to a mouthful of mouthwash. Her spare tooth-brush was in the bathroom in the other wing of the house, off of "her" room.

Though she was now pretty sure Nancy Callahan was not a romantic connection, Lexie's doubts had been roused, and instead of climbing back into bed with Gabe, she decided to go for a run. Maybe she could sweat out some deep-seated insecurities or pound the pavement hard enough to bounce them out.

Saint was waiting on the other side of the bathroom door, and together, they left Gabe's room to face the day. She let the dog out the patio door, then made her way to the other side of the house.

She'd worn her running shoes when she'd come over yester-day, and she found everything else she needed in the spare bedroom. Within a few minutes, she was dressed for a run and had Saint back inside with full bowls of kibble and water. She left Gabe a note on the kitchen counter and exited the house to run out her annoying, pesky fears.

When she came back forty-five minutes and four miles later,

she was drenched with sweat and had gotten her self-doubt a little better under control. It would take a lot more than exercise to dislodge the underlying fear that this new thing with Gabe was too good to be true, but maybe she could keep it buried deep enough until it had no power over her.

As soon as she came in the front door, the aroma of coffee, bacon, and pancakes hit her, and again, she thought, *Too good to be true*, but this time it was more of a lighthearted, *oh my God he's amazing* thought instead of a heavy, insecurity-based one.

Saint wandered up to her as she entered the kitchen, where bacon sizzled in a large skillet and chocolate chip pancakes bubbled on a griddle.

"Hey, boy," she said, patting his head as she sought out Gabe's gaze at the stove.

His hair was damp, and he wore gym shorts and a North Brothers Sports tee that stretched just right across his chest, and she guessed he'd already showered. When their eyes met, he lifted his brows and smiled. She melted down to her toes, because the smile was somehow different today. Somehow more *I've seen you naked and want to do it again.*

"There you are." Gabe set down the bacon tongs and turned off the burner, then stepped over to her, reminding her a little of a hungry predator, in the very best way. He palmed the back of her neck, leaned down to her, and kissed her slowly, thoroughly, the most tantalizing good morning ever. When he eventually pulled back a couple of inches to look her over, Lexie smiled shyly, realizing she must stink to high heaven. "You could've woken me up. I would've gone with you," he said.

"I thought maybe you'd want to go to the gym with your brothers." Which was half the truth. It was what he did most mornings.

Gabe sputtered out a laugh. "With a gorgeous girl in my house? Not happening today." He kissed her again, pressed his body into hers suggestively. "Waking up alone was very sad. Lonely." His voice was a sexy growl.

There was still a part of her, deep inside, that struggled to believe he was attracted to her. It was just her screwed-up psyche, because he'd proven that attraction several times over last night, and she could feel his arousal pressed against her right now.

Stupid psyche.

"Lex?" he said, as if he could tell her thoughts were muddled. "You okay?"

Of course he could tell her thoughts were muddled. He knew her better than anyone on the planet. Which meant it would take some effort on her part to convince him she was fine, way more than fine. Because mostly she was.

"Question. Who's Nancy Callahan?"

"You saw her text," he said, seemingly to himself. He pressed a kiss to the top of her head and pivoted to the griddle to turn off the heat, then started scooping pancakes onto a plate. "She's one of our lawyers for NBS. Some shit went down at the end of the day yesterday and she needed to fill me in. She left a message on my work phone early in the evening and was concerned when I didn't call back."

"You're not Mason," Lexie said dryly.

"And I was definitely distracted." There was heat in his eyes.

"Is everything okay?"

"A former employee filed a lawsuit. Could get ugly, but we've got a good team on it."

"I'm sorry, Gabe. That sounds bad."

He shrugged, though she could tell he wasn't as nonchalant as he was going for. "We'll see what happens. No reason to let it spoil our morning."

In other words, that was all he was going to say about it, maybe all he *could* say about it right now. All she could do was be there for him if and when he needed to talk about it.

At least she'd figured out Nancy Callahan was no threat to her personally on her own. Yay, her.

"That smells amazing," she said, eyeing the food. "You're going to spoil me."

"That's the plan. Grab some plates. Everything's ready."

She put two plates on the island, served herself a large cup of cold water from the spigot on the fridge, and gratefully grabbed the mug of coffee he'd brewed for her. As she slid her beverages across the counter to the stool side, she said, "I should shower. I'm fragrant."

"You're perfect. And if you play your cards right, maybe I'll help you in the shower after we eat."

"You already took one," she pointed out.

He shrugged. "I'll take a dozen a day if it means getting my hands all over you."

"News flash," she said. "You don't need a shower to get your hands all over me."

With the plate of bacon in one hand, Gabe drew her in close yet again. "Sexy Lexie, you are killing me."

Not knowing what to do with that, still trying to process the *sexy* label for herself, she laughed and stole a slice of bacon and slipped away, to the other side of the island, and sat on one of the stools. "I need food and sustenance. And lots of coffee. Some guy kept me up most of the night."

"Didn't hear you complaining," Gabe said as he set all the food down, then came around the island to her side with an oversized mug of black tea. Once he'd taken the stool next to her, he said, "Confession: I've called you Sexy Lexie in my mind for ages, but I was always terrified it would slip out."

Lexie narrowed her eyes and said, lightly, "I call bullshit."

He set his fork down emphatically, straightened, and turned to pierce her with a direct gaze. "You'd be dead wrong."

The intensity in his eyes took her aback, and she grinned to lighten things up. "Okay, okay. I'm working on believing you."

As she looked at him from the side, she saw him lock his jaw, as if biting down on a comment. Definitely not lightening up at all.

"What?" she said. "Whatever you're thinking, just say it. We can't stop leveling with each other now."

In silence, Gabe poured syrup over his pancakes, then jabbed a hefty bite with his fork. Shoveled it in, still looking intense. Pissed?

Apparently he wasn't going to say more, so Lexie nibbled on

her bacon, took a few bites of pancake, and tried to figure out if she'd said something wrong.

Gabe set his fork down again. "Here's the thing," he said emphatically. "I've sat by all these years, met the guys you've dated, tried to like them, because you're the most important part of my life and that's what friends do. But whatever they have done, as a group or individually, to your self-image is un-fuck-ing-forgivable, and I want nothing more than to track them all down and smash their heads together." He spun on his stool to face her, took her chin in his hand so she had to look at him. "Lex, you're beautiful inside and out. You are desirable, tempting, and sensual. You, Lexie Gallagher, are sexy. As. Fuck. I'm going to do everything in my power to help you unlearn what shitheads like Raleigh Clarke made you believe, even if it takes me years."

The determination, the conviction in those cornflower eyes as he peered down at her sent a shiver through her and left no room for any doubt that he meant every word he said. Lexie sucked in a deep breath, trying to get it to sink in, wishing it could somehow erase everything that had come before.

She reached out and palmed his freshly shaven cheek. "You are"—she shook her head, laughing quietly—"going to get a big head. You're incredible, amazing, and I'm not just talking about last night. If anyone can do it, you can," she said with a half smile. "I'm trying, Gabe. I've just…got a lot of years of crap to work through. Everything from the guys I've been with to my childhood." She dropped her hand and swallowed hard, finding it difficult to even say the word *childhood* because it was fraught with so much garbage that was still affecting her today. "I'm working on believing you—"

"You think I'm lying?"

"No. Not at all." Lexie blew out a heavy breath. "Last night was magical, Gabe."

"Yeah?" There was a hint of a grin, finally.

She leaned over and kissed him. "Yeah. Duh. Like, the best sex of my life."

With a cocky grin, he sat up straighter and said, "Duh."

Lexie swatted his shoulder and shook her head, grinning. "Guys and sex aside, there's a lot of baggage in this head of mine."

"Your mom?" he said, flipping back into serious mode in a blink.

"She's a part of it." A part she hated thinking about, let alone discussing. "Among other stuff. Gabe, you're this guy everyone loves, from little kids to old ladies and everyone in between. You can have any girl you want—"

"I want you, Lex. I have for years."

"I'm the luckiest girl in the world." She smiled, meant that with her whole heart. "I just hope you can be patient with me, because on one level, I know you mean everything you say. On another level, one night with you can't undo thirty-some years of conditioning. It's going to take some time."

"I'm in for the long haul, Lex. Just let me know how I can help you."

"There is something," she said hesitantly. She'd thought of it on her run as she'd tried to wrap her brain around the astounding turn her life had taken in the past twelve hours.

"Name it."

She met his gaze directly, worked up the courage to say it, knowing it was a lot to ask. "Can we keep *us* to ourselves for a while?"

He reared back as if she'd slapped him, and she cursed her insecurities once again. "You want to keep it a secret that we're more than friends?"

"Just for a little while. While I get used to it. And to let more time pass from my crash and burn."

"The wedding?"

"That wasn't. It wasn't even a month ago that I was going to marry Raleigh," she said quietly, fervently, "and you know and I know that it would've been a huge mistake and never should've gotten that far, but everyone else…doesn't."

"The people who know you best do."

She didn't know if that was good news or bad. "Let's just take some time to get used to this, to us. To savor it. No outside influences, no having to answer questions or make explanations. Just for a little while. Please?"

Gabe turned back toward the island, rubbed his hand over his eyes, and let out a short, humorless laugh. "There's a big part of me that wants to shout out to the entire world that you're mine, Lex. Finally, truly mine after all these years of wishing for it. I don't fully understand all of your deep issues and fears. You haven't really let me in on them completely, but"—he looked at her again, earnestly, grabbed her hand, and wove their fingers together—"yeah. For you, I'll go along with it. For a while. Whatever you need, sexy Lexie. If I can give it to you, it's yours."

She slid off the stool and worked her way between his legs, wrapped her arms around his neck, pulled his face down to hers, and kissed him, not quickly this time. She poured her gratitude into the kiss—gratitude and everything else she felt for him.

"Thank you," she said quietly when she finally came up for air, her voice lower than normal because every cell of her body was heavy with need for this man. "There is something else I need."

"Oh, yeah? What's that?" He peered at her under heavy, half-closed lids, and the lust in his eyes made her breath catch.

"I need a shower," she said, paying no heed to their half-finished breakfast or her cooling coffee or the rattle of Saint's tags as he rolled over wherever he was dozing nearby. "And I might need some help with it. If you still feel like getting your hands all over me."

He stood and hoisted her several inches up in a single motion, and Lexie curled her legs around his waist.

"Sexy Lexie, I will always feel like getting my hands all over you."

He knocked his stool over with a loud clatter as, in a hurry, he carried her out of the kitchen and straight to the master bath.

CHAPTER SIXTEEN

Two weeks later, Lexie was on a twelve-foot-high scaffolding in the East Nashville North Brothers Sports store, adding detail to a red-tailed hawk with a paintbrush. Two weeks might as well have been two years for all the changes going on in her life, most of them good. She tried—perpetually—not to let that make her nervous.

As she touched up the hawk's eye to get the reflection just right, her mind went where it camped out nearly all of her spare moments—to Gabe. They'd been spending most nights together, usually at his place because of Saint but a couple at hers, and that right there, his willingness to compromise for her, said it all. She was sure he remembered Raleigh's insistence that they stay at his place, and Gabe would never be so unbending.

Lexie tried not to compare them, but she couldn't help it every once in a while because the differences were so marked, so…right. And for the record, Gabe had no rules about what nights they could sleep together or have sex, and his hunger for her hadn't dimmed at all since that first multi-orgasm night.

She was so not complaining.

Below her, a few customers and employees went about their business, but she'd gotten used to them over the past week since she'd started the project. When she worked on the floor level, people were more apt to stop and chat her up, ask her what she was doing or whether she was going to paint every wall in the store or, in the case of the cutest little girl a couple of evenings ago, whether she could do face painting too. Up on the scaffolding, they generally left her alone to get lost in her Tennessee forestland.

After coming up with the idea of painting the walls around the Outdoor Department, Gabe had made it a reality faster than Lexie would've believed possible. North Brothers Sports was paying her what seemed like an astronomical sum, five figures, more than she made in two months, for work that would end up taking her less than a month—and that was just working evenings and weekends, fitting it in around her day job. But Gabe had done his research, and she'd done hers separately and was a little shocked to learn that the fee they were paying her was well within the range of the going rate for corporate murals.

"Holy crap."

The familiarity of the female voice from below took a few seconds to penetrate Lexie's brain as she assessed the hawk and the leaves of the tallest white oak, where it was perched. She glanced over the edge of the platform to see Sierra and her sister, Kennedy, standing several feet back in a wide aisle and taking in the nearly finished left side of the mural.

"What are you two doing here?" Lexie asked as she set her brush down and wiped her fingers on a rag.

"Hey," Sierra said with a big smile. "Gabe was going on and on about your project at the family dinner tonight, and I had to come see what you've been up to. It's amazing!"

Lexie had skipped the weekly dinner at Mrs. N's for the past two weeks, in part because of the mural and in part because it would be so hard to hide her status change with Gabe.

Kennedy walked closer to the finished part of the wall. "Lady bugs," she said. "And look at this caterpillar. It looks real. Please tell me there aren't any spiders."

"Or snakes," Sierra added.

"No snakes or spiders," Lexie said as she hopped to the floor from the bottom ladder rung on the end of the scaffolding. After a glance down at herself to make sure she wasn't covered with wet paint splotches, she stepped forward to hug Sierra. "I can't believe you two drove all the way over here."

Sierra shrugged. "It was only fifteen minutes from Kennedy's. It's good to see you. It's been a while."

"I know. This has kept me busy." Lexie gestured to the wall, knowing full well the mural wasn't the only reason she'd been less social. Mostly she was spending her extra time with Gabe, but there was also an element of avoiding her friends so as not to have to lie about her and Gabe. Which made her realize how hard it must be for Gabe, seeing his brothers and cousins every day at work and at the baseball foundation and not being able to level with them. She had to remedy that soon.

Kennedy ended her up-close examination of the left side, which centered around a fat, old oak tree with numerous knots and branches in its trunk for critters to lurk in, and came over to them. "This is looking incredible, Lexie."

"Thanks. It's been sort of…incredible is a good word." So incredible that her mind had been spinning night and day with all kinds of possibilities. "Can you guys sit for a few minutes? There's a bench outside and I'm due for some fresh air."

When they went out the side door, the humid summer evening was a welcome contrast to the air-conditioned air where Lexie had been for hours now. She was surprised to see how low in the sky the sun was and realized it was nearly time for her to start cleaning up her supplies to leave.

"How is it this late already?" she said as they walked toward the bench at the end of the sidewalk. "It's like a time warp up on my platform in there."

"Gabe said you were pulling some long hours," Sierra said.

She'd started when the store opened this morning at eleven. Pulling out her phone from her back pocket, she checked the time and laughed. "I guess I have. Just over nine hours, but that's the thing. It doesn't seem like nine hours. I get lost in what I'm doing and lose all track of the time."

They reached the bench, and the two sisters sat next to each other. Instead of sitting beside them, Lexie lowered herself to the warm concrete, stretched her legs out in front of her, and sat facing them.

"When you love what you do…" Sierra said, and Lexie knew she spoke from experience. As owner of a remodeling company, she put in long hours, but she was passionate about her work. Any time she talked about it, you could hear it in her voice.

"I do love it," Lexie said, "and it's got me thinking hard. Wondering if I could do this full-time."

"You absolutely could," Sierra said enthusiastically.

"It's not if but how," Kennedy said more practically, and that's what made Lexie sit up straighter.

"Exactly," Lexie said. "*How* could I do it? Would I be stupid to try?"

"Never." Sierra's tone was adamant. "As long as you do your research and have a plan. Tell us what you're thinking exactly, and between my business experience and Kennedy's marketing chops, we can help you figure it out."

"Well," Lexie said, trying to organize her thoughts as excitement buzzed through her veins, "I'm thinking it's risky to start a business, especially a creative one, when I have a perfectly good job that I spent five years of college preparing for."

"Starting any business is risky," Sierra said, "creative or not. But let's back up. You have a 'good' job. What do you like about it?"

"The paycheck," Lexie said with a laugh. "The security. The benefits."

"All good things, for sure," Kennedy said. "Anything else?"

Lexie closed her eyes and imagined for a moment if she no longer worked for Martin and Baines. She sat there on the hard pavement and waited for a twinge of…anything. Regret. Sadness. Disappointment.

There was none.

"Honestly, I wouldn't miss it. A few people, sure, but I could see them outside of the office. It's not a bad job, it's just…"

"It doesn't light you up like this does," Sierra said, gesturing toward the store.

"It never has. Not the same way."

"Plus, who wants to work with their ex?" Sierra said.

"Actually, Raleigh got a new job," Lexie said, grinning. "In Atlanta."

"What?" Sierra's brows rose on her forehead and Kennedy sat forward on the bench. "He quit?"

"He gave his notice on Friday." Once it was public knowledge, Lexie had heard it from Judy in HR, who'd been concerned that Lexie would take it hard. It turned out she hadn't. She'd taken in the words, waited for a gut-punch feeling, but it had never come. In fact, the main thing she'd felt was relief. And a twinge of sadness that that was what two years of her life had come down to.

"That was fast," Kennedy said. "He didn't have that in the works when you were together?"

Shaking her head, Lexie said, "He must have started searching right away, probably the week we were supposed to honeymoon."

"This tells me he's not a factor in your wanting to quit," Sierra said.

"I'll admit it sort of sucked to work at the same place, but nope. Not a factor."

"So what are you thinking?" Kennedy said, pulling her legs up on the bench to sit cross-legged. "You've got murals and your online store. How's that going, by the way?"

"I sold two pieces!" Lexie said. "The setup you taught me apparently works."

"And your artwork is beautiful," Sierra said. "Congratulations! We should be celebrating with ice cream."

"Definitely. That's awesome," Kennedy said. "So one of the most important things in setting up a business is knowing who your customers will be and how to reach them."

"I was thinking..." Lexie pulled her knees into her and draped her arms around them, working up her courage. "One market is corporate customers. Like North Brothers Sports. This is just a simple spruce-up job, but the store they're building on the west side... So many possibilities."

"You could paint something in every department," Sierra

said. "The view from home plate in the baseball section. A stadium of fans in the football and soccer sections. A collage in footwear. Possibilities are endless."

"That's true. A little daunting but intriguing," Lexie said, easily visualizing what Sierra suggested.

"And they're opening new stores all over the country, aren't they?" Kennedy asked. "Keeping Cole busy?"

"He leaves for Lexington on Tuesday," Sierra said.

Ideas bubbled up in Lexie's mind like water boiling in a pot. "I don't want to take up a bunch of your time tonight, and I need to get in there in a few minutes and start shutting down, but I'd love to talk specifics. Could we meet sometime this week to talk more, Kennedy? A paid consultation?"

"Definitely. I'll text you tomorrow and we can find a time that will work for both of us." She and Sierra shared a look that Lexie noticed but couldn't quite decipher as the three of them fell silent for a moment, the only noise the buzz of the streetlight that illuminated the parking lot. "Question for you," Kennedy finally said. "Have you thought seriously about nursery murals?"

"I have. Not in-depth the way you're thinking, as in how to reach that market of parents-to-be, but creatively, I think nurseries could be the most fun of anything. The possibilities for subject matter are endless, from forests to underwater to outer space to—" She was rambling excitedly but paused, noticing an odd half smile on Kennedy's face.

Again, Kennedy glanced over at Sierra, who raised her brows at her sister. Kennedy lowered her legs to the ground and leaned forward, looking almost…conspiratorial?

"I have a secret. I'm expecting." Kennedy kept her voice low and glanced around as if looking for eavesdroppers.

"What?" Lexie sat up straight. "Kennedy, congratulations! That's so exciting! Oh, my goodness. So, when we were unpacking the kitchen and Sierra asked you—"

"She was preggers then," Sierra said. "But she didn't fess up to me until a few days ago."

Lexie popped up off the ground and threw her arms around Kennedy. "I'm so happy for you!"

"Thank you." Kennedy hugged her back, laughing. "It wasn't planned, and I'm scared shitless, but we're excited." She sobered. "It's early. I'm only eight weeks, so we're not telling people yet, but Sierra knows and Cole knows and now you know, because if you're doing murals, I want to get on your list. I was thinking some kind of stars-and-moon theme."

"A gray and blue and yellow palette," Sierra added, which told her they'd discussed it.

"I'm in. Whether I go into full-time business or not, I'd be honored to help with your nursery." Lexie sat at the end of the bench, next to Kennedy. "So Hunter's excited?"

"He's quite proud of himself," Sierra said. "Strutting around like a peacock, bragging on his 'swimmers.'"

"All for Cole's benefit. Men." Kennedy shook her head, still grinning. "He's super excited. Of course, he doesn't have to give birth."

"Men," Lexie parroted, laughing. "Your secret is safe with me. We can talk more about due dates and timelines when we meet. You'll be first on my schedule. Are you feeling the pressure now?" she asked Sierra, leaning forward to look at her.

"The only pressure I'm feeling is pulling off this wedding. There can be no other whoopses in the Lowell family." She cringed. "One thing at a time."

"I get it," Lexie said. "Planning a wedding is so much stress. But it'll be worth it for you," she said, finally able to grin a little bit about the topic. "So much more worth it when the wedding actually happens."

"I didn't really know your ex," Kennedy said, "but his loss is so one hundred percent your gain, Lexie. Your turn will come, and one day we'll be talking about what you're putting on your nursery walls."

"Yeah." Of course, Lexie's mind went automatically to Gabe. He would be the best father ever.

She was riding such an emotional buzz right now, from working on the mural all day, from discussing exciting business options with these two, from the bond that was forming between them, Kennedy included, especially now that she'd entrusted

Lexie with such a big secret. Lexie wanted to build on that, to strengthen the friendship, and without letting herself think too hard, she barreled forward.

"I have a secret of my own. I'm not pregnant," she rushed out with a laugh. "Thank you, sweet baby Jesus." She sucked in a deep breath, about to burst. "You girls can probably guess it."

"You and Gabe," Kennedy said, with zero question in her tone.

"Really?" Sierra leaned forward to better assess Lexie, who laughed again, the pure joy of her feelings for Gabe finally able to come out to someone else.

"Really. We're together."

"Finally!" Sierra said. "When did things change?"

"Sixteen days ago, not that I'm counting. Much."

"Seems like your turn is coming sooner than I even guessed," Kennedy said. "That's great news. I'm so happy for you and so not surprised."

"His family doesn't know yet, do they?" Sierra asked.

Lexie shook her head. "No one does. Except you two. I... made him agree not to tell anyone for a while."

"Because you're scared," Kennedy said.

"Yes."

"I get it. So much." Kennedy nudged their shoulders together supportively.

"I also just got dumped at the altar," Lexie reminded them, as if anyone could forget. "I'm worried that people might think it's too soon."

"Screw what people think," Sierra said.

"It's your life and your happiness," Kennedy agreed.

"Besides, you and Gabe have known each other for thirty years. I'd say, if anything, you're long overdue."

"Nailed it," Kennedy said. "I've seen you together. You know each other inside and out. Well, probably now he *really* knows you inside and out."

"Kennedy." Sierra swatted her sister. "No shame."

All Lexie could do was blush and nod. "She did kind of nail it." She fell into a fit of laughter, at the double entendre, at the nervousness of sharing so much, at the exhilaration of finally letting out her and Gabe's secret, and the other two joined her.

When they'd mostly recovered, Lexie leaned forward, propped her elbows on her knees. "Gabe has been so patient with my neurosis. He says he wants to yell the news to the world. I guess it's probably time."

"His family will be ecstatic," Sierra said. "His mom, especially."

"I know. You're right. Maybe I told you two as practice," Lexie said. "I need to figure out how to spread the news without making a big honking deal out of it."

"I know the perfect solution," Sierra said. "You're going to the foundation's gala with him, right?"

"I am." The inaugural event to raise money for Cole's foundation was next Saturday, a formal affair with dinner, dancing, and a silent auction.

"You show up there and dance together, sit together, hold hands..." Sierra said. "No need to announce it or do anything that will make you feel awkward. Just be yourselves and make a point not to hide your relationship."

"Great idea," Kennedy said. "And then sit back and wait to see which nosy Nelly questions you first for confirmation."

"If they have to ask, you're not doing it right," Sierra said. "What do you think, Lex?"

"I think you're right. It's the perfect opportunity." And somehow still scary as all get out. She nodded slowly anyway, letting the idea sink in. It would be harder *not* to show her feelings, truly.

"A little glass of bubbly to kick things off will help," Sierra said.

"Or tequila," Kennedy added.

"You Lowell girls are wise." Lexie grinned, then a thought occurred to her. "Do you need to tell Cole before then?" she asked Sierra.

"Maybe. Probably. Honestly, I'm dying to tell him. But he'd keep it to himself. Would you mind?"

Lexie shook her head, figuring that the more people who

knew ahead of time, the less pressure she'd feel Saturday night. "Tell away. Hunter, too, if you want, Kennedy. But yeah, nobody else before Saturday. And then it won't be telling. It'll be showing." She shot up off the bench in a surge of nerves. "And I should get back inside and clean up. So I can go home to Gabe."

"So you can go home to Gabe." Sierra rose and hugged her tight, full of nearly tangible love and support. "Saturday will be okay. Better than okay. We'll be there with you. And then it'll be out, and you can move on to kicking off this amazing business of yours."

Kennedy walked alongside them, offering a quick side hug and a genuine smile. "You've got this."

As they walked back toward the door, Lexie bit her lip and tried to decide which scared her more—quitting her job and starting an entirely new career or going public with her feelings for Gabe.

CHAPTER SEVENTEEN

"Good evening," Gabe's mom said into the microphone at one end of the Wentworth Hotel ballroom on a small dais.

She looked radiant in a classic black evening gown, and Gabe was relieved to see her color was good, even under the spotlights. She'd been adamant about speaking tonight, at the inaugural benefit dinner for the Harrison North Baseball and Softball Foundation, named, of course, for Gabe's father.

"Thank you, everyone, for joining us. My family and I and everyone at the Harrison North Foundation genuinely appreciate your time and your support. We're blessed to have among us numerous local celebrities, a couple of big names in country music, lovers of baseball, from the truest blue of fans to some former professional players, and, just as importantly, lots of everyday folks who want to help a good cause."

Light applause broke out throughout the darkened room, where a few hundred people sat around dinner tables and the waitstaff distributed dessert. Gabe's table had been among the first served, and they were already nearly through with their strawberry cheesecake.

"So here's a question for you," his mom continued. "How do baseball players keep in touch?" She waited a beat and then said, "They touch base every once in a while." She paused and received the collective laugh she was hoping for, with a couple of lighthearted groans mixed in.

Lexie, whose chair was next to him at the table but in front of him in relation to the dais, turned and flashed him a gorgeous smile, and if his physical need for her wasn't already ramped up, that would've done it.

She was breathtaking tonight, and he meant that literally. When he'd picked her up at Sierra's, where she'd spent the afternoon prepping herself for the gala with Sierra, Mackenzie, and Hayden, he'd stood there for several seconds with his jaw gaping like a bumbling idiot, unable to form words.

Her gown was coral-colored and one-shouldered, a slender floor-length sheath with a killer slit up the side that Gabe found himself watching for flashes of her sexy leg in her fantasy-inspiring four-inch silver heels. Her hair was done up in some sort of complex do that included braids and a sexy, tousled bun and strands framing her face. Her makeup was flawless, her eyes smoky and sultry and absolutely working for him.

On the drive to the Wentworth, she'd suggested casually—though he knew her well enough to recognize it wasn't at all a casual thing—that they stop hiding their more-than-friends status tonight. He was over the moon about being able to let his feelings show—and strangely had found himself overcautious about doing exactly that now that they'd agreed to.

Knowing how big of a step it was for her, he wanted to make sure she was comfortable, and so, thus far, throughout the mini red-carpet arrival setup, the pre-dinner drinks and mingling, and dinner, he'd not made their new relationship obvious. Sure, he'd touched her—how the hell could he not touch this stunning woman?—but that was the extent of the PDA, and anyone who knew them was probably used to them being physically close and comfortable together.

But now…the lights were down, everyone's attention was riveted on Faye North, and Gabe was dying to subtly stake his claim. They'd both finished their dessert and her full focus was on his mom. He leaned forward to her ear from behind and whispered, "You…in that dress…make me want to do dirty things to you later."

He pressed a lingering kiss to her neck, just below her ear, noticed her head tilted almost imperceptibly toward him, then straightened away from her and tried—and mostly failed—to tune in to his mom's words.

Lexie kept her gaze on his mom, playing it off, which he figured was better than her gasping in shock or shying away. She seemed to be on the same page. He couldn't wait to peel her gown down her body and tend to every inch beneath it.

As he picked up his wineglass, he noticed Drake across the table, eyeing him, and when he met his brother's eyes, his knowing look told Gabe he'd seen him kiss Lexie. Drake's brow went up in question, and all Gabe could do was grin and lift his glass slightly in acknowledgment. Drake gave a subtle thumbs-up.

Satisfied, and with his blood humming through his veins just from that little contact with Lexie, he forced himself to listen to his mom.

"I think you'll agree," Faye was saying, "that each and every one of these programs can be life-changing for a kid, and I know that's one of the objectives my son Cole had in mind when he created this foundation. Another was, of course, to honor Harrison North, his father, my beloved husband." Faye pursed her lips and lowered her head, obviously and unexpectedly overtaken by a surge of emotion, and that had Gabe's throat swelling up as well.

His mom lifted her chin, looking determined. "Oh, how I wish Harry were here today to see this, to see his boys, who've become big, overgrown, pretty fantastic humans if I do say so myself."

Gabe broke into a smile, torn by the bittersweetness of her words.

"Harry," his mom continued, and she smiled and shook her head, as if she was momentarily overcome by memories and thoughts of him. "My Harry would've been so greatly honored to be the namesake of what these boys, these men, these *people* are building—because don't get me wrong, Calista St. James, the office manager at the foundation, pulls the weight of five people."

Another smattering of laughs rang out, the kind of laugh that was half relief when humor followed a heavy moment.

"Harry would have been so honored, because to him, baseball was life and baseball was love. Baseball was a precious thing he shared with his boys from the time they were born. I'm fairly certain at least one of my children held a baseball before he even held a bottle."

Gabe moved his chair a couple of inches closer to Lex and sought out her hand with his, entwined their fingers, rested them on her thigh.

"Harry taught his boys to throw, how to catch, how to hit, how to pitch, how to steal bases, and in the process, he taught them how to be caring, considerate, compassionate people. There wasn't a weekend in the summertime when you didn't find Harry at the city park with his boys, working on the fundamentals or playing a pickup game, and he was always coaching at least one Little League team. He was perpetually in the heart of it, and that man adored every second of it, of sharing what he loved dearly with the people he loved even more.

"It's that connection, that powerful give-and-take between those boys and that man, that this foundation seeks to create for kids who don't have a father to teach them to hit, or kids whose father works two jobs to put food on the table and can't spend weekends at the park with them, or kids whose 'father' is a single mother who wants to give them the world but doesn't have the funds to make baseball a part of their lives. That, dear people, is what we're asking you to contribute to tonight.

"So please check out the silent auction in the next room, bid on a fabulous new something for yourself, and help us make a difference in local children's lives. Do baseball and softball make the world go around? No, probably not, but folks? The connections and relationships that come out of these sports sure the heck can. I know they have for my family. Thank you."

There weren't many dry eyes at the table as the applause

drowned out everything. Mason escorted their mom down the two steps and back to her seat, and gradually, the lights came up slightly, to more of a dessert-and-dance atmosphere and less of a pay-attention-to-the-speaker one.

"Let's go spend the big bucks," Lexie said, laughing as she turned to face the table. "Your mom is good."

"Heartstrings, check. Desire to buy something, check," Gabe said. Desire to buy this woman whatever her heart desired, double check.

Later, Gabe and Lexie had browsed the auction, and Gabe had insisted on Lexie choosing what she was most interested in. He put in bids on a Nantucket getaway, a Cardinals fan package, and a full-service spa package from Bliss on Hale Street. In addition, Lexie had thrown in a bid for a framed photograph by Asia Knowles.

As they made their way through the brightly lit auction room, Gabe savored the feeling of holding Lexie's hand in public. Up ahead, his mom was standing in their path, staring at them, her brows raised, a half smile on her face. As he met her gaze and smiled back, her eyes darted down to his and Lexie's joined hands and back to his face. She tilted her head.

"Gabriel? Drake said you have something to tell me."

Gabe couldn't help laughing at his pain-in-the-ass brother. "Most times I'd say Drake needs to mind his business." As they reached her, he kissed his mom's forehead and said, "Your speech was perfect, Mom."

"It was," Lexie added. "It got me...and everyone else in the room."

"Thank you," his mom said distractedly as she glanced between him and Lexie, obviously trying to decide if there was cause for celebration. "Am I reading this right?" she finally said.

"Reading what right?" Gabe said, putting on an innocent, don't-know-what-you're-talking-about act.

"Gabe," Lexie scolded softly, laughing and shaking her head. "You're awful. Tell her."

The right words failed him, so he leaned down and kissed Lexie on the lips. Nothing too hot or risqué, just enough to let his mom know things had changed for the better, without making her uncomfortable.

"You've been holding out on me!" his mom said excitedly as she squeezed Gabe's upper arm.

"It's my fault, Mrs. N," Lexie said. "It's new and I was worried about going public. But now we are." She smiled up at Gabe and her happiness radiated from her eyes.

"Heavens," his mom gushed, "come here." She pulled Lexie into a warm, tight hug, beaming at Gabe over her shoulder. "I've been waiting years for my son to pull his head out and see what's right in front of him." She winked at Gabe, then ended the hug and held on to Lexie's upper arms, looking her in the eyes. "I am so, so happy to hear this, Lexie Lou. You're already like a daughter to me, and if you two can make each other happy, there's nothing better for this mother's heart."

"Thank you. That means the world to me." Lexie looked close to tears, happy, relieved ones.

Before she could say more, Gabe's mom turned to him. "You don't have a lot of practice with this kind of thing, but you've got a big heart, Gabriel. You treat her well or you'll be answering to me." With a laugh, she hugged him too.

"My mom is siding with my girlfriend," he said. "I see how it is."

"Darn straight. I'm absolutely ecstatic for you kids. And there's Liz and Geraldine. I've got to tell them the news!"

Before they could say more, she was off on her mission, and Gabe and Lexie laughed.

"That's all we had to do," he said. "Let Mom know, and everyone else will find out before the night's over."

"That was fun," Lexie admitted as her hand found his again.

"Not bad. And for a damn good cause," Gabe said lightly, "but what I'm really dying to do get you on the dance floor. Will you dance with me?"

"In a heartbeat. Lead the way."

They continued toward the door, but when they were nearly there, he felt a hand on his arm on the opposite side from Lexie.

"Gabe?"

He turned toward the familiar feminine voice and smiled automatically when he recognized the blonde. "Ava, hello."

"I suspected you'd be here tonight," she said, all smiles, her hand still on his arm. "How are you?" Her eyes darted to Lexie and back to him.

"I'm good. Ava, I'd like you to meet my girlfriend, Lexie Gallagher. Lexie, Ava Summers."

The two shook hands, and he could see the moment Lexie made the connection. "Wait. Ava Summers of 'Heart's Alive' fame?"

"Guilty as charged," Ava said, managing to look humble and unaffected by her recent rise to a household name for her first country music hit. "It's nice to meet you, Lexie. Gabe, did you have a hand in organizing this impressive evening?"

"Only peripherally," he said. "Cole's hired quite a staff, and my mom and aunt have gotten heavily involved."

"Your mom did a bang-up job on the stage. I marched right over here and put in some bids. I'm hoping for the Joey Bloom signed guitar. She's been one of my idols for years."

"As long as you're not going for the Cardinals fan package," Gabe said, laughing.

"Baseball?" Ava cringed. "Not a chance. Lexie, your dress is gorgeous. I love that color."

"Oh," Lexie said, seeming slightly flustered. "Thank you. Yours is too."

Ava's dress was emerald green and highlighted her eyes. She was a beautiful woman who Gabe had gone out with a handful of times a couple of years ago. He'd enjoyed his time with her, but she was an ambitious woman who knew what she wanted, and back then, in addition to fighting to make a name for herself in a cutthroat industry, she'd wanted a more serious relationship with Gabe. He'd let her down easily and they'd parted on amicable terms, because Ava was also gracious and full of class. She was really quite a woman, but she just didn't do it for Gabe. Not then and sure as hell not now, with Lexie on his arm.

"Well, I don't want to keep you two. Gabe, it was so good to see you." She squeezed his arm again. "Nice to meet you, Lexie. Y'all enjoy your evening."

They said their goodbyes and Gabe led Lexie out of the room, desperate to get her on the dance floor as a ballad started playing. He wasn't wild about dancing, but if it meant he'd have Lexie in his arms, up against his body, he could dance all damn night.

"Come here, you," he said in her ear as they found a spot on the dance floor. Lexie glided into his arms as if she, too, couldn't wait to be closer. "Been waiting all night for this."

"Same," she said, her arms around his neck, eyes peering up at him.

A camera flashed mere feet from them, and Gabe glanced over to find one of the numerous members of the press who were here tonight—which was an ideal situation for the foundation— aiming her cell phone camera at them and clicking away. "Smile pretty," she said. "You're Gabe North, right?" He nodded. "And your pretty dance partner is…?"

"My girlfriend, Lexie Gallagher," he said, still getting a rush every time he called her his girlfriend.

The twentysomething girl clicked a few more times, then said with an easy smile, "Enjoy your evening—though it looks like you've got that covered," and moved on.

"Celebrity life," Lexie teased him.

"I'm not a celebrity." He shuddered at the thought.

"Tonight you are. One of the illustrious North brothers." She hesitated. "So how do you know Ava Summers? And why haven't you ever mentioned it?"

"Friend of a friend kind of thing," he said. "I went out with her a few times. I'm sure I mentioned her name but maybe not the music part. Ancient history."

Though she kept any reaction from her face, he felt her hesitation, just for a moment before she swayed closer to him.

"How many is a few?" Lexie asked.

"Four or five."

"She's beautiful."

That wasn't what he'd expected her to say. "She is."

"And friendly," Lexie continued. "And she seems genuine, especially in light of her success."

"I'd agree with that."

"I'd like to hate her," she said.

"But you're not a hateful person."

"And she doesn't seem at all hateable." She frowned momentarily, then pulled him down to her and kissed him, a possessive, passionate but brief locking of lips, as if to say, *I'm the one with you now*, which was spot on.

He knew she had insecurities, understood why she did, so her bravery in this moment made him love her all the more.

Yes, *love*.

He'd been biding his time with such a declaration, letting Lexie get used to being with him, trying not to rush her, but he had to say the words soon.

The DJ played two more slow songs, giving Gabe a good, long opportunity to savor the woman in his arms. It was no small thrill, as well, to watch the reactions of their friends and family as they spotted them and either figured out or had already heard Gabe and Lexie were more than friends.

As Kennedy and Hunter Clayborne danced nearby, Hunter gave him a subtle, "Way to go, man."

Connor, dancing with a brunette Gabe didn't know—and probably never would, knowing Connor—gave him a wide-eyed "Yessss" from across the way.

And Hayden steered her date—a bartender from Clayborne's named Pierce—up next to them and high-fived Lexie.

When the third love song in a row came to an end and the beginning notes of a classic up-tempo Timberlake song began, he leaned down to Lexie's ear and asked, "Fresh air?"

She nodded, and he whisked her out of the ballroom, to one of the side doors of the Wentworth.

The night air, though still warm and humid, was refreshing compared to the indoor heat of so many people in spite of the air conditioning. A faint breeze played with the strands of Lexie's hair as they eased up alongside the historical building. It was dark on this less-frequented side, no benches, but it was still a relief to take a break from the noise and chaos inside.

"Why did you and Ava break up?" Lexie said out of nowhere.

"We weren't together enough to break up."

"You know what I mean. Why did you stop seeing her?"

The self-doubt he'd expected earlier made her voice waver now, and he was almost glad it had surfaced so that he could extinguish it once and for all. She was leaning her back against the rough wall, and Gabe moved so he faced her, his palms flat against the light-colored surface, framing her face as he peered down at her.

"I stopped seeing her because we had nothing in common. I didn't want to go out with her anymore."

"Most guys would want to go out with her, I think."

"Lexie," he said, nudging her chin up with his knuckle to ensure she kept eye contact. "I don't know, because I'm not most guys. What I do know, though, is that Ava, just like any other woman I've been out with in my adult life, was merely a place-holder, a way to pass the time. None of them could ever be the one woman I've always wanted."

He kissed her because he couldn't stand not touching her lips for another second. When he finally pulled his mouth away from hers, his breath was uneven and his insides were shaky.

"Lexie, I'm going to tell you something, but I don't want you to feel forced to react in a certain way. In fact, I don't want you to say anything back. Just hear what I'm telling you."

"Okaaaay," she said, dragging it out like a question, holding on to the lapels of his tuxedo jacket.

"You are literally the girl of my dreams. You have been for years. I love you, Lex."

As she peered up at him, her lips parted, and he lowered his mouth to hers again before she could say anything. Because there was a part of him that was worried he was rushing this or wanting too much from her. A part of him that, at times, still couldn't believe that Lexie was finally his.

If Lexie did love him, he wanted her to say it when she was ready, not just because she felt pressured to say it back.

They kissed like a couple of teenagers for several minutes, and he was pretty sure, based on the way she kissed him, that she did love him, whether she could say it out loud or not.

When they finally made their way back inside, though, he thought, for the first time, maybe he was an idiot to always put Lexie's needs above his, because he could really stand to hear that she loved him back.

CHAPTER EIGHTEEN

*L*exie had loved Gabe forever.

Maybe she'd only ever let herself acknowledge the platonic love she had for him, hadn't dared to even think about anything more, but there was no question she'd felt love and affection for him for years.

They'd never been the types to say *I love you* to each other as friends, and even when she signed emails or birthday cards, she hadn't used the *L* word. It was just…there. Underlying their friendship.

From the passenger seat of his car, she glanced over at his handsome profile as he drove them from his mom's house to his place and felt a thrill down to her toes, especially knowing what she had in store for him tonight. A thrill…and some definite nerves.

The whole extended North family had been at his mom's house for the weekly dinner this evening—all of his brothers, except Zane, of course, and their significant others, plus the cousins and Aunt Liz and Geraldine, the honorary non-blood-related third matriarch of the North clan. It was Gabe's thirty-seventh birthday, and the North family did birthdays up right.

She hoped to cap it off and make it an unforgettable day for him.

And that had her mind wandering back to the *love* debate.

Now that their friendship had deepened into more, something amazing and fulfilling and better than her wildest dreams, her feelings for Gabe had absolutely increased, become multidimensional and exponential. She was pretty sure she *love* loved him.

And yet last night at the gala, when he'd told her not to respond, she'd been grateful. Because it took the pressure off.

Weirdly, it also put the pressure on.

Good lord, did she feel the pressure.

Because now she had to figure out the right time to say she loved him. And before that, she had to be sure she really, really meant it. It should be a no-brainer, but hello. She'd thought she loved Raleigh. When her ex had said the *L* word to her, she'd zinged it right back. Just like expected.

Look where that'd gotten her.

If she was honest, telling Gabe she loved him scared the daylights out of her. It was one more step out onto the vulnerability limb, and that limb had been tested and was bowing hard from the gala and "going public."

Their friends and Gabe's family had been excited for them and supportive to a T, and his mom's reception meant the world to Lexie, but still, it all made her nervous. Because now, if she blew it with Gabe, everyone would know, just like they all knew with Raleigh. Even though she and Gabe had years and years of friendship behind them, she was scared she could still mess it up somehow or that Gabe might figure out she was too needy or too emotional.

After worrying nearly nonstop since last night about her inability to say what Gabe wanted to hear—and acknowledging that she was on a quest to not do or say things just because it was what someone else wanted—she'd come up with an alternate solution to make his birthday special. She was going to *show* him how she felt. Between that and the present she'd wrapped up, she was giving him a big chunk of her heart, and she hoped he would see that. Feel that.

"So..." Gabe said, jolting her out of her thoughts as he pulled the car into his driveway. "What's my present?" He was grinning like a little kid at Christmas. "Did you really get me something or is it you I get to unwrap?"

"It's a surprise," she said coyly as he killed the engine. "You get Saint taken care of and I'll bring it out to you."

Once inside, she went to "her" spare room. She had more than a few extra pieces of clothing stored there now, since she was staying at Gabe's more often than not. She wasn't moving in, and using the master closet felt a little like an encroachment on Gabe's space, so she'd just continued to use this one. It was also where she'd stowed his gift.

She pulled the large wrapped package out, leaned it against the spare bed, and checked her appearance in the mirror.

Her dress choice for dinner at his mom's was a strategic one, and she grinned to herself as she surveyed the casual summer dress, in a super-soft, flowy aqua fabric. The short sleeves were loose and cool, the neckline was a V but not too deep, not too sexy, and the thigh-length dress tied on one side. Very girl-next-door.

She'd kept her long hair down in a wavy, tousled style, and it needed a finger comb now. Her makeup was light enough it didn't need a touch-up except for her lip gloss, and she applied a coat of medium pink, hoping that would be kissed off soon.

In the other room, she heard Gabe and Saint come inside and shut the door, Gabe talking in a low, affectionate voice to the dog, which made Lexie melt a little. Who could resist a sexy man sweet-talking his overgrown beast of a dog?

"Time to do this," she said to her reflection. "Time to do *him*." With a quiet, nervous laugh, she hoisted up the present and headed out to the living room.

"There she is," Gabe said in his talking-to-Saint voice, and the dog came over to her to see if he could "help" or maybe get an ear rub.

"Hey, Saint. How's the big baby?" She presented the gift to Gabe, who was sitting on one end of the sectional, relaxed and taking up a lot of room with his long limbs semi-sprawled. He sat up straighter to take it from her. "My first gift to you is *not* singing 'Happy Birthday.'"

Gabe laughed. "I'd listen to it and love it even if you were a little off-key."

"How do you feel about a lot off-key?" she said, grinning. "Anyway, I hope you like that." She nodded toward the present, anticipating his reaction.

He flipped it over to expose the seam in the wrapping paper and tore it open. The back was facing him, so, still smiling, he flipped it again.

He suddenly went serious, his eyes transforming from humor to disbelief to a wave of emotions. She thought they were good ones, but she held her breath.

"Oh, God. Lex..." Balancing the framed artwork on his legs, he reached out and dragged her, still standing while he was sitting, over to him. When he met her gaze, his eyes were damp and full of love. "You're giving this to me?"

Unexpectedly, she was overcome by emotions too, and it was suddenly hard to speak, so she nodded. Her eyes teared up at the look on Gabe's face as he studied the colored-pencil painting like he hadn't before. Yes, he'd seen it before, the one of the Adirondack chair, the bat, the mitt, and his dad's hat.

"This is incredible," Gabe said. "Best gift anyone has ever given me."

Lexie sank down next to him on the cushion, relieved, gratified, overwhelmed by the feelings this piece evoked in her—from nostalgia to grief to the closest thing to parental and family love she'd ever experienced.

"You've always given so much to me, shared so much goodness, and your family's near the top of that list. I just wanted to give something back to you. I hope this feels like a tiny part of your dad, because when I started working on it all those years ago, he'd made me the happiest girl in the world that day by including me. Treating me special. Taking time from his busy life to teach me something that was so important to your whole family." She stopped and wiped her eye before a tear fell, smiling at the same time because the memories were good ones.

"That's my dad." Gabe's voice was raw with love and memories too as he studied the artwork some more. "And the chair is so much my mom. You got my whole family in this, Lex. I'm…" He shook his head, clearly at a loss for words. He pulled her in close to his side and she felt his appreciation and affection in every cell. Closing her eyes, she drank it in, savored the moment.

Gabe squeezed her and then straightened. As he stood, he grasped the sixteen-by-twenty-inch frame and walked to the fireplace. The only decor on the mantel was three small framed photos, one of his family, one of Saint, and a candid of him and Lexie from several years back. He set those out of the way and propped Lexie's gift in the center. "I've needed something here for years," he said and nodded as he stepped back to admire it. "I love it, Lexie. It's perfect in every way. Thank you."

She came up beside him, agreeing that it looked great on the mantel—just the right size, and the colors stood out against the light-colored stonework, but not so much that it looked garish or out of place. "You're welcome."

"Come here." He turned to her and wrapped his arms around her and lifted her up in the very best thank-you hug of her life. Then, still holding her, he kissed her, and Lexie locked her legs around him and sank into the kiss. She got lost in it as his tongue probed at her lips and he deepened it, showing her exactly how happy he was about his present.

A couple minutes later, he came up for air and turned, looked around, as if deciding where to take her, and that brought her back to herself enough to remember her plan.

She unhooked her legs and slid her feet to the floor. "Sit," she said, pointing to the sectional.

"Sit?"

"It's time for your next present."

"There's more?"

"There's more. I'm hoping it's your favorite part."

With a smile, he tilted his head, shot a glance at the art on the mantel, and said, "I don't know. That's pretty tough to beat."

She pointed to the sectional again, hand on her hip, trying not to grin. Seduction was not exactly her strong point, but she had learned that Gabe would respond to whatever awkward attempts she made, unlike some people she knew. But she was so not thinking about anyone but Gabe today.

With an expectant grin, Gabe sat and focused his knowing blue eyes on her. Lexie went to the kitchen and flipped on the lights over the island seating area and dimmed them, then flipped the living room lights off, leaving them in a romantic low light. She glanced around at the windows to make sure they had privacy. As she made her way back toward Gabe, she felt his eyes on her the whole time.

She stopped a couple of feet from him, faced him, and his expression as he watched her... *Hungry* was the best word she could come up with. And not for food, because he'd consumed pounds and pounds of that at his mom's, and then birthday cake afterward.

With a courage-reinforcing inhale, she reached to her side, untied her dress, and let it drop to the floor, revealing the teddy beneath. It was made of the palest pink mesh, with lace-up sides and exquisite pink flowers and sage-green leaves and stems embroidered in a trail down the front, from her breasts to her nether bits, where it snapped between her legs. The flowers sort of covered things but not really. Just enough that, she hoped, it was an alluring tease. Though she didn't normally wear such elaborate lingerie, she had to admit it was a gorgeous piece.

"Holy—" Gabe's eyes popped all the way open as he ate her up with his gaze, and her nervousness dissipated.

Wearing this lingerie under her innocent-looking dress all evening, especially around his family, she'd felt a little nervous, but this moment made it all worth it.

He blew out a shaky breath and leaned forward. "You are so beautiful, Lex."

"Thank you," she said demurely.

"You bringing that here?" he asked, his voice rough.

"In time. First you need to take your shoes off."

He had them kicked off just about before she finished the sentence.

"Next, your shirt."

He was wearing a royal-blue polo and reached back and

whipped it over his head just as quickly, giving her a view of his delectable chest and abs.

"Shorts next?" he asked eagerly, making her laugh.

"You've always been above average in intelligence. Shorts next."

He unbuttoned and unzipped them, then rose enough to slide them—and his boxer briefs—off, leaving him gloriously naked for her to feast her eyes on. Her body reacted to the sight, inside and out.

Slowly, she stepped toward him, letting her gaze burn into him as she approached. She bent over him and kissed him, not touching the rest of him yet even though she was dying to.

The groan that came from deep in his throat turned her on even more and verified he was totally into this—in case she'd missed the impossible-to-miss erection jutting toward his abdomen.

Gabe's hands were on her sides in a flash. As she continued to kiss him, he tried to pull her down on top of him but she resisted. Then he grasped one of her thighs and attempted to pull it up beside him, as if he wanted her to straddle him, but she prevented that, too, and straightened for a moment.

"Nope," she said. "You are going to be a good birthday boy and sit there and let me do what I want to do to you. No taking control this time."

He let out a low, sexy chuckle that resonated through her and turned her the rest of the way inside out. "You drive a hard"—he glanced between his legs—"bargain."

"Best kind," she said, and then she proceeded with her plan and spent the next eternity trailing her lips over his body, from his mouth to his ears to his neck and chest, over the hard ridges of his pecs, into the dip in the middle, down toward his navel. When she was nearly to his Mr. Friendly, she did an about-face with her tongue and worked her way back up, spending inordinate amounts of time on his nipples because that seemed to make him the squirm the most.

"You...are...killing me," he gasped out after trying, more than once, to guide her, and her returning, more than once, his hands to his sides with a wicked grin. "It would be bad…for me to die…on my birthday…wouldn't it?"

She lifted her mouth from his chest and pressed a kiss to his lips. "You're not"—she kissed him again—"dying. I promise."

His response was a long, low groan.

Slowly, she worked her way down again, and this time, she took him into her mouth and swirled her tongue around him, tasting salt and musk and sex.

"Sweet mother of God," he said as he watched her.

She spent the next few minutes loving him with her mouth, and judging by his movements and sounds, he was as turned on as she wanted him. The next thing she knew, he was pulling out of her mouth and lifting her up to kiss his lips.

"What…?" she managed as she found herself on top of him with his shaft pressing into the part of her that was throbbing with need.

"I love what you're doing to me, but I want to be inside of you when I come. I'm not trying to take control," he added quickly, "but can we do that?"

Breathing hard, as was he, she gazed into his eyes from inches away, and honestly, him inside of her… "Yes." She kissed him briefly again, then managed to stand up. "But you have to wait just a second."

"What? Where are you going?"

Lexie walked across the area to the pantry, ducked in and grabbed what she wanted, and then came back out to find Gabe not far behind her.

She held up the canister of vanilla frosting she'd bought for exactly this. "Every birthday boy deserves to have frosting. Am I right?"

With a growl, he lunged for her, picked her—and the frosting —up, and carried her into his bedroom.

CHAPTER NINETEEN

*I*t'd been a hell of a day already, and it was only 10:25 a.m. on Wednesday.

The good news was that Lexie was due to show up any minute.

Gabe looked up from his desk at North Brothers Sports, where he'd only just sat down a few minutes ago after returning from the hospital, as Mason entered his office with Melody from Marketing.

"Are you ready for us?" Mason asked, pausing inside the door.

"Come on in."

"What's the latest on Brad?" Melody asked.

"He's in surgery as we speak," Gabe said.

The company's benefits specialist had been in a serious car accident on his way to work early this morning and was in critical condition.

Mason walked around the table in the corner of Gabe's office and stood behind one of the four chairs, his attention focused on his brother. "Is he going to be okay?"

"They don't know at this point," Gabe said grimly. "Multiple internal injuries." He shook his head, still reeling. "His wife's understandably a mess."

"Let us know when you hear more, would you?" Melody

said.

"Of course."

"Even assuming the best," Mason said, "he's going to need an extended absence to heal. You guys on top of that?"

"We'll figure it out." Covering Brad's work was the least of Gabe's worries after spending a couple of hours in the waiting room with the guy's family.

Jalisa, Gabe's assistant, appeared in the open doorway and rapped on the door. "Guess who's here," she said. "Are you ready for Lexie?"

"We are." *More than*, he thought as he came around his desk and soaked in the sight of Lexie as she walked in, instantly feeling more centered.

She might be small, but a quiet confidence exuded from her. She wore navy dress pants that ended above the ankle, heels that matched, and a white shirt with a fancy neckline. Last night, she'd debated jacket or no jacket as she tried to figure out what image she wanted for her new venture, and he applauded the decision to go without. She looked professional but not overly banker-like, perfect for a creative entrepreneur.

"Hey, Lex," Gabe said, and he resisted the urge to kiss her in welcome, endeavoring to be professional since this was an official meeting and one that meant the world to her and her future.

She'd been closed-mouthed about exactly what she was presenting to them regarding mural work. One evening last week, once the east-side mural was completed, she'd met with Kennedy for several hours to hash out ideas, and he'd be lying if he said he wasn't dying to hear her business proposal.

"Hi, Gabe," she said with an intimate smile. "Hi, Mason."

His brother stood and came around the table and shook her hand, which was weird as hell, but Mason would never slip from the utmost in professionalism. "Hey, Lexie. It's good to see you. This is Melody Schafer, our marketing VP and branding guru."

Melody stood and the two women shook hands. Gabe took the chair next to Mason's, Mason returned to his place, and soon they were all seated around the table, making small talk.

"Well," Mason finally said, "we're intrigued by what you'd like to present to us, Lexie. Are you ready to get into it?"

"I am. First, thank you for meeting with me. I know how busy you all are."

"You're part of the family," Mason said. "We'll always take time for you. But after what you did with the east-side store, we'd be crazy not to talk to you regardless. The buzz for that store has been tangible—as in dollars-and-cents tangible. Traffic's been up for the past week plus, and sales have followed. People want to see the changes, and they're spending money in the process."

"That's great news," Lexie said with a nervous smile. She'd set a folder on the table and was resting her hands in her lap. She took in a big breath, and Gabe couldn't help himself. He grabbed one of her hands under the table, not trying to hide it from anyone.

"It's just us, Lex. Nothing to be nervous about," he said.

"I saw the finished mural last weekend," Melody said. "It's fantastic! I can't wait to hear about your ideas."

"Thank you," Lexie said. She squeezed Gabe's hand before releasing it, then rested her palms on the folder, and he noticed her nails were freshly coated with silver polish. "I'm excited about the possibilities. And I trust that you two won't go easy on me just because I've known you since you were in Little League." She laughed, and Gabe could still hear the nervousness. She'd forge through it soon enough, he knew.

"No leniency," Mason said. "I might think of you as a little sister, but you know when it comes to this company—"

"He's a hard-ass through and through," Gabe said lightly, although he meant every word of it.

Nodding as she eyed Mason across the table, she said, "Okay. Hard-ass Mason I can handle," making everyone laugh.

Gabe listened as Lexie launched into her proposal and gathered steam. Once she started, her experience with presenting to clients was undeniable, and her passion for the topic shined through. She explained the benefits of murals on business and cited research that showed that the east-side store's sales spike after her mural was finished was no fluke.

Her energy and ease built up as she got into the meat of her proposal, and Gabe realized he was holding his breath. He wanted this to work on so many levels—for the company and for Lexie.

First, she presented Part A, which consisted of painting multiple murals in the west-side store, one for each department. They would add interest, color, and branding opportunities, and it was such a good idea that Gabe didn't know why they hadn't thought of it before. With his mind still spinning on possibilities, Lexie moved on.

"Part B of what I'm proposing for the brand-new, under-construction west-side location is, indeed, a mural," she said, "but it goes beyond a pretty picture on the wall that will add ambience and excitement and branding. Yes, murals have been proven to increase traffic and sales, but I want you to think even bigger than that. I want you to imagine a mural that could become an interactive attraction in and of itself."

She paused, opened her folder, and distributed pages to all three of them. "Imagine a giant outdoor forest-river-camping scene along a forty-foot wall, a draw on its own, but what if it was also something for families to do? What if it was a giant hidden-pictures game that customers could play at their leisure? The *Where's Waldo* of North Brothers Sports, except instead of looking for one guy in a striped shirt, they're searching for a lady bug and a hatchet and a fishing bobber and a mouse, for example."

An audible breath came from Melody as she looked over the sketches of what Lexie had in mind, examples of different types of hidden pictures.

"Say we put one hundred hidden pictures in the mural," Lexie continued. "You could have ten different lists of ten items. A customer can do one per store visit, and if they find all ten on the list, maybe they get a prize or a discount on a certain item. Or what if they won a free fitness class or some other benefit to encourage their participation in exercise and sports? It's a win-win-win. The specifics are for you guys to figure out," Lexie said, "but the possibilities are endless. And the cornerstone is the hidden-pictures mural."

"We'd have kids begging their parents to go to North Brothers Sports," Melody said.

Gabe was blown away, and his mind was reeling as he imagined, as Lexie had suggested, all the things they could do with this idea. What he wanted to do was jump out of his seat, pump his fist, pick up Lexie, and spin her around in celebration of a seriously badass concept that could not only boost their business but be the heart of a community presence like they'd only dreamed of. What he actually did was remain calm in his chair and try to maintain an air of professionalism, as if he wasn't bursting with pride and enthusiasm.

He listened as Lexie outlined the different levels of projects and the fees involved with each. Though he hadn't known details about her proposal before today, he'd been well aware of her ongoing research into pricing her services, and he'd done extensive research for the east-side project, so he knew she was spot on with the industry. The boyfriend side of him jumped ahead to think about the potential for Lexie's new company in the North Brothers stores alone. With nearly twenty locations in the southeastern quadrant of the country and several more slated to open yet this year, if this idea went over well and became a North Brothers signature thing, they could keep her busy—and paid—for a good while.

He reined it in and stuffed his business hat back on his head, took a hard look at the proposal as a member of senior management. Mason and Cole knew the construction budget better than he did and would be able to say if there was room for this kind of investment. And of course, Melody's take on the branding opportunities and challenges would carry a lot of weight.

A few minutes later, Lexie was finishing up when Ruby, Mason's administrative assistant, knocked lightly on the door, then stuck her head in.

"Cole's on line two. Says it's urgent," Ruby said to Mason.

With an exhale and a glance toward Gabe that hinted at *what now*, Mason stood. "I'll take it in my office, Ruby. Lexie, thank you for all the time and thought you've put into this. Gabe and Melody can finish getting any questions answered, and we'll get back to you when we can."

And then he hurried out. They both knew if Cole, who was their special projects manager and the point person for their various building projects, said it was urgent, it was, and probably not good news.

"Sorry about that," Gabe said as the door shut.

"I've pretty much covered everything anyway." Lexie smiled, unflustered by the interruption. "The last part is potential time tables, which, of course, would depend on the construction schedule on your end."

They briefly went over that section, and then Lexie asked if they had further questions.

"You've been really thorough," Melody said as she flipped through the printed-out proposal and the sketches again. "I need some time to absorb all the potential for this, Lexie. It's an exciting idea with so many possibilities. I assume Gabe can get me in touch with you if we have questions later?"

"He knows where to find me," Lexie said. "I'm waiting on business cards, but my cell number and email are right here." She pointed to the header of the proposal. "Contact me anytime."

"Thank you," Melody said as they all stood. "This is such an exciting concept." She shook Lexie's hand.

"I'd love to work with you on it," Lexie said.

"Thanks for joining us, Melody," Gabe said as the marketing VP went toward the door. "Let's set up a time to get with Mason and whoever else needs to be in on it to discuss it more."

"You've got it." Melody walked out the door, leaving it ajar.

Gabe gave half a second's thought to closing it and ravishing Lexie, but with the kind of day he was having—and Mason on the line with Cole—there was no doubt they'd be interrupted a dozen times. He knew she'd only taken a half day off from work anyway. "I wish I had time to take you to lunch, but I'm playing catch-up. One of my HR people was in a serious accident this morning," he told her.

"Oh, no. Are they okay?"

"He's in surgery right now, fighting for his life."

"I'm so sorry, Gabe. I hope he pulls through."

"Me too."

As they walked out of his office, through the halls, past the cubicles, and out of the building, he filled her in on the few details he had until they reached her Subaru.

"Between covering for Brad and prepping for the court hearing for the lawsuit, the next couple of weeks are going to be a challenge," he said.

"It all sucks, Gabe. I'll try to keep out of your way as much as possible."

"Don't you dare," he said, opening the driver's-side door for her. He'd been professional for long enough, and now he pulled her into his body and kissed her the way he'd been dying to. Well, the shortened, PG-rated version of it, anyway. "You knocked it out of the park in there. The spin you put on the mural idea is genius, Lex."

"I can't take all the credit. Kennedy was a big part of it." She fiddled with his tie and the lapels of his suit jacket. "I couldn't get a read on Mason. Any idea what he's thinking?"

"He's good at the stone-faced thing," Gabe agreed. "I'm pretty sure he likes the idea, but I don't know where he's at with the investment and logistics. We'll be talking about it in depth, and I'll see if we can get to it soon. If it were up to me, I'd have hired you on the spot."

She pressed a brief kiss to his lips. "You're biased."

"I'm biased as hell, but I also know a damn good idea when I see it. That'd be a good one even if it was my archenemy presenting it."

"Who's your archenemy?" she asked, her head tilted flirtatiously.

Gabe laughed. "No one. Everybody loves me. Well, except the guy suing my family's company."

"In my opinion, he's a crazy-pants." Her expression went serious, and she looked thoughtful for a few seconds, her gaze pointing off to the side, in the distance. "Can I ask you a question and get an unbiased, not-my-boyfriend-and-not-even-my-best-friend answer from you?"

"I can try," he said curiously.

"Not taking my presentation today into account, because I fully realize it could be turned down because of budget or whatever…" Lexie pursed her lips as she inhaled deeply, then finally hit him directly with her gaze. "Would I be crazy to quit my job?"

His eyes popped open wider.

"I want to do this, Gabe." She lifted the presentation folder. "I've had a sampling of selling online, and there's potential there, maybe a lot. Lord knows I have the material even if I never draw or paint another thing. I have two home-nursery murals booked without really trying, and even if NBS says no, I think I have a solid business idea in the corporate murals. I have enough savings to live on for over a year if I cut back on expenses, and I could cut down on my shopping hobby." She let out a self-deprecating half laugh.

"Drastic measures," he said, only half kidding as he thought about her question.

"I've been thinking a lot about what I want for my life, for me," she continued, "like we talked about in Colorado, and this is something I want to do. I want to own my own business. I want to be my own boss. I want to do something creative and get paid for it."

Gabe had known she was seriously considering making this a full-time thing; he just hadn't realized how far along in the thought process she was.

"Wow." He ran a hand over his face, letting everything she'd said sink in. His first instinct was *hell yeah*, but he wanted to be sure he was giving her sound advice based on his business experience, not just reacting as the man who loved her and thought she'd hung the moon. "Have you thought more about a business plan?" he asked.

"I've done more than thought. I've been reading up on them, researching online. I started jotting down notes this morning."

And that was why she'd succeed. Not only was she talented but she was intelligent as hell. Her career in landscape architecture used both sides of the brain—creative and analytical—and she excelled in both.

Between his business sense and his belief in her, his second and third instincts were also *hell yeah*.

"I believe in you, Lex. You're not crazy. If you want, I can help you with your plan."

"Thank you." She stretched up on her toes and kissed him again. "But no. You have enough on your plate. If I run into problems, I'll ask you for help, but otherwise, my goal's to not bother you. And right now, I don't want to keep you from work any longer, so"—another quick kiss—"off with you. Tell Mason thanks and I look forward to hearing back. I'll see you tonight."

He barely managed to get out a "Bye, Lex," before she had her door shut and car started.

Backing away, he watched her drive off and wondered how and when he would convince her the only kind of bothering she did to him was the good kind and that she would never be in his way.

CHAPTER TWENTY

*L*exie had had only three swallows of her lemon drop martini Friday night, but she was flying high. It was a good day, a fantastically good day, and she couldn't think of a better way to top it off than to celebrate the engagement of Mackenzie Shaw and Drake North.

The party was being thrown by Sierra, Sloan, Hayden, and Lexie and was at Mackenzie and Drake's new home. Drake didn't live there yet, wouldn't until after their wedding, but it was important to them to break it in with their engagement party.

The guests had started arriving a few minutes ago, close to seventy expected, and they gathered in the spacious living room and poured out into the backyard. The house was now buzzing with a din of happy people, and Sierra, Hayden, and Lexie were in the kitchen, plating up more of the appetizers they'd had catered in and pouring drinks. And sipping their own. Sloan was outside, circulating with a cheese tray and one of antipasto bites.

Mackenzie floated in from the entryway, where she'd been greeting people as they arrived, wearing a cute party dress that showed off her long legs and looking on top of the world.

"Everything going okay?" Mackenzie asked.

"You're not supposed to be in here," Hayden chided as she popped a stuffed mushroom into her mouth.

"Aww, who knew you were such a bossy party planner?" Mackenzie said, winding an arm around Hayden and pressing a kiss to her cheek. "I just wanted to tell you girls thank you again. This is so awesome. Best party ever and it's only getting started."

"You're welcome again, crazy girl," Sierra said. "You're so happy your face is going to split in two—as you should be!"

"I also came in because I heard our quiet girl here has news," Mackenzie said, coming over to Lexie, putting her arm around her, and peering at her expectantly.

With her own wide smile, Lexie admitted, "I do. I've been dying to tell you guys, but it's your night, so I've been biding my time."

"Well, quit biding! What's going on?" Mackenzie leaned against the counter and took the wineglass Sierra handed her, obviously having lost her previous beverage.

Lexie put the last mini cupcake from the Sugar Babies box on the plate and turned to face the trio. "This afternoon, I gave notice at my job."

Sierra grabbed her arm, her brows raised, eyes wide. "Did NBS say yes?"

"They did," Lexie gushed. "Lock, stock, and barrel." She filled the other two in. "They're hiring me—my new company—to paint multiple murals in their brand-new store here in town."

"Like what you did in the east-side store?" Hayden asked. "Sierra showed me a pic. It's incredible."

"Like that but more." Lexie briefly told them about the hidden pictures and the multiple department murals and the prospects for doing the same in the other stores around the country eventually. "It blows my mind that they want to pay me at all, let alone the going rates."

"You're so worth it," Sierra said. "And that could take you months, right? So job security for quite a while?"

"Months or even years, depending on how fast they want to go. I'm up for anything."

"Plus the murals for Kennedy and Lena, right?" Sierra asked.

"Plus those. I hope to get to work on those in the next month or two since the new store won't be ready for me right away."

"That," Hayden said, picking up her wineglass and coming closer, "is fantastic news! I'm so happy for you. How about a toast? To woman-owned businesses, to the North brothers for being smart enough to hire you, and to you, Lexie."

"Hear, hear," Mackenzie said, and the four of them clinked glasses and took a drink.

"Thank you, girls." The words seemed so lame in light of what was a doubly momentous occasion for Lexie. Not only the career change but the girlfriends to celebrate it with.

Sierra glanced toward both doorways, as if making sure they were still alone in the kitchen. Seeing that they were, she lowered her voice. "I have something quick too. I wasn't sure tonight was the right time, but here we four are together, and it's the perfect opportunity."

With the four of them still gathered in a tight circle, Lexie and Mackenzie leaned closer, while Hayden smiled knowingly, as if she was in on the secret.

"Do tell," Mackenzie said, her copper highlights catching the overhead light just right and making her look redder than usual.

"It's ask, actually." Sierra's gaze hit each of them briefly. "Cole and I, now that we're all moved in, started getting serious about wedding planning. Hayden has already accepted, and I was wondering if you two would also be bridesmaids."

Lexie's hand flew to her mouth as she let out a happy laugh. Happy but quiet when compared to Mackenzie's reaction—the willowy girl at her side squealed joyously and said, "Yes, yes, yes, of course! I'd be honored."

"Same," Lexie managed, nearly speechless because she was so touched. "I'd love to." She swallowed, debated her next words, decided to be honest. "I've never been in a wedding before. Not even the one I planned for myself." She let out a genuine laugh, because finally, she could joke about it.

"Then I'm doubly lucky to be your first," Sierra said. "Kennedy and Asia will round out the group. Bigger than I ever expected, but you're all special to me, and no way could I narrow it down."

"Plus Cole has all those brothers," Hayden said.

"They're going fast, but there's still a couple left if you want me to set you up," Sierra told her.

"Ha. Still no. Not ever. But thanks. I know your heart is in the right place." Hayden bumped hips with Sierra to soften the rejection. To the other two, she said, "I made her promise no awful colors for the bridesmaid dresses. She agreed in theory. We'll see if that holds up."

They all laughed and started suggesting the worst colors from a Crayola box, from Asparagus to Macaroni and Cheese to Raw Sienna.

When Drake called out for Mackenzie from the French doors that led outside, she fluttered away happily, hugging Sierra on the way and promising she'd have the best wedding ever.

"I guess we should get back to work," Sierra said, "but thank you, girls. It means the world to me."

Lexie found herself tugged into a group hug and knew right then and there, between her career, her friendships, and Gabe, her life couldn't get much better, and she said a silent thanks to the powers that be, remembering how low she'd felt just weeks ago on the day her wedding had been called off.

As they pulled away, her phone, which was resting on the counter where she'd been plating desserts, started vibrating, and she walked over to check it, thinking just about everyone she knew well enough for a phone call was here at the party. The caller was listed as unknown, and she almost let it ring, normally would have, but something had her picking it up and answering.

"Lexie?" The voice was hard to hear over all the noise, but she still thought she recognized it.

"Hello?" Lexie said, her heart speeding up as she hurried out of the kitchen and around the corner, to the stairs going up, where no one could see her.

"Can you hear me?" the voice said.

Lowering herself to the carpeted stairs halfway up, Lexie said, "Mom? Is that you?"

"It is," her mom said, her voice matter-of-fact. "Is this a bad time?"

At a loss, because her mom had only called her a handful of

times, and those whenever she was back in the States, Lexie held the phone away from her face for a moment and checked the time, as if that would answer her mom's question.

"N-no. It's fine. Is everything okay?"

"Everything's fine. I'm in California."

Lexie shouldn't care. She knew that. She knew Gabe would suggest she not take the call in the first place, because talking to her usually left Lexie upset and wanting. Wanting a mom who cared about her, who was in her life. But still, every time her mom reached out, few and far between though the calls were, it lit that little spark of hope inside of her that was smaller than a pilot light. Hope that maybe this time would be different.

Her mother's next words knocked her for a loop.

"I'll be in Nashville by Thursday. I'm renting a car and driving from San Diego."

"Really?" Lexie heard the words but it took several seconds for them to sink in. "You're coming to Nashville?"

"I am."

She hadn't been back since Lexie's dad's funeral, nearly ten years ago. Before that, it'd been when Lexie was four. As far as Lexie knew, she hadn't come back once in all those years between, but then, maybe she had and Lexie and her dad just didn't know it. Or maybe her dad had known, had talked to Jean, the woman he'd been married to for all of four and a half years when she walked out on him, and he just hadn't told Lexie. Nothing would surprise her. Not more than her mother's news now.

"That's a long way to drive," Lexie said, as if that was the most important thing.

"I'll get to see the country," her mom replied. "I won't keep you now, but I was hoping we could meet. How about lunch on Friday?"

"In Nashville?" Lexie said again stupidly, still unable to wrap her head around this conversation.

With a short laugh, her mom said, "That seems most logical, since we'll both be there. You'll be in town?"

"Of course," Lexie said. "I'll be here. Um, I don't know about lunch. I'll have to check my calendar and I'm at a party right now."

It was an excuse, a way to buy time, because there was a battle going on inside of Lexie. As much as she ached for a real relationship with her mom, history had taught her that wasn't in the cards, and the woman had done nothing but let her down. When they'd reconnected at the funeral, Lexie had gotten her hopes up that things would be different, but Jean Gallagher had returned to South America and her beloved monkeys.

"Why don't I call you Thursday when I get into town. We can hammer out the details if you're available." Her mom made it sound like a business appointment, and wasn't that always the problem? Lexie wasn't a daughter to her but more like an afterthought whenever she was geographically close, relatively speaking.

And yet Lexie wasn't sure she'd be able to say no.

Since her mom had just offered her time to decide, nearly a week, she took it and agreed to talk to her on Thursday.

Once they hung up, Lexie sat there, alone on the stairs, for several minutes, her mind spinning and her elation dimmed significantly. Because there wasn't an easy answer. There never was with her mother.

Finally standing, she vowed to put the dilemma out of her mind for the night, go finish her martini and pour another one, and get back to feeling on top of the world, Mom or no Mom. Somehow.

CHAPTER TWENTY-ONE

hursday evening, it was nearly eight o'clock when Gabe got home from work. He pulled into the garage, cut the engine, and closed the door behind him, realizing that Lexie and her car weren't there. Realizing how odd that was.

He didn't like it.

He'd gotten used to having her around most evenings, unless one or both of them had something going on. Coming home to her was not a hardship, didn't make him feel penned in in the least. It felt natural. Easy. Right.

Except for the last week. Something had been bugging her for days now.

He'd tried to get her to open up about it several times, with no luck. To be fair, he had his share of a shit show going on at work, so maybe he'd been distracted and missed something obvious. Gabe leaned his head back against the headrest and breathed fully in, maybe for the first time all day.

The pre-trial hearing was tomorrow for the age discrimination suit filed against NBS. A former employee, Raymond Polanski, was in his early fifties and had worked in the IT department for eighteen years. He'd always been a likable guy, competent, loyal to the company—until he was passed up for a promotion a few months ago. Olivia Kirk, in her early thirties, was a go-getter who could pull rabbits out of hats. One conversation with her and you knew she was going places, and it'd been a unanimous opinion that North Brothers Sports management wanted those places to be within the company. They'd be stupid to let her get away.

Raymond had resigned when Olivia was granted the promotion and was suing for age discrimination. It should be an open-and-closed case, but then, as their legal team had reminded them countless times, nothing was ever guaranteed. The time and money being spent on preparations were no joke—not only for the lawyers but for Gabe and Connor and Mason and several others.

Brad Morris had made it through his first surgery, started to recover, then taken a turn for the worse two days ago and undergone an emergency second surgery. He was apparently stabilized and hopefully on the road to healing. It wouldn't be a short road, and Gabe was still trying to figure out how best to handle his extended absence at work.

And the latest crisis, the situation with the employee with the prescription drug problem had come to a head. This week, the problem had become impossible to ignore because of work performance issues. After Gabe and the employee relations manager had met with the guy and his direct supervisor, there'd been drama and blowups and breakdowns and a family intervention and the guy eventually announcing that he was entering an eight-week inpatient rehab program. Encouraging news for the employee and his family but yet another challenge for the HR department.

The dim light on the garage opener had gone out, leaving Gabe in the dark, and he soaked in the quiet for a moment before pulling out his phone, sending Lexie a text to check in, grabbing his messenger bag, and getting out.

Saint met him at the door with enthusiasm and, undoubtedly, hunger. Gabe let him out to the backyard, then filled his bowls and checked for a reply from Lexie.

Nothing.

With a kernel of worry forming, he changed out of his suit, then let Saint back in. While the dog beelined for his dinner, Gabe tried texting again and watched his screen, waiting for the three dots to appear to signal Lexie was typing.

She wasn't.

His concern increased when he called her and got no answer, and that pretty much sealed it. Fifteen minutes after he'd pulled in, he gave Saint a good ear rub and was back out the door, heading to her apartment.

Traffic in the downtown area was a hassle, as it usually was at that hour on a Thursday, but he finally parked in one of the visitor spots and headed up to her apartment.

After he knocked, he checked for texts again, making sure he hadn't missed any.

"Come on, Lex," he said under his breath as he knocked a second time, and then the door opened, and there she was.

He pulled her head gently to him and kissed her hair—her messy, sleep-tousled hair, he realized as he got a good look at her. She still wore her work clothes, minus shoes, and her shirt was wrinkled. When he spotted the sleep lines on her left cheek, he said, "I woke you up."

Rubbing one of her eyes, she nodded drowsily, looking disoriented. "I fell asleep on the couch."

Seeing her had eased some of his worry, but finding out she'd fallen asleep—in her work clothes—had the cloud of concern that had hovered over him all week coalescing as if a storm was rolling in.

Lexie had never been the napping type. He was all too aware she hadn't been sleeping for the past few nights. Two nights ago, he'd woken up in the middle of the night to find her out on the patio, staring into the darkness. When he'd asked, not for the first time that week, what was wrong, she hadn't given him a concrete answer, just alluded to changing careers. Which could be legit—but he didn't think that was the full story.

As she stepped back to let him in, she glanced at the clock on the microwave in the kitchen and cringed.

"Sorry to wake you up. I texted several times and was worried when you didn't answer," he said.

"My ringer is probably off," she said with a scowl toward the couch. "Phone must have fallen between the cushions. Sorry to worry you."

She went into the kitchen, opened her freezer, and rummaged around. Gabe followed her. He put his hand over hers on the freezer handle. "Lex." It took a little doing to get her to let go of the handle, but finally she did, and he closed the door. "What's going on?"

"I wanted to make dinner for you. I came home because I have everything I need for spicy stir-fry chicken. You're having a terrible week, and I wanted to make things easier for you by doing one stupid little thing like cook dinner, and I screwed it up."

"Hey." He nudged her chin up so she would meet his gaze. "Dinner's not important. Tell me what's really wrong. You haven't been yourself all week."

She blinked back the tears that suddenly filled her eyes. "I'm sorry. You have so much on your plate, so much work crap going on, and the last thing I want to do is add to it."

Taking a gentle hold of her upper arms, he peered down at her and said, "You're not adding to anything. It doesn't matter what else is going on in my life—you're the most important thing. You come first. Before any work crisis or life crisis or anything."

A tear rolled down her cheek. He caught it with his finger and wished he could so easily erase whatever was upsetting her. "I want to be supportive of you, not too needy or too emotional or…" She sucked in a shaky breath and looked away.

Gabe studied her, confused and so damn frustrated. "What's bothering you, Lexie?"

She stepped past him to the opposite counter, leaned forward on it with her back to him. She ran her hands over her face and into her hair, where she kept them in a tight grasp that looked painful. He put his hand on her back, tried to soothe her.

"I'm having lunch with my mom tomorrow," she blurted out.

Silence fell between them as Gabe tried to wrap his brain around that. "Say what?" He dropped his hand and stepped back to lean against the counter opposite her, still processing. "Your mom— She's in Nashville?"

As unprecedented as that was, it was the least of the WTFs going through his mind.

Lexie nodded but didn't offer more.

"Why?" was what came out of his mouth next.

They didn't disagree on many things, but her mom was one of them. All the woman did was hurt her daughter repeatedly. Gabe had met Jean Gallagher once, when she'd showed her face at Lexie's dad's funeral, and she'd done nothing during that five-minute interaction to convince him she had anything to offer Lexie except disappointment.

Lexie expelled a long breath and shook her head. "Because she asked, I guess."

"When did she call you?"

"Last week, when we were at Drake and Mackenzie's party."

That was when she'd started acting out of sorts, he realized. She'd been practically bubbling over with happiness when they'd driven to the party but quiet, almost sullen on the way home. He should've figured out sooner that something big had happened. Dammit, he would've thought she would tell him something as significant as her mother calling her.

"And you didn't bother to mention it?"

She turned and narrowed a look at him that said she thought he might not take it well if she'd told him.

Damn straight.

"I told you I didn't want to lay one more thing on you when you've got so many issues going on at work. I was trying to be considerate."

He believed that was true…but not the whole truth. He swallowed and tried to dial back his irritation. "So you told her yes?"

"I told her maybe. I've been trying to decide what to do all week—"

"Which I could've helped you talk through had you told me about it."

"Or talked me out of it?" she asked, straightening, facing him full on. "I know your opinion, Gabe. I know you'd advise me not to see her. I know that, from your standpoint, that seems like the smart thing to do, but there's more to it than that. Things are complicated between my mom and me." She paused, swallowed. "I don't expect you to understand."

"You're right," he bit out, unable to fight down the utter frustration any longer. "I don't understand. How the hell can I understand when you've never told me anything about what happened with your mom?"

She looked like someone had slapped her. "I've never told *anyone* about that and I'm not about to now. Not with lunch tomorrow staring me in the face. I need to go in fresh, try to put the past behind me."

He suddenly had a sinking feeling in his gut, like... Shit. After all this time? After everything they'd been through together? His dad's death, her dad's death, his mom's heart attack, her wedding-day breakup, plus all the good stuff, like graduations, parties, jobs. All of that and more, and she still couldn't open up fully to him?

"Look, Lexie, I understand that tomorrow will be rough," he said, his words measured as his frustration built, "but I have to say..." He shook his head, weighing what he said carefully, wanting to get through to her but not out of anger. Though there was definitely anger. More than a little. "I don't know how we can make this work if you're never going to let me all the way in."

"Make what work?" she asked warily.

"Us."

"I'm doing the best I can, Gabe," she snapped, turning away from him and busying herself with transferring several dirty dishes to the dishwasher.

"You can trust me with anything."

Lexie didn't respond for some time, just rearranged the nearly full dishwasher, keeping her back to him.

"If you can't tell me the stuff that's troubling you for days at a time, keeping you awake at night, then what do we really have?" he pressed, desperation to get through to her clawing at him. "Good sex? Is that all you want?" He didn't give a shit whether he was playing fair or not. He needed to get her to see they had a big, fat, ugly problem that they had to address or they weren't going to last.

She shoved the lower tray all the way in and closed the dishwasher hard, then spun around to face him. "That's not all I want and you know it." Her eyes flashed anger. "That's a shitty thing for you to say."

He took a step back, knowing she was right, but fuck… He was afraid this could be the beginning of the most important thing in his life slipping away.

Forcing himself to take several slow breaths to rein his shit in, he leaned back on the counter, gripping it with both hands.

"What did she do to you, Lex?" he asked in a rough, quiet voice.

Arms crossed over her chest, without looking at him, she merely shook her head, her jaw clenched.

"She's been off-limits for thirty-some years, Lexie. When will you be able to let me in?" he persisted.

"I don't know. All I know is not today," she said firmly.

He studied her, firm jaw, leave-me-alone body language, and all, for a long moment. "It's not that I specifically need to know the story of your mom leaving your family. It's the principle. It's that you went six days torn up inside over something and didn't speak a word of it to me. Didn't even give me the chance to try to help you work through it or make a decision. Might I have reacted badly if you told me? Chances are good. But if we can't be honest with each other—I mean full-out honest with no holds barred—then I don't know how we can have a future."

Her eyes met his briefly and then fluttered closed. In resignation? What was she resigned to? Trying harder? Or letting *them* go?

"Lexie?"

She didn't say a thing, didn't budge, didn't flinch…nothing.

Fuck.

This was going nowhere tonight, and if he didn't get out of there, it could turn ugly.

"I'm going to go," he said resolutely, and then her eyes did pop open, but she didn't move to stop him.

That, he was afraid, said it all.

He shoved off the counter and headed for the door. When he reached it, she said, still standing in the kitchen but facing him now, "Gabe…"

He paused with his hand on the knob, mid-twist, hoping…

"I'm sorry," she said. It was more a dismissal than a plea to give her another chance.

Dammit, he'd give her infinite chances if she'd just try.

"Yeah," he forced out around the emotion balled up in his chest. "Me too."

He opened the door, walked out of her apartment, and headed toward the elevator, the blood in his veins going ice cold with the fear that he was going to lose her.

For once, he was putting his needs first, and what he needed from Lexie, he wasn't sure she could give him.

CHAPTER TWENTY-TWO

s Lexie walked from her car to Frank's Diner on Friday, she wished for a deserted tropical island to run away to —one with no snakes or spiders.

In the span of a week, she'd gone from being on top of the world with hope and excitement to, well, crashing and burning hard.

Watching Gabe walk out of her apartment last night had been devastating, made worse because she knew his points were valid. Maybe she should have told him days ago that her mom had called. Maybe he would've helped her reason through her decision of whether to meet for lunch. Maybe she should've told him everything about her history with her mom years ago. Maybe, maybe, maybe.

But she hadn't. Because it was hard and it hurt. And now she was left to handle the fallout—and handling it was not going so well.

As she walked past the florist and the wedding dress shop on the end of Hale Street, toward Frank's Diner, she was so lost in her thoughts and bone-tired she barely noticed the bright colors in the summer window displays.

Last night, between fretting over her meeting with her mom and crying her eyes out about the argument with Gabe, she hadn't been able to turn her mind or her emotions off. She'd slept for no more than an hour, and that was only dozing, right before her alarm went off.

She'd done her best to disguise the bags under her eyes, but there wasn't much she could do to get rid of the bloodshot, worst-night-of-her-life look. Then she'd been ten minutes late for work, and naturally, she'd run into her boss in the elevator—that elevator was *so* not her friend—on the way up to the fourth floor.

As she'd been walking out to meet her mom for lunch, her boss had called her into her office and told her to forget about working the last week on her notice. It'd been a punch in the gut, because when she'd resigned a week ago, the same woman had gone on about how much they would miss her and everything she brought to the table and had asked if more money could keep her there.

Funny how things could change in a week.

Her boss had been tactful and empathetic in explaining that Lexie's head hadn't been in it at all this week, that she could tell she was distracted and no longer dedicated to her usual quality of work, and that they would all be better off if they parted ways early.

She'd been kind in allowing Lexie to go to her lunch with her mom and then come back afterwards to collect her belongings and say any goodbyes. Lexie had seen people ushered out immediately before, and she was thankful that wasn't her fate, but… she'd just been dismissed early from her job.

As she arrived at the door to the diner, she paused for moment on the brick sidewalk, took in a deep, cleansing breath, and did her best to set the work blow aside so she could deal with the potential mom blow she was about to walk into.

A couple walked out holding hands, and Lexie took the glass door from them and went inside.

The place was bright and cheery and hopping, and before an employee could glance her way, she recognized her mom in the corner booth along the front windows.

Her heart pounded as she headed in that direction, and as she got closer, before Jean Gallagher looked up and spotted her, Lexie was stunned at how old and worn-down she appeared compared to the last time she'd seen her. As if more than time had beaten her down. She looked a decade and a half older than her fifty-eight years.

Her mom glanced up when Lexie was only a few steps away, and even when Jean's mouth eased into a smile, her eyes seemed somehow flat, like her spark for life was missing.

Maybe she'd never had one. Lexie wouldn't know.

Her mom scooted out of the booth. "Lexie, look at you," she said, extending both arms as if she meant to hug her daughter. Lexie didn't have a chance to ponder the oddness of that—a hug from her mother—before her mom did indeed pull her awkwardly to her and held on for a few extra seconds.

As foreign of a gesture as it was, Lexie didn't pull away. Instead, without thought, she soaked it in, the thinness of her mom's frame, the scent of her no-frills soap, the fact that they were about the same height—something she hadn't realized they had in common. Lexie's guard was admittedly up, but being hugged by her mom twisted something deep inside, some deep longing. She tamped down on it, determined not to be hurt or let down again today.

They slid into seats on opposite sides in uncomfortable silence. Though tempted to break it with pleasantries, Lexie held back, waiting, letting the burden of conversation fall on her mom's shoulders, wondering what her mom's goal was.

As soon as the sixty-something red-haired server with the kindhearted eyes had filled their water glasses and promised to be right back for their orders, Jean said, formally, "Thank you, Lexie, for meeting with me today."

"You're welcome," she replied stiffly.

Her mom flashed a half grin, then averted her gaze. She grasped on to her water glass, lifted it for a drink, set it down. Her eyes darted around the diner, not landing on any one spot for long enough to really see anything, if Lexie had to guess, and she wove her fingers together, released them, wove them together again, repeatedly.

Her mom was nervous, Lexie realized. Jean dared another

direct glance at her and said, "You look so professional and lovely and...tired."

"Oh. I am tired today." And there was the brutally honest, mother-to-daughter *you look like hell* comment she'd never had before. Between the hug and that, the milestones were coming nonstop.

The server, who introduced herself as Tilly, came back and took their orders, then rushed off to the next table and flirted with a guy half her age and winked at the curly-haired brunette who was with him. Both the man and woman laughed with Tilly and obviously knew her well.

In the next few seconds, Lexie's mom looked so lost and ill at ease that Lexie was starting to feel bad for her, so she threw her a conversational crutch. "How was your trip from San Diego?"

"Long," her mom said. "But I got to go through some beautiful parts of the country I'd never seen."

Lexie listened as her mom described the dramatic rock formations in the West and the vast flatlands of the Midwest and the grandeur of the Mississippi. She told her about her route and the places she'd stayed the past few nights—cheap, run-down roadside motels.

It gave Lexie the chance to listen to her mom's voice, her diction, her choice of words and phrases—all things she had so little knowledge of. It was clear she was an intelligent woman, but she seemed rough around the edges socially, conversationally, just as she had during her few-and-far-between phone calls. Lexie wondered if she'd always been that way or if three decades of living remotely in a rainforest had caused it.

When Jean finished talking about her cross-country trip, silence once again fell between them, and Lexie was becoming more and more sure this was a mistake. There was no relationship to rekindle here. There was nothing but awkwardness.

Tilly broke the silence for a good two minutes when she delivered their burgers and fries with some friendly conversation, and then she hurried off again.

Lexie's mom cut her burger in two, exhaled, and said, "So tell me about your life, Lexie."

Her life. Lexie held in a sardonic laugh at the absurdity of trying to sum up the thirty-three years of her life since her mom had left.

As if her mom sensed her thoughts, she frowned self-consciously and studied her plate, and Lexie relented mentally. She had so many mixed emotions toward this woman, and she couldn't deny that pity for her was creeping in.

"I'm in the midst of changing careers, actually," Lexie finally said. "I was a landscape architect since college, but I just started a mural-painting business and landed a sizable contract with North Brothers Sports to paint murals in their stores."

"Ah, yes. You're dating Gabe North, isn't that right?"

"How did you know that?"

Her mom looked momentarily flustered and then smiled sheepishly. "I confess I looked you up online to learn more about you. I realize it's not right that I had to Google my daughter. And acknowledge that it's my fault." She frowned, and the lines in her face deepened, making Lexie believe her regret was genuine, at least a little. "Anyway, I saw the most beautiful photo of you and Gabe at a charity event of some sort," she said. "Baseball, I believe. You were wearing a coral dress."

"It was for the Harrison North Baseball and Softball Foundation," Lexie told her, realizing she shouldn't be surprised that photos from the gala were online, due to all the press coverage the event had received. "It was just a couple of weeks ago."

"It was obvious in the photos that you two are in love." Jean's expression was kind, curious, bordering on affectionate. "Tell me about him. Is it serious?"

It felt like a knot tightened in Lexie's gut, because after last night, she didn't know how much longer she could rightfully call Gabe her boyfriend. She forced a smile, determined to keep her troubles to herself. "I've known Gabe since kindergarten. He's my best friend. He's the VP of Human Resources for North Brothers Sports."

"He's very handsome," Jean said, and Lexie considered that an understatement. "And those Norths, they seem to be well-off. What a catch, Lexie. I'm impressed."

Lexie stiffened and narrowed her eyes, instantly wary. The one thing she knew about her mom was that she and Dr. Lightfoot, her partner in monkeys, were always in search of funding for their life's work. Every time she'd called since Silas's funeral, Jean had been in the States to secure another grant or other contributions. "His financial status is none of my business."

Her mom flinched at the rebuke, and Lexie studied her, suspicious now. Were her ties to Gabe and his finances the reason for this unprecedented in-person meetup?

"Is that..." Lexie said, eyeing her hard. She knew the odds of her mom wanting any sort of true relationship with her. The woman had gone for three decades plus without making any motion toward truly knowing her daughter.

"You're looking for money, aren't you?" Lexie said after pushing her plate away. "That's why you called. That's why you wanted to meet."

"I'm not—"

"I'm such an idiot." Lexie dug into her purse and took out a twenty, tossed it next to her lunch, her face burning with shame that she'd been dumb enough to get her hopes up that she and her mom could ever build any kind of true relationship. Gabe had been right...again. "I have to go."

She slid out of the booth, and as she headed toward the diner door, she heard her mom calling out, "Lexie, wait. Please. Lexie!"

Lexie wasn't one for public scenes, and she was done trying with her mother.

She shoved the door open and headed down the sidewalk, making a point of looking in the opposite direction as she passed the window where she and her mother had sat. Tears blurred her vision, and she hurried past the rest of the businesses on this side of the street and nearly jogged across Hale when she got to the corner.

Without a coherent thought, she veered off the opposite sidewalk into a small park with towering trees, lush greenery, and a picturesque gazebo. On the left side of the winding walkway she found herself on, she spotted an empty bench, and she detoured to it. Sat down, her mind sputtering with shock and hurt and mortification that she'd been dumb enough to fall for her mom's bullshit. Desperate enough to believe her mom had reached out to her for the sake of getting to know her better.

"Lexie!"

As soon as Jean's voice reached her, she realized her error in pit-stopping in the green space to collect herself instead of continuing to her car and getting as far away as she could. She'd been on autopilot and had reverted to the age-old habit of finding refuge in the peace and majesty of nature, and wasn't it coincidental that the cause of her problems hadn't changed much at all after all these years?

"Lexie," her mom said, winded, as if she'd been running. "Please, could you hear me out?"

Feeling trapped, Lexie closed her eyes and craned her neck back against the low back of the bench. She could either run away and then likely have her mom contact her until she said her piece, whatever that was, or she could get it over with.

"Fine," Lexie said coldly. "Say whatever you need to say. I have places I need to get to."

Her mom sat down next to her, and Lexie increased the space between them as if she was still four years old. Maybe, in part of her heart, she was.

"I'm not looking for funding," Jean said in a quiet, solemn voice. "My project is over. My life's work is done."

Lexie eyed her from the side, taken aback and yet still wary. "What do you mean?"

Her mom looked away and let out a measured, slow breath, as if she was trying to hold her emotions in check. When she faced forward again, she looked sad down to her bone marrow. "Four months ago, Dr. Lightfoot died."

In spite of herself, Lexie let out a gasp. She didn't know the man, but she'd heard his praises sung when she was four or maybe even before. He'd been Jean's mentor and partner and sole colleague ever since she'd left home and, by Lexie's estimation, the one person her mom had left in her life. "What happened?"

"Cancer. It wasn't treatable, so we were in a race against time," her mom said somberly. "We almost made it…"

"Almost made what?"

Jean blew out another breath, this one shaky and less controlled. This one filled with heaviness and grief. "The goal was always to get the monkeys off the endangered list. After all these years, we were so close, knew we were close." She swallowed. "Two months after he died, the news came through. We'd done it. They're officially off the list. But Arthur never got to experience that moment. He never got to know what it felt like to hit our decades-long goal."

Lexie's throat tightened at the tragic timing. Even though her feelings toward her mother were ambiguous on a good day, she couldn't help but feel sorrow on her behalf. It sounded like she'd been on a roller coaster for the past several months.

"So they took the monkeys off the list, and just like that, you're out of work?"

"Oh, there's always more to be done," her mom said. "But funding becomes a lot harder to attain once they're off the list. I thought about continuing the work, in Arthur's honor, but as much as I loved it, I don't have it in me. It's a losing battle to make more progress, especially by myself. So I'm back in the States for good, with my whole life to figure out."

Lexie nodded. "I'm sorry I jumped to the wrong conclusion," she said quietly, feeling foolish yet again. Even when her mom had been in pursuit of contributions and funding, she'd never hit up Lexie or anyone she knew, and yet the mention of Gabe's money had apparently been a trigger. Because she herself had never been enough for her mom?

"It's okay. You've probably been trying to figure out what I could possibly want after so many years. I understand that. Know that it's my doing." She was trying to sound matter-of-fact, but Lexie could hear the underlying defeat in her voice.

"I don't know what I wanted or what I expected to find." Jean shook her head slowly. "The fact is, I'm fifty-eight years old, and I don't know what's next." Her voice climbed higher at the end of her sentence, and she sat there for several seconds, her lips pressed together. "My life's work is done. My colleague and closest friend is gone. I deserted my family and lost touch with what few friends I had years ago. It's all on me. I realize that. I spent the two-thousand-mile drive to Nashville trying to figure out where to start, and I'm still at a loss. But I think... I was thinking I'd start here. In Nashville."

The flatness in her mom's eyes... Now Lexie understood. This woman beside her truly had nothing left. No family, no friends, no job, no home. Yes, she'd made it that way herself, but the sympathy it stirred in Lexie was undeniable.

"I know we don't have a relationship, Lexie, but the first thing I set out to do when I got back to US soil was touch base with you." Her mom again paused, seemingly overcome, and swallowed hard. "Of all of my regrets, you're the biggest. I'm so sorry for what I did to you." She clamped her jaw down as if fighting off tears, her regret nearly tangible.

After several seconds of battling to keep her composure, she continued, "I know I have no right to ask, but is there any way you could give us a chance to get acquainted? To start from scratch?"

Lexie chewed on the inside of her cheek as she thought it over, but there wasn't a lot of thinking to do. She had no illusions that they could build a healthy mother-daughter relationship. Too many years had passed, with too many emotions. But Lexie wasn't heartless, wasn't at all immune to the sad plight this woman who'd given her birth was now in, and while she couldn't be her mom's savior, she could give her a small bone to chew on, a sliver of hope in her regret-filled life, while at the same time doing something for herself as well.

"I'd like to get to know you better," Lexie said. "Slowly, because there's a lot of baggage I can't just throw overboard, but" —she nodded, becoming more sure of what she wanted—"yes. If you're staying in Nashville, I'd be happy to meet with you again, maybe another lunch or dinner sometime."

Lexie's hand was resting on the bench between them, and her mom reached down and put her own hand over it. "Thank you." Her voice was barely more than a whisper, thick with emotion.

Lexie gave her a tentative smile and nodded back. Then she inhaled deeply and straightened. "I need to get back to work. I'm glad we talked more. Once you get settled, give me a call."

"I'll do that, Lexie. You take care."

"You too," Lexie said as she stood. "Bye."

She went back down the winding trail and made a beeline for her car, not noticing her surroundings, too lost in her thoughts.

There were a lot of things about her mom that she needed to process, but the one thing she was crystal damn clear about was that she never wanted to end up like Jean Gallagher. She never wanted to push the people she loved away and find herself all alone.

Also clear as a sunny day was how very fortunate she was to have a chance with a man like Gabe North, who was loving, caring, supportive, and yes, handsome on top of it all. She'd made some mistakes with him, and it was time to remedy those before she lost him for good.

She wasn't about to let the rest of the day pass without fixing things with the man she loved.

CHAPTER TWENTY-THREE

$\mathcal{I}$t wasn't yet three p.m. Friday when Gabe walked out of Mason's corner office after a celebratory finger of scotch. In spite of the spirits and the morning's news that Raymond Polanski had dropped the lawsuit, Gabe wasn't much in the mood for celebrating.

He hadn't heard a word from Lexie since he'd walked out of her apartment last night. Had he really expected to? Well, no, not considering he'd been the one to get frustrated and leave, but dammit, he was climbing the walls not knowing how she was doing, how her lunch with her mom had gone, that she was okay.

It was habit. Thirty years of habits that he might have to learn to do without if they couldn't work things out. He wanted them to work out more than anything, but Lexie was the one up to bat.

He couldn't remember ever feeling so powerless in something so crucial.

On his way into his office, Jalisa stopped him to go over some calls that had come in. As she was finishing up the list, his phone vibrated in his pocket. When he saw the message that Lexie's key had been used to enter his home, he waited until Jalisa finished her sentence and then said, "I need to take off. Clear my calendar for the rest of the day?"

He was already heading into the inner office to get his bag when she acquiesced, as he'd known she would.

"Everything okay?" she asked.

"I hope so. Issue at the house." That wasn't a lie, as misleading as it was. "See you on Monday," he remembered to say before he hauled ass out of there.

"Hey, Gabe," Prisha, the receptionist, said as he hurried past her desk toward the outer door. "Coming back?"

"I'm out for the weekend," he said over his shoulder. "Have a good one." He didn't even slow his step, unwilling to get caught up in conversation or, worse, another problem of some kind.

As he sped toward home, relieved the weekend rush hour hadn't really gotten going yet, he wondered what Lexie could be doing at his place. The fact that it was the middle of the afternoon concerned him. Why wasn't she at work? Was she packing up all her belongings to take home for good?

It was suddenly difficult to get his lungs full, and he opened the window, as if that would help.

Lexie leaving was too awful to contemplate, and yet, after last night, he wasn't convinced that wasn't where they were heading. He couldn't figure out how to help her, didn't know what more he could say or do to let her know she could tell him anything and he would never stop loving her.

And dammit, all the times she and Mason and his mom and anyone else had accused him of putting his needs last, well, this time he wasn't. He needed her to let him in completely, wasn't sure he could stay in a relationship where there wasn't complete openness and trust. Did he need to know all her innermost thoughts and secrets? No. Not by any means. Hell, there were times he knew he was better off not completely understanding what was going through her mind. But when it came to the deep-seated issue of her mother, who was one of the only ongoing sore spots between them, openness and communication were the only way to handle it.

In record time, he pulled into his driveway, past Lexie's Subaru, noting she'd parked it in the driveway instead of the garage and not liking what that might signify.

When he entered the house, silence met his ears. No dog, no Lexie, nothing. On some level, he realized they must be in the backyard, but even so, he went to the master bedroom and into the bathroom to check that her shampoo and soap were still in the shower—they were—and then he went to the other side of the house, to the guest room where she kept her clothes. It didn't appear she'd taken anything out.

He threw his suit jacket onto the sectional as he passed it, then went out the back door. On the opposite side of the pool, Lexie was stretched out, eyes closed, dressed in a tank top and shorts, on the double lounger, next to Saint, who perked up at the sound of the door, then hopped down and trotted over to greet him.

"Hey, boy." Gabe gave him a good, fast, distracted rubdown, then the two of them headed out toward Lexie, who'd opened her eyes and watched their progress. He tried to gauge her thoughts by her face, but her expression gave away nothing.

Saint beat him to her and nailed her with an overzealous lick of his giant tongue across her face, making her laugh and roll to one side.

"Your manners suck, Saint," she said as she sat up straight and crossed her legs in front of her. "Hi," she said to Gabe.

"Hi. What are you doing here?" He didn't smile, didn't lower his guard. She wouldn't just act like last night hadn't happened, would she? Because that wouldn't work for him.

"Hanging out with Saint," she said, then leaned over and hugged his big lug of a lucky-ass dog, who'd climbed back up and flopped by her feet. "I was hoping to talk to you eventually, just didn't expect you home this early."

"I saw you were here," he said with no further explanation, towering over her. "What'd you want to talk about?"

Lexie hugged her knees to her chest, facing him. "I'd like to start with some old business," she said, sounding unsure of herself, her gaze averted as she tapped her chin on her knee a few times.

He walked around to the single lounger closest to her and sat on the edge of it, facing her, his feet remaining on the concrete pool deck.

After several seconds passed, she made eye contact. "I'm sorry, Gabe. Sorry for all the years I've shut you out of some parts of my life. I know I can tell you anything. I trust you with my life."

"I don't take your trust lightly," he said, trying not to let her words soften him.

"Sometimes I've felt, I don't know, unworthy, I guess. Not because of anything you've ever said or done, just...because. You have such a big, loving family, and mine was always a train wreck. You're the guy everybody loves, and I'm the girl nobody really knows. From the very first day I came to your house, I felt so lucky to be included, sort of like a charity case—"

"God, Lexie, you're not a charity case. You're my friend. Best one I've ever had."

"I know that, but some days I felt like a tagalong, because of stuff in here"—she pointed to her head—"not because of anything you did." She paused, took a deep breath, her whole upper body rising with the inhalation. "It's just...admitting my parents didn't seem to want me, to the guy who everyone loves..." She shook her head and let out a laugh-scoff. "Who wants to do that?"

Yet again, his heart broke for the neglected little girl she'd been, and his defenses crumbled. He reached out and took her hand in his.

"Anyway, I'm ready to tell you about the day my mom left my dad and me. Not because you're mad that I haven't yet—"

"I'm not mad."

"Upset, disappointed, whatever," she said. "I want to tell you because, until I do, it's holding power over me. I think maybe it will until I let it out, tell someone about it, and I'm tired of letting it."

"Okay." He suspected she was right. He wove their fingers together, hoping to reassure her.

"It's not a long, dramatic story," she said, clutching his hand tighter. "There was no big fight. She didn't beat me or do anything outwardly horrible like that."

"But she left you," Gabe said. "When you were four years old."

"I don't have a lot of memories of her. I don't think she was home very much. I remember Miss Alice, my babysitter, better. She stayed with me every day, was there when I woke up in the morning and often stayed until my bedtime because my mom was a grad student with an irregular schedule. My dad, he came home earlier than my mom some nights, but he always kept Miss Alice there until I went to bed. Looking back, knowing what I know now, I'm sure it's because he didn't have a clue what to do with me."

"I don't think he ever did," Gabe agreed.

"There were times my mom would come home for dinner, but I remember she would leave again, go back to campus to work some more. I remember when she got hooked up with Dr. Lightfoot, who was a professor in California specializing in her area of interest."

"The monkeys," Gabe said.

"The stupid rat-sized monkeys that were on the endangered list. Only found in the Amazon, and only a very few were left," Lexie said. "My mom was so excited when Dr. Lightfoot initially invited her to go to the rainforest on a research trip. She was gone for a month and came back with dozens of pictures of the monkeys, and of course, I loved that. She was spending time with me, and the monkeys were adorable. What I didn't know then was that she would always choose the monkeys over me. Over our family."

Noting the dampness in her eyes, Gabe reached between them and put his other hand on her knee and squeezed, wishing he could erase all the pain that woman had caused her.

"One day, Miss Alice brought me home from preschool and my mom was home, which was unusual, but I was happy, excited to show her the picture I'd drawn of a family of monkeys. When I walked in, I noticed the suitcases by the door—three of them—and I thought we were going on a trip. There was a suitcase for each of us. Logical conclusion."

She swallowed hard, and the tears spilled over and flowed down her cheeks. "I was such a foolish little girl, not seeing until later how much she didn't care about me. She was busy. I made excuses for her all the time, probably because she made excuses for herself. *I wish I could go to your preschool music program, Lexie, but I've got a very important paper I have to work on. I can't play with you this weekend, Lexie. The monkeys are depending on me, but maybe next week we can go to the zoo.* We never went to the zoo."

He fought off the urge to pull her into his arms and stop her from saying more in an effort to assuage her pain. Whether she told the rest of the story or not, the pain was already there, a steady, unwanted companion for most of her life, and like she said, maybe speaking of it would help her release a little of that.

"I remember the look on my mom's face when we came in. She wasn't happy and she glared at Miss Alice and said, *That was faster than I expected.* And Miss Alice told her, *Pickup never takes long.* I remember Miss Alice's tone took me by surprise, because she was mad, and she never got mad. I asked my mom where we were going, because of the suitcases, ignoring the tension in the room, and that's when she told me *she* was the one going. She'd just gotten back from her first trip with Dr. Lightfoot not too long before, and I asked her how long she'd be gone this time. I remember the silence, and I caught her and Miss Alice looking at each other, seeming to tell each other things without words, but I didn't understand what things. My mom finally let out a big sigh and sat me down on the couch and told me she was going for a long time to a place very far away."

Lexie's tears kept streaming down her cheeks, and Gabe couldn't stand it. He leaned closer and brushed them away—a fruitless gesture since they kept right on coming.

"Eventually she admitted she wasn't coming back," she continued, "that she was going to live in that faraway place. And then she said, *I'm sorry, Lexie, but you need more than I can give you.*"

"Jesus," Gabe said. "She said that?"

With her eyes closed, Lexie nodded. "I can still hear her voice. I've never forgotten those words."

"Son of a bitch. She should've thought about that before she had a child."

"Years later, my dad admitted I was an oops."

Gabe bit out, "Too bad. Accidental pregnancies happen all the time. If you have that baby, you figure out how to put the kid first."

"You would think," she said quietly, wiping at her eyes. "And then, I got to know the Norths, saw how a family could be, and" —she squeezed her eyes shut, unleashing another torrent of tears —"I was too ashamed to admit how it was in my family."

"Lex, I'm so sorry." His voice came out raspy with sadness. "No kid should have to go through any of that."

"I realized recently I've been mad at my mom my whole life —for all the things she never gave me, did for me, was to me, all the things your family gave me but she couldn't. But today…the woman I saw at lunch…she's full of so much sadness and regret, and I realized I couldn't be mad anymore. All I can feel toward her is pity. It's taken her thirty years to figure out what she's been missing. Her monkey project is gone. Dr. Lightfoot is gone. She admitted she has nothing left. She apologized for leaving all those years ago, for what it's worth, and it's obvious she's weighed down by tons of regrets."

"As she should be."

Lexie nodded. "She made no excuses. Took full blame for our non-relationship. I don't know if I've forgiven her or if I can forget. I'm still processing everything."

"Understandable." Gabe was pretty damn sure he'd struggle with both, maybe for the rest of that woman's life.

"I do know one thing," she said, sitting up straighter.

"What's that?"

"When we were in Colorado, all that stuff about figuring out what I want for my life, instead of what everyone else wants or needs from me? Remember that?"

"Of course."

"I've been turning that over in my mind for weeks, trying to come up with some answers."

"Any luck?"

"I know what I don't want, and that's to be like my mom."

"You could never be like your mom," Gabe said with conviction. "And what about what you do want?" He barely breathed after asking the question, hoping so damn hard that he was on the list.

"Three things so far. The first you already know. The career change. I'm scared of all the changes, scared to be a business owner with no backup income, but just thinking about it invigorates me. I wasn't unhappy with landscape architecture, but it never made me feel so alive. Sparked."

"I can see it in your eyes when you talk about it. Mason and Melody saw it when you presented to us."

"Second, I want to try to get to know my mom. No mother-daughter expectations. It's too late for that, but I'd like to know her as a person. And if you don't support that, well, that's your prerogative, but I'm doing it anyway."

Gabe didn't, in fact, like the chances that Jean Gallagher could hurt Lexie again, but he would do his best not to stand in her way, and if she'd let him, he'd be there for her if her mom ever let her down again.

In response, he merely nodded and then asked, "You said three things. What's the third?" still hoping beyond hope it had something to do with him. Them. Something good.

Lexie shifted to her knees, facing him, and said, "Unequivocally you. Gabe, I love you. I love you as my best friend, and I'm in love with you as the man I want to be with forever, and I know that might be premature and you don't have to say anything about it, but you wanted to know what I want, and that's it. You're it."

He felt like letting out a roar of victory and joy so the whole universe would know how unequivocally happy this woman made him. Instead, he went up on his knees and drew her into his body, then, burrowing his fingers into her hair, he brought her mouth to his and poured all of his love into kissing her.

"You're it for me too, Sexy Lexie," he said when they broke for air, and then he was going on instinct alone when he barreled forward. "I want to marry you, Lex. I don't have a ring, didn't plan this for today, and this is probably the lamest proposal ever, but will you marry me?"

She stared at him for a long moment, her eyes wide and sparkling, her mouth open in an expression of shock and cautious happiness, as if gauging whether he meant it or not, and then she figured it out and said, "Yes!" He wouldn't forget the utterly ecstatic, joyful sound that came after it for as long as he lived.

He pulled her tightly into him again, held on for all he was worth, and said, "Thank God."

EPILOGUE

*B*uying this sprawling lodge-style home burrowed into the side of a mountain was the second-best thing Gabe had ever done.

The best, of course, was convincing Lexie Nicole Gallagher—soon to be North—to marry him.

The three weeks since he'd proposed had been a whirlwind on all fronts. Once he'd closed on the Colorado house, he'd persuaded Hayden Henry—and paid her well—to fly out and begin decorating. She had that well underway and had even managed to make it comfortable and furnished enough to host the whole family this weekend for the nuptials.

The bedrooms and the bunk room had brand-new beds, enough for all fourteen of them, and Hayden had worked her magic to somehow secure most of the furniture for the living areas and dining room, as well as the expansive deck, though she promised she had a long way to go with the decor itself. He'd decided not to put the place up for vacation rentals after all. Instead, it would be at the North family's disposal for getaways and holidays.

While Hayden had worked the house miracle, he and Lexie—along with Sierra, Mackenzie, and his cousin Miranda—had worked their own miracle by planning a private, one-step-removed-from-elopement wedding to take place here, in the next few minutes.

The site of the simple ceremony was on the wraparound deck, which had a jaw-dropping two-hundred-forty-degree vista of forested mountain peaks and the picturesque valley that included Caribou Creek. The officiant, who'd be here soon, would perform the ritual in the very spot Gabe was standing, with the perfect angle on the tallest peak, which still had patches of snow at the top, even now, in August.

The small, intimate ceremony had been his idea, as he wanted to avoid any hint of what Lexie had gone through with her ex, and when he'd suggested the possibility of a family-only wedding in Colorado, she'd responded with tears—happy, relieved tears.

The whole family had been able to finagle their schedules to make it, with the exception of Zane, who couldn't get leave at the drop of a hat. Drake and Cole had brought their fiancées, Mackenzie and Sierra. Mason was alone as always, and cousins Connor, Miranda, and Logan were stag as well. The matriarchs, Gabe's mom, Aunt Liz, and Geraldine, were in full mothering force.

The final member of their party was Lexie's mom. Lexie had been getting to know her better, helping her get settled. When she'd asked Gabe to join them for dinner, he'd agreed, knowing how important it was to Lexie, and gone in with an open mind. What he'd discovered was a woman full of regrets who wanted to be better, love her daughter better. When Lexie had later brought up inviting her to the wedding, he'd embraced the idea —and had since pulled aside Jean and had a heart-to-heart about not hurting Lexie or she'd have him to deal with. They had an understanding now, and Lexie would have her mom at her wedding.

Behind him, the door to the house opened, and his loud-ass

brothers and male cousins spilled out onto the deck, dressed in suits and carrying cocktail glasses with an inch or so of amber liquid in each. Logan carried a guitar, as he'd offered to strum some background music for when the bride walked outside.

Mason held a spare glass and a bottle of his favorite high-dollar scotch that he saved for celebrations. He ambled over, held the empty glass up to Gabe, then poured him a finger.

"Aren't we supposed to wait till after the ceremony to celebrate?" Gabe asked, taking the glass anyway, never opposed to a dose of Macallan 30 if it was his older brother's treat.

"Champagne is for afterward. This is to toast the purchase of this place," Mason said, sweeping the hand with the half-full bottle out to encompass the house. "This is a hell of a find. The house itself is ideal for a group like ours, and the setting... unbeatable. Good call."

They'd all arrived last night, after the sun had set, so while they could tour the four-thousand-square-foot home then, the view had been a surprise for today, in daylight.

"Lexie's the one who spotted it," Gabe said. "Though I don't think she had any thought of ever seeing the interior, let alone owning it."

"You always have to take things to the extreme, huh?" Cole joked. "I'm with Mason. Good move."

"To holidays and celebrations in the mountains," Logan said, holding up his glass. The afternoon sun glinted off his hair, making him look nearly blond.

"To family," Gabe said, mimicking his gesture.

The six of them clinked their glasses, then sipped.

"Thank you all for making the trip," Gabe continued. "And for being here for Lexie and me."

"Wouldn't miss it," Connor said, coming up alongside Gabe and bumping shoulders. "This is looong overdue."

"I can't argue with that," Gabe said with a laugh.

"Good things come to those who wait, and all that," Drake said with a shit-eating grin that likely translated to *about time you grew a pair*.

Gabe couldn't agree more.

A text alert sounded, and Mason straightened, dug his phone out of his pocket.

"Put the phone away," Drake scolded. "You're in the mountains. It's disconnect time."

"It's never disconnect time," Mason said, and Gabe knew he meant it. He was always plugged in for the sake of North Brothers Sports—always. As he read whatever was on his phone, he frowned and then muttered, "Fuck."

"What's wrong?" Cole asked.

Connor, who was standing next to Mason, leaned in to read the message himself, but Mason stuck his phone in his pocket before he could.

"It's from Ruby," Connor said. "Something wrong at the office?"

Mason shook his head, seemed to be leaning toward not saying another word, then admitted, "Apparently one of the Nashville rags released their most eligible bachelor list today and put me on it. Ruby's being bombarded by phone calls and messages." He shook his head like he didn't have time for any of it, and that was probably the truth.

"Which rag?" Logan said, pulling his own phone out.

"I don't know. Who cares?" Mason said. "It's all garbage."

After tapping something into his phone, Logan said, "Found it. *Nashville Heat*. Ooh, Mason, you're number one. Will you sign a print copy for me?"

"Asshole," Mason said with a chuckle. "Ignore it. It'll go away."

"Hate to tell you," Drake said, "that's not going away. Not for the next while."

"That's right, you were on that list a few years ago, weren't you?" Gabe said to the youngest North.

"I only made number eight." Drake shook his head as if it was truly troubling. "The CEO title will give you an edge every time."

"We can't all be at the top," Mason said with a smirk, and

that, if Gabe had to guess, was the extent of the attention Mason would pay to the "honor."

"Unfortunately for you, when Ruby says bombarded, she means it. You wouldn't believe how many people follow that shit. The women will be coming out of the woodwork for weeks." Drake didn't look sorry at all but rather amused.

"Get some quality dates that way, did you?" Connor asked Drake, who, before Mackenzie, had been the most chronic serial dater of them all, hands down.

"I don't know about quality, but I could've had my pick. Marriage proposals, paternity claims, nude photos posted to my social media… It brings out all the whackos and the desperate ladies."

"Dammit," Mason said, pulling his phone back out. He tapped something, then raised it to his ear as he walked off toward the other side of the deck, and the rest of the group joked and made predictions about their top-dog brother/cousin.

"Guess I'm dodging that bullet for good," Gabe said, laughing, appreciating for yet another reason that he was getting hitched to the girl of his dreams today—in just a few minutes, he realized as his aunt led the officiant they'd hired out to the deck.

"Hey, everyone," Aunt Liz said. "This is Claire Caldwell. She'll be performing the nuptials today."

Gabe introduced himself, shook Claire's hand, and welcomed her. He'd booked her via email so hadn't met her face-to-face before. She was tall and willowy, younger than him, with a genuine smile that had him instantly liking her.

"It's a pleasure to meet you," Claire said. "You picked a gorgeous day to get married."

The rest of the guys introduced themselves, with both Connor and Logan turning on the charm.

"Look at you boys," Aunt Liz said, standing back and taking them all in. She wore a flattering taupe dress and had her chestnut hair pulled up in a fancy do. "So handsome, every one of you. Finish up your beverages. It's almost time. I'll take your glasses inside."

"You look beautiful yourself, Aunt Liz," Drake told her, handing her his empty.

"But only one of us is the most eligible bachelor of Nashville, Tennessee," Connor said with fanfare. He nodded toward Mason, who was still on the phone, then explained to his mom what had transpired.

"He *is* eligible," Aunt Liz said, "and I consider myself an optimist, but I'm not sure anyone will ever pry his bachelor status out of his tight-fisted hands."

"Mason?" Geraldine said, obviously overhearing as she waltzed outside, looking elegant in a silver dress and taking several of the empty glasses from Liz. "He'll find a girl. Someone who will break through his single-minded focus and sweep him off his feet."

"I'd pay to see it," Cole said.

"Ante up then," Logan said, looking at his phone again. "The comments on the bachelor article are already in the thousands. Even our boy Mason could get lucky with all this attention."

Liz and Geraldine took the glasses inside, then returned. Liz fluttered over to Gabe and straightened his bow tie. Though their wedding was informal in a lot of ways, he'd chosen to wear a tux, and Lexie had found a dress she loved. He couldn't wait to see her in it.

"Are you ready to do this?" Liz asked, her hands on his shoulders as she gazed up at him.

"Aunt Liz, I've been ready for twenty years."

"Well, not quite, or he would've gotten the balls to make a move long before now," Drake said.

"Timing is everything," Gabe said.

The door opened again, and Gabe's mom stuck her head out. "The girls are ready," she said. "Are you guys?"

"Speaking of timing..." Liz squeezed Gabe's wrist, her eyes sparkling as her brows rose in question.

Gabe glanced around, made eye contact with Claire, received a nod from her and no objections from anyone as Mason made his way back to the group, his phone returned to his pocket.

A slow smile spread over Gabe's face as he looked back at his mom and said, "I am so damn ready. Let's do this."

As he moved next to Claire to await his bride, his mom nodded, smiling widely, and she ducked back inside. Logan stood at the edge of the group and started softly strumming "All I Want Is You."

When the door opened again, the ladies came out—his mom and Jean together, then Mackenzie and Miranda, and then the door closed most of the way and Gabe's heart raced in anticipation. They'd closed the blinds on the door so he couldn't get a peek.

Then the door eased open, and there stood the most beautiful, incredible woman in the world, smiling back at him as his breath caught in his chest and his eyes blurred with tears of gratitude and love.

He was the luckiest man in the universe.

———

Lexie made eye contact with the man she was going to marry, and it hit her that, during all the preparations today, she hadn't felt a single twinge of nerves. Only excitement and promise and love.

Holding the door open, Sierra whispered from behind her, "Go get your guy," and Lexie moved forward, holding his gaze with every step she took toward him and their future.

She barely noticed the woman there to join them legally, barely noticed the stunning scenery, barely noticed their beloved family gathered around them in a semicircle. It was as if she was in a bubble with Gabe, and everything around them was white noise.

She managed to get through the simple vows, the exchange of rings, lost, the whole time, in his eyes—his beautiful, so-familiar cornflower-blue eyes. As the officiant wished them a life of love and happiness, the simple truth seeped into Lexie's soul—the love she'd been searching for her entire life was right there, looking back at her, accepting every bit of her, loving her completely, radiating from Gabe's eyes.

"And with that," the officiating woman said, "I invite you to seal the promise between you with a kiss."

They leaned toward each other for the first time as husband and wife and did exactly that.

———

NOTE FROM THE AUTHOR

Thanks for reading *True Blue*! I hope you loved Gabe and Lexie's story.

You can read Mason's story now! He's a workaholic CEO who likes to control everything. Eliza has a four-year-old secret that will send his life into chaos.

———

If you liked *True Blue,* I hope you'll consider leaving a review for it. Reviews help other readers find books and can be as short (or long) as you feel comfortable with. Just a couple sentences is all it takes. I appreciate all honest reviews.

———

True Blue is part of the North Brothers series, which includes these stand-alone stories:

- True North
- True Colors
- True Blue
- True Harmony
- True Hero

Don't miss my new small town romance series, the Henry Brothers of Dragonfly Lake! Dragonfly Lake is a small town on a picturesque lake in Tennessee, where the waters run deep, the neighbors are nosy, and the Henry brothers are stealing hearts.

- Untold (prequel)
- Unraveled
- Unsung
- Undone

ACKNOWLEDGMENTS

Thank you to Nicki J., Roxana L., and Jaime G. for answering my many questions on your areas of expertise. I appreciate your patience and willingness to help me better understand my characters' professions and interests.

Thank you to my beta readers for the time you've taken to help me make my story as strong as possible. Your ongoing support means the world to me.

Thank you, Kay Lyons, for being my alpha reader and a sounding board on story, marketing, and the thousand other details that make our jobs both challenging and rewarding.

Thank you to my family—my parents, who continue to peddle my books to anyone who will listen, and my sons, Colton and Camden, and husband, Justin, who are my rocks, who have always been so supportive of me and my writing career. My three guys may not be romance readers, but you are my biggest cheerleaders. You celebrate the high points with me and pick me up at the low points, and I truly couldn't do this without you. Love you always.

ALSO BY AMY KNUPP

<u>Henry Brothers Series</u>
Untold (prequel)
Unraveled
Unsung
Undone

<u>North Brothers Series</u>
True North
True Colors
True Blue
True Harmony
True Hero

North Brothers Box Sets:
North Brothers Books 1-3
North Brothers Books 4-5
North Brothers: The Complete Series

<u>Hale Street Series</u>:
Sweet Spot
Sweet Dreams
Soft Spot
One and Only
Last First Kiss
Heartstrings

<u>Hale Street Box Sets:</u>
Meet Me at Clayborne's

Clayborne's After Hours

It Happened on Hale Street

<u>Island Fire Series</u>:

Playing with Fire

Heat of the Night

Fully Involved

Firestorm

Afterburn

Up in Flames

Flash Point

Fire Within

Impulse

Slow Burn

Island Fire Box Sets:

Sparked (books 1-3)

Ignited (books 4-6)

Enflamed (books 7-10)

OR

Island Fire: The Complete Series

Themed Box Sets:

Friends to Forever (Friends to Lovers Romance)

Working It (Workplace Romance)

ABOUT THE AUTHOR

Amy Knupp is a *USA Today* Best-Selling Author of contemporary romance and a freelance copy editor. She loves words and grammar and meaty, engrossing stories with complex characters.

Amy lives in Wisconsin with her husband and has two sons, four cats, and a box turtle. She graduated from the University of Kansas with degrees in French and journalism. In her spare time, she enjoys traveling, breaking up cat fights, watching college hoops, and annoying her family by correcting their grammar.

For more information:
www.amyknuppbooks.com